Such a Dance

Books by Kate McMurray

Such a Dance

Ten Days in August
(coming March 2016)

Published by Kensington Publishing Corporation

Such a Dance

Kate McMurray

LYRICAL PRESS
Kensington Publishing Corp.
www.kensingtonbooks.com

LYRICAL PRESS BOOKS are published by

Kensington Publishing Corp.
119 West 40th Street
New York, NY 10018

All Kensington titles, imprints, and distributed lines are available at special quantity discounts for bulk purchases for sales promotion, premiums, fund-raising, educational, or institutional use.

Special book excerpts or customized printings can also be created to fit specific needs. For details, write or phone the office of the Kensington Sales Manager: Kensington Publishing Corp., 119 West 40th Street, New York, NY 10018. Attn. Sales Department. Phone: 1-800-221-2647.

Lyrical Press logo Reg. U.S. Pat. & TM Off.

First Electronic Edition: October 2015
eISBN-13: 978-1-61650-799-2
eISBN-10: 1-61650-799-3

First Print Edition: October 2015
ISBN-13: 978-1-61650-800-5
ISBN-10: 1-61650-800-0

Printed in the United States of America

For Sean

"And I have been able to give freedom and life which was acknowledged in the ecstasy of walking hand in hand across the most beautiful bridge of the world, the cables enclosing us and pulling us upward in such a dance as I have never walked and never can walk with another."

—Hart Crane

Chapter 1

"Are You Lonesome Tonight?"

New York City, 1927

Left, right, left. Left, left, right, right, hop. Step forward, step back, hop, tip hat, blow the lady a kiss.

The steps were easy enough, the routine so committed to memory that Eddie could let a dozen other things swim through his mind without missing a beat.

He tossed his cane in the air and let it twirl. Light bounced off the polished silver shaft of it as the audience murmured appreciatively. Eddie caught it deftly, bowed a little, and moved his feet to the left, right, right, left, left, hop. He grinned at Marian, who stretched her arms above her head with grace, betraying her ballet training. Then she shuffled over to him, evidence of her years spent on the vaudeville circuit. She sang her lines in her trademark style, which sounded a bit like a goose honking, and the audience roared with laughter. She smiled and winked at him, and he grinned back and sang the end of the song. Left, right, forward, together, a flourish from the horn section of the orchestra. Then there were deep bows before the curtain fell. Applause erupted throughout the James Theater. Eddie and Marian did their goofy curtain call before retreating backstage.

Thus ended Eddie Cotton and Marian France's act in *Le Tumulte de Broadway*, more informally Jimmy Blanchard's Doozies of 1927, the variety act that was competing with George White and Flo Ziegfeld for ticket dollars and popularity. The song-and-dance team of Cotton and France was among the more popular acts. They were a comedy duo who told jokes, danced their way through physical comedy, and sang funny songs in funny voices. That year, they preceded the Doozy Dolls, fourteen barely-dressed chorines hired more for their looks than their dancing or singing skills.

While the Dolls paraded around on stage, Eddie walked back to his dressing room, Marian trailing behind him. She was already pulling off her shoes, and she padded past Eddie in stockinged feet. "I cannot wait to get out of here tonight," she said.

"Hot date?" Eddie asked.

"Hardly." Marian rolled her eyes, and then paused near the door of her dressing room. "I'm exhausted and my tootsies are killing me. I'd cut my feet off if it didn't mean Mr. Blanchard would fire me." She looked at Eddie, who chuckled. "What about you?"

"Nothing planned for tonight. Figure I'll just go home and sleep so we can do all this again tomorrow."

Marian smiled and kissed his cheek. "Good night, Eddie." Then she retreated into her dressing room and slammed her door in his face.

Eddie went to his room to change. He wasn't the least bit tired. No, his ailment was much worse: he was horny.

His restlessness had been building for days, starting as an itch and progressing to an all-out yearning, an uneasiness that wouldn't be quenched by Eddie pushing his needs aside.

He considered his options as he changed out of his costume and slid into a pair of brown trousers and a white cotton shirt. He could go home and forget about it. He could keep his regular appointment with his right hand. Or he could find someone who would help him take the edge off.

He washed the stage makeup off his face and examined his reflection in the mirror. He hadn't shaved in a couple of days, something Mr. Blanchard had taken exception to before showtime that day. The stubble looked like bronze dust on his otherwise pale jaw. His eyes looked tired. Eddie let his fingers dance over the black powder he kept on hand for the occasions when Blanchard wanted him to do blackface—thankfully, rare these days—and then dusted some over his eyes. He liked the effect, which created rings around his eyes and made him look a little less rosy and innocent, as he tended to present in his normal life. He grabbed his fedora from the shelf in the corner and plopped it on his head. He pulled the brim down so it hid his eyes. He thought himself hard to recognize as he posed in the mirror, his eyes hidden, his chin shadowed.

Mind made up, he slipped out of his dressing room and then out of the stage door, onto 41st Street. The cool spring air bit his exposed skin, but he liked it, liked the contrast to the sweltering lights of the stage. He adjusted the brim of his hat and walked.

He fingered the money clip in his pocket, tried to remember how much cash he had on hand. Behind him, he could hear a roar of applause from one of the theaters, though whether it was from the Doozies or one of the productions in the four other theaters nearby, Eddie couldn't tell. It didn't much matter. He was about to leave that world—the dancers, the lights, the laughter, the applause, the cute little families out for a night of entertainment—to go to a much darker place.

He walked east. The lights of Times Square seemed to fade as he left them behind, and then he was standing on one side of Sixth Avenue, the elevated train platform separating him from Bryant Park. He pulled the brim of his hat down a little farther and looked around. There was a man standing against a pillar, the train platform above casting striped shadows over his body. He was tall and thin with an elegant stance. A cigarette dangled from his long fingers, and he would occasionally lift it up to his lips and take a drag. He wore a dark coat and had a bright red scarf tied around his neck.

Julian, Eddie thought. *Maybe this will be easier than I expected.*

He approached slowly. Julian was looking at something in the distance, but he turned his head when Eddie got close. There was something wary in his eyes. Eddie lifted his hat so Julian could see his face, and something like relief showed over those delicate features before a wide grin spread across Julian's face.

"Dearest Edward. Funny meeting you here."

"How are you, Julian?"

"Marvelous." He took a long drag from his cigarette before dropping it and smothering it with the tip of his shoe. "You looking for something?"

"I am."

Julian nodded. "There's a new boy in my employ. He fancies himself my apprentice. He's over by the library. I can fetch him, if you like."

"I don't want a boy," Eddie said.

Julian smiled. "I know, darling. I was just offering." He reached over and stroked Eddie's arm.

Up close, Eddie could see the makeup caked on Julian's face, designed to make him look much younger than he really was. Eddie had known Julian for a while, but had never been able to ascertain his actual age. If he had to guess, he'd put Julian in his late thirties. Under the makeup, Eddie knew, there were crow's feet and frown lines. Strands of silver ran through his body hair, though the hair on his head was, of course, bleached blond.

Eddie looked at the aging fairy and saw that he was tired and underdressed for the weather. "You want a warm place to sleep tonight, Julian?"

"I would, yes," Julian said quietly.

Eddie crooked his finger so that Julian would follow. Julian pushed off the pillar and fell into step next to Eddie, who walked back toward Times Square along 40th Street.

"Dinner?" Eddie asked.

"No, darling, I already ate. An older gentleman named Roberto takes me to Sardi's every Thursday and buys me dinner just for the pleasure of watching me eat."

Eddie glanced at Julian. He could imagine that watching him eat would be quite a pleasure. He thought Julian beautiful, but of course couldn't say that. Men were not beautiful. Julian would probably joke that he was something else, but Eddie thought him a man in all the ways that counted, in all the ways that he needed to ease the tension and longing that had built up in his body.

"You're still at the Knickerbocker?" Julian asked.

"Yes. I'd prefer to go in through the Broadway entrance." Which was not through the main lobby where everyone could see what Eddie was up to.

"Of course." Julian fiddled with his scarf. "Fancy digs or not, my usual fee still applies. Don't stiff me." Julian paused and then chuckled. "Well, not monetarily, anyway."

Later, as Eddie lay awake in bed, contemplating the décor in his relatively modest room with Julian sound asleep and snoring softly beside him, he reflected on how he felt physically satisfied but empty at the same time.

The loneliness was familiar, was a comfort in its way. The knowledge that Julian would be gone in a few hours, that this room and its silence would be waiting for Eddie after the noise of the theater the next night, that life would carry on as it had been, these were all things he could trust and rely on, and a thousand days played out before him in his mind, days of the same. Eddie liked routine, thrived within the confines of it, but could he really go so long without change?

Julian stirred in his sleep. Eddie shuffled over in the bed and pulled the quilt up to his chin, careful not to let their bodies touch.

He chastised himself for his own fear of change. He glanced over at Julian's sleeping form and let himself imagine what it would be like if they forged some kind of partnership. He'd met other men like himself over the years, men who lived together or had some kind of permanent relationship. He even knew a few husbands. Having worked in the theater for a number of years, he encountered homosexual men almost daily, and often they acknowledged each other without much fanfare, which was just as well. Eddie wanted people to notice him for his dancing or his comedic chops; he didn't want them to notice after whom he lusted.

So he kept his little secret tucked away in the hidden corners of the city.

Julian stirred again. He woke and looked at Eddie. "You're awake."

"Just thinking."

"Such heavy thoughts you must have to be wearing such a serious expression." Julian leaned over and ran a hand down Eddie's chest. "Maybe I can help unburden you."

Eddie sighed. He gently moved Julian's hand back to the other side of the bed. "Thanks, but not right now."

Julian rolled onto his back. "You should know, I might have to move."

"What?"

"I adore you, you know that I do. I'm always glad when you wander over to the park. But I'm not sure how much longer you'll be able to find me there. Some club on Sixth didn't pay off their local law enforcement, so a raiding party got themselves worked up into a good frenzy a couple of days ago. They came to the park and arrested everyone who wasn't dressed like he was on the way to a funeral."

"You too?"

"No, I was visiting with a gentleman at the Hotel Astor, but my dear friend Jesse told me all about it. You'll know Jesse, of course. He's the fellow with the proclivity for violet."

Eddie had no idea to whom Julian referred, but he nodded.

"Not that I haven't been arrested before," Julian added.

"So where are you moving to?"

"I don't know yet, darling. And it may not even be a problem. But should you come to the park looking for something, you may not find it there for much longer." Julian rubbed a hand over his face. "Can I leave word for you somewhere?"

That seemed like a terrible idea. "No. I'll find you, I'm sure." But even if he didn't, Eddie was surprised that the prospect of not seeing Julian again was not too dire.

And what did that say about Eddie?

"Maybe I should go," Julian said, sitting up.

In the moonlight streaming through the window, Julian appeared to be an entirely different creature, less an effeminate affectation and more an actual man in his late thirties, a man who worked for a living, who had dreams deferred and given up on, who had come here tonight to do a job. Eddie wondered how much of Julian was real and how much was an act. As a rule, Eddie had long been fascinated by the fairy men who occupied the streets of New York, the queens who talked like women and dressed like them sometimes, too. He had never found them especially attractive—in fact, looking at a fairy sometimes brought shame, because Eddie, behind all other things, was a man who lusted after men the way he was supposed to lust after women. But here was Julian, thin and willowy, but with short blond hair on his head, and long limbs and broad shoulders. He had a pattern of blond hair on his flat chest that was unrelentingly masculine, and a large cock, of course, which was part of his appeal to Eddie just to begin with.

And Eddie found himself lusting again.

"You don't have to go," he told Julian, and he reached over and ran a hand over Julian's shoulder. "I'm sorry, I don't mean to be mean, I just have a reputation . . ."

"I understand, darling. Of course I understand. I didn't mean to imply . . ."

"I just . . ."

"I know."

Eddie frowned. "I need to keep my job. I've worked so hard."

"I need to keep mine, too."

Eddie sighed. "If you have to leave the park, I will find you. Or you can find me. I go to the club at the Astor sometimes."

"Where the sailors hang out."

"Yes."

Julian smirked. "I suppose that you are a man of sophistication. You like the trade. The big brawny men, the soldiers of fortune."

Eddie couldn't deny that. "I like to look at them, yes."

"And fuck them. I like to, too."

Eddie sighed. It was hard to believe he was having this conversation.

"But you don't want me to find you," Julian said. "It doesn't matter, I just thought . . . well, I figured you liked me."

"I do like you, Julian." Or Julian was a good companion for tonight. For any night. He had a working knowledge of men's bodies that could not be rivaled, and he could make Eddie forget his problems and his loneliness.

But was there anything more lonely than lying in bed next to a man who would take your money and leave in the morning?

Eddie sat up and pulled his legs up to his chest. He knew, too, that part of Julian's seeming affection now was borne of the fact that, when their encounters were over, Eddie didn't beat the shit out of Julian. In the thin white light that flooded the room, Eddie could see the bruises on Julian's torso from the last john who'd felt the need to prove his masculinity by pounding his fists into the effete object of his affection. Eddie wasn't sure if he should feel reassured by that, if it was a good thing that he made Julian feel safe.

"I'm sorry," Julian said softly, as if maybe he wasn't sure about that, either. "I do care about you. I won't come after you. If after tonight we don't see each other, I hope that things go well for you. Maybe I'll come see that show of yours sometime."

"Sure. It's very good. Or so I've been told." Eddie wasn't sure how the usual crowd at the James Theater would deal with a man like Julian.

"I'm sure that you are perfectly marvelous in it." Julian reached over and caressed Eddie's hair. He smiled affectionately. "But if I don't see you, good luck."

"You too."

"I don't need luck. I make my own." Julian grinned. "Perhaps you would like one last tussle with me. Free of charge."

When Julian reached for Eddie, Eddie let himself be pulled into those long arms. He wasn't feeling especially affectionate. If anything, the encounter felt more than anything like a good-bye. Would he ever see Julian again? He wondered as they moved and moaned and sweated together, and when Julian cried out at the end, something in Eddie's heart closed off.

Eddie got up afterward and went to the restroom. On his way, he left Julian's fee on the dresser. When he returned to the bedroom, Julian was gone and so was the money. Just as well, Eddie thought, returning to bed. The sheets smelled like sex and Julian, and it was enough to let Eddie sink into sleep.

Chapter 2

"Nobody Knows You When You're Down and Out"

In 1922, three important things had happened to Lane Carillo: he got engaged, he broke his engagement, and he ran off to New York with his bride's brother.

They were still in New York eight months later when shame and guilt finally drove Scott off the side of the Brooklyn Bridge. And it was the moment Lane saw the police drag Scott's bloated, lifeless body out of the East River that confirmed for him what he already suspected: he'd never be able to go home again. The scandal was bad enough, but he could not face his family now that he had essentially killed Scott.

The next year had been equally momentous. In his numb haze, he'd reached out to a cousin for a job, any job, and he'd been given a gun and enough money to buy a new suit. It was later that year that Jimmy Ribello had pulled a gun on Lane and told him a faggot had no place in the family business.

That was the first and last time a member of the family challenged Lane's masculinity. Sometimes when he closed his eyes, he could still see Ribello's blood pooling on the floor.

Now he sat at a corner table at Lenny's, a restaurant on Broadway near Times Square that was something of an art deco explosion on the inside, and he contemplated the bowl of soup before him as he listened to conversation buzzing through the dining room. David Epstein held court at the table in the opposite corner. Lane kept an eye on Epstein as he carried on meetings, but tried to focus more on his soup.

Mickey Maroni slid into the chair across from Lane. "I need fifty simoleons."

Lane rolled his eyes. "What for?"

Mickey leaned forward and lowered his voice. "Legs says we gotta pay Hardy again or we're gonna get raided. Plus I heard Mook say he's got a delivery of white lightning coming in next week that we want to be in on."

"Why do you think fifty dollars will accomplish all that?"

Mickey frowned. "Well, see, I got a little here, and I thought . . ."

Lane grunted his disapproval. Mickey was a relatively new soldier, and a real amateur at that. Lane thought him more like a bee buzzing around his ear. "I'll talk to Legs," Lane said, effectively cutting Mickey out of the equation. He casually lifted the edge of his jacket so Mickey could see the gun hidden there.

"Oh. Thank you, sir." Mickey moved to stand up, but then he settled back into his chair. "And Mook's delivery?"

"I'll take care of it."

Mickey slapped his hand on the table. "You're darb. I owe you one."

"Get out of here, Mickey."

When Mickey had left, Lane raised his hand slightly. Timmy, one of Epstein's runners, appeared at his side. "Get me Legs Aurelio. Then go find Callahan and ask if he knows anything about a shipment coming in next week."

"You got it, boss."

Timmy ran off, so Lane went back to contemplating his dinner. The soup was light and creamy, but Lane didn't have much of an appetite, thinking now instead about cops and shipments, which he supposed was an improvement over thinking about Scott or poor, dead Jimmy Ribello. And still, he went back to trying to recall the details of Scott's face, that look in his eye that had convinced Lane they should hop the train in Chicago that took them to New York. It was difficult to do; the finer parts of Scott's features were faded like a blurry photograph from his memory.

Legs showed up then. Before he even opened his mouth, Lane said, "Did you send Mickey to ask me for fifty dollars?"

Legs's eyes widened. "That idiot asked you for fifty rubes?" He sat, looking chastened. "No. Sorry, boss, but no, absolutely not. I told him to tell you that Hardy's been making noise, and I'm thinking that if Epstein wants to get this new venture off the ground, I'm going to need to make arrangements." He shook his head. "For a lot more than fifty dollars."

"I figured." Lane considered. "I don't have much cash at hand, but let me talk to Epstein."

"Great. Thanks, Carillo."

"You know anything about a shipment coming in next week?"

"Mook said something about some rotgut coming in from one of the boats off the coast." Legs leaned in and lowered his voice. "Between you and me, I think it's more of that hooey from New Jersey that tastes like formaldehyde. You can't give that stuff away."

Lane dismissed him. He rubbed his face and looked around the restaurant. At this time of night, nearly everyone in Lenny's was affiliated with either Epstein or Giambino or Joe the Boss Masseria or someone else lurking in the shadows. Lane had, in fact, caught sight of Arnold Rothstein earlier in the evening, though he seemed to have moved on to somewhere else in the interim.

Epstein shooed away the man he was talking to, some flunky Lane recognized but couldn't name. The flunky came over to Lane's table and said, "Mr. Epstein wants to see you."

Lane looked at his soup. He lifted the bowl to his mouth and intended to sip some but realized it had gone cold. He put it back on the table and stood up.

When he got to Epstein's table, Epstein gestured for him to sit.

Lane sat and looked over Epstein. He was a corpulent man with dark hair streaked with silver and several extra chins. He looked very much like the well-fed fat cat he was, and his large size made him an imposing figure when he had to do business. Half the city was terrified of him, and Lane had to admit that he would never have wanted that dark gaze looking at him with disdain.

"Hello, Lane," Epstein said cheerfully. "I see you've been doing business tonight. Is everything all right with you? Your dinner okay?"

"I'm fine, sir. I wasn't very hungry tonight, but, you know, everything here is good."

Epstein nodded. "Yes, well. What was your business?"

Lane sighed. "Well, we have to pay Officer Hardy. He's making noises about raids again."

"All right. What else?"

"Rumor has it that Mook has a shipment coming in from some rum runners, but it sounds like it's tainted or not good. I don't think it's worth buying. Mook has never been reliable anyway."

"I agree. Anything else?"

"No. Just that my soup got cold."

Epstein chuckled. "That's a damn shame. I'll take care of Hardy. I have a different job for you."

Lane had been expecting this for a while. Epstein had been dropping hints for weeks that he wanted Lane to do something related to his new business venture, but he'd been cagey about the details. "What is the job, sir?"

"As you know, I'm looking to open a new nightclub. I think you'd be in a unique position to run it."

Lane frowned. "Run it, sir?" Lane wondered what his unique qualification was. Probably loyalty. He'd been working for the Giambino family, and Epstein specifically, for a long time now. He and Epstein were not exactly friends, but Epstein seemed to respect him. Lane had regrets about some of the things he'd done over the years, but the job meant he could continue to afford to live in his apartment on 26th Street, with Scott's memories. "I don't know anything more about running a nightclub than Legs Aurelio does." And Aurelio, at least, had the advantage of being a close cousin of the Giambino family's underboss.

Lane's family connection was a little more tenuous. The Carillos were Sicilian, at least, which had been Lane's ticket in when he'd needed a job, and he had a cousin who was a favored son. Yet much of *La Cosa Nostra* considered Lane an outsider, since he hadn't run around with the gangs downtown in his younger days like everyone else had. Hell, even Epstein had once been a member of the Eastman gang and grown up on the same block as Carlo Giambino himself. Epstein was always doing special favors for his old friends, which was how he'd come to be an associate of the Giambino family, despite the fact that he had no Sicilian roots.

But Lane was good with money, kept a level head in a crisis, and, more to the point, had made it clear that anyone who dared call him a cocksucker would meet the same fate as Jimmy Ribello. He'd been working his way up the family leadership hierarchy ever since.

A smile spread across Epstein's face slowly. "This is not just any club. I'm looking to fill a niche. One left open when such venerable establishments as Paresis Hall closed."

Lane bit back a groan. It immediately became clear to him what Epstein was doing, and he wanted no part of it. He shook his head. "Sir, some of those clubs got shut down for a reason, and if you really think that—"

"This is a brilliant idea. And I want you to run it."

"Why me, sir?" As if that weren't obvious. Lane, of course, knew why he'd been chosen.

Epstein sat back and scratched his chins. "We've known each other a long time. I like you. I admit that the way you are, I don't understand it. I love women. I love how they look, I love how their voices sound, and if I'm in a club, I want to be surrounded by beautiful women. But you. I know all about you, Carillo. And I know that you could find a way to make a club for men like you work."

Lane looked at Epstein and wondered what would possess him to think such a thing. Surely Epstein knew that just because Lane had certain proclivities, it didn't mean he could run a whole club on his own. "You realize you're limiting your clientele."

"A clientele not currently served by many other clubs in the city. I've looked around."

Lane sank into the chair and contemplated the pros and cons of the offer. On the one hand, wasn't this what he wanted? He'd been a little bored for a while, and this was an excellent opportunity. Running one of David Epstein's nightclubs was certainly a step up. It was a chance to prove he deserved to be a *caporegime*. On the other hand, did he really want to be associated with a club that catered to queers? Would that be advertising his own queerness?

"How much control would I have?" Lane asked.

Epstein laughed. "I like how you think, Carillo." He looked at the table for a brief moment. "You still report to me, and we run things my way, but you would have some discretion over the entertainment, and you'd be the person on hand to solve problems."

Lane still wasn't sure what to say. He stayed silent as he thought it over.

Epstein tapped the table to get his attention. "I'm surprised you're this hesitant. I thought this project would be right up your alley. I know you go to places like the Hotel Astor bar. Mook told me he saw you there with a sailor. I know you're a fag. Do I care? Not a whit. I don't get it, but I believe in personal liberty, let's say. Just as I should be able to make a dollar in the way I choose, so too should you be able to choose how you find your pleasure. Just like any man should be able to choose how he wishes to spend his time."

"It's not that I disagree . . ."

"You're a smart fella, Carillo. You can do this job. I want you for it. And I am going to open this club with or without you, so you might as well take it. I can't guarantee I've got anything else for you to do."

Lane rubbed his forehead. "In other words, I take this job or I'm fired."

"I did not say that." Epstein's face went hard and stern. "It is in your best interest to take the job, though."

So there it was. Lane didn't have much of a choice.

"Why are you holding out?" Epstein asked.

Lane struggled with the most succinct way to sum up how he was feeling. "Everyone will know, sir."

Epstein furrowed his dark brow, but then he all of a sudden seemed to get it and his eyes widened. "They would know your secret."

Some secret, though, if Lane's boss already knew. Who else mattered? What jeopardy would come to him if the whole city knew he was queer? It's not like he'd be arrested for indecency again. Epstein would protect him. That was the other advantage to being a member of this organization: the cops wouldn't touch him.

"I'll do it," he said.

Epstein laughed. "Of course you will."

Could he run a club? Did he want to? Lane shook his head. "Do I have any power over who works for me?"

"All right. Yes. You can choose which of these guys you want to work with you, although I want Legs in there, and Callahan."

"To keep an eye on me."

"Legs is dumb as a brick, but he's good at what he does." Epstein crossed his arms over his chest and scanned the room. "Callahan's good with money. He'll help you keep the joint open."

Lane wanted to hold out for something else, but he nodded. "You have a name for this club yet?"

That slow grin spread across Epstein's face again. "Of course! It will be called the Marigold Club."

Lane should have known. It was a good name in many ways, but it sounded feminine. So Epstein intended for it to be a pansy bar, something that didn't really appeal to Lane. It was a hard sell, for one. There were a dozen speakeasies in Harlem and Greenwich Village that catered to effeminate men and female impersonators and the like, so what reason would they have to come to Times Square? But Epstein's opinion ruled, and there wasn't much room for Lane to argue.

Also, Lane preferred his men masculine. Rough trade, as they called it, definitely appealed. It had been a while since Lane had been with a man. The last time the Navy had been in town was the last time Lane had gotten anywhere near sex. He'd met a bunch of sailors at the Hotel Astor bar and, yes, had taken one of them home with him.

"It's a good name," he said, trying to focus back on the issue at hand.

"I knew you'd approve." Epstein looked smug. Lane thought him a clown in many ways, and it was hard to remember that this man controlled a substantial portion of the city. "I have a deal going with a man to keep the place wet. I'll have him talk to you. Did you ever get that telephone installed in your apartment?"

"Yes, two weeks ago."

"Good, good. We're in business, then."

They shook on it. Lane let Epstein talk his ear off for a while about details and then reminded him that something needed to be done about Al Hardy, a cop and self-appointed Volstead Act enforcement agent. Lane was pretty sure Hardy didn't care about alcohol one way or the other, but he liked getting his palm greased.

Lane coughed.

"I hope it's not the flu," Epstein said, although Lane didn't detect much genuine concern behind the sentiment.

"I'm fine. Getting over a cold. It's much better than it was a few days ago."

"Go home. I can handle things for the rest of the night."

"Are you sure?"

Epstein grinned and spread his arms wide. "Yes. Go home and rest up. We'll meet in the morning to start planning."

That suited Lane fine. "Great. I look forward to it."

They shook hands again and then Lane excused himself. He was happy enough to go home. He opted to walk; the spring night was nice enough. On the way, he thought about this new venture and thought of all the ways it could go horribly wrong. Paresis Hall had, in its last days, been largely a place men went to pick up working boys. Lane wondered if the queer community wouldn't be better served by a place where men could meet each other instead of paying teenagers for sex. As he walked, he came up with many ideas and possibilities. Yes, it was probably a disastrous idea and they'd get shut down by the cops inside of a month, but this place had the potential to be something really great. *If* Lane could figure out how to make that happen.

Chapter 3

"In a Mist"

Eddie sat in Marian's dressing room and watched her clean off her makeup. She smiled at him in the mirror and picked up a jar of cold cream. "How are you, Eddie, really? You've seemed sad the last couple of days."

"I'm all right."

"You want to go out tonight? I heard that there's a good band playing tonight at the Shay Club on Fifty-third."

Eddie did want to go out. Part of him was still thinking about Julian. Eddie was doubtful he'd see Julian again; if the cops were after the merry band of boys who occupied the park, it probably wasn't safe to seek him out. Eddie wondered where he would go the next time the need struck, though. He said aloud something that had been on his mind. "I heard a new club opened on Forty-eighth, right off Broadway."

"Really? I hadn't heard." Marian leaned closer to the mirror and appeared to inspect her face to make sure the makeup was gone. "Usually Walter Winchell or Lois Long writes about those places in their columns, but I don't remember any mention of a new club recently. What's it called?"

Eddie hesitated. He wondered if Marian would get it or if she would judge him. Or both. He suspected that she had some notion of what his inner life was like, but they'd never had a real conversation about it, despite their many years of friendship. "The Marigold," he said.

Marian dropped the cloth she'd been wiping her face with and turned around. "You don't want to go there, do you?"

So she did know about the club. "I just wanted to look at it," he said.

Marian shook her head. "First of all, that's an Epstein club, isn't it?"

"So are a dozen clubs around Times Square."

"He's a real sleaze. I'm not so naïve that I don't know most of the joints in this city are owned by the Mob, but everyone knows Epstein will do anything to make a buck, including swindling his customers. Second, that's a . . . you know."

Eddie raised an eyebrow.

Marian whispered, "It's a club for fairies."

Eddie bristled. That actually was contrary to what he'd heard. The buzz he'd overheard from a couple of the stagehands at the James Theater was that this place, like the Hotel Astor, catered to a wide variety of men who were interested in other men, so sure, there were female impersonators and probably a few fairies, but there were also rougher sorts, sailors and what he'd heard called wolves, the masculine men who liked to prey on the fey youths that often populated the seedier parts of the city. Eddie had been able to eavesdrop on those stagehands undetected long enough to hear one of them mention the password to get into the club.

"I'm not a fairy," he said. It came out more defensive than he intended.

"I know." Marian sighed. "That's why I don't think you should go there."

"Fine, I won't. Let's go to the Shay. Which band is playing?"

"Not sure. A new one, I think. The pianist worked for Gershwin, I heard."

When Marian finished applying fresh makeup, they left the theater together and walked arm-in-arm up Broadway to the Shay Club. The band was competent though not exceptional, but Marian made the most of it, talking Eddie into dancing even though her feet must have ached after the performance that night. Eddie's certainly did.

Close to midnight, Marian said she was tired. Eddie offered to walk her home, but instead, she got in a cab and headed uptown. Eddie watched the cab disappear up Broadway before he walked back down to 48th Street.

He was greeted at the door of the Marigold Club by a woman in flapper garb—a long, shapeless dress covered in shiny fringe, chin-length curly hair, and a long string of metallic beads hanging from her neck. "Hello," she said in a deep voice when Eddie smiled at her. "What can I do for you tonight?"

"Flo sent me," Eddie said.

"Well, why didn't you say so?" The woman—the impersonator, Eddie clarified in his own head, for this woman had stubble and an Adam's apple and an unmistakably baritone voice—pulled back the curtain behind her. "Go ahead in, my dear. My name is Etta, if you decide you need someone to dance with later."

Eddie took a cautious step forward and was immediately pulled into a room full of hot air and cool tempers. Everything was draped in red velvet and blue fabric. Men around him danced and sang and cavorted. It was everything he expected and nothing like he could have anticipated.

He pulled down the brim of his fedora, took a look around, and tried to get a handle on the situation. Did anyone recognize him? It didn't seem so; his arrival was unheralded and no one so much as spared him a glance. Was there anyone he recognized? Not for certain. A few faces seemed vaguely familiar, like they might have been stagehands or people he worked with at the theater. No one whose name he could recall. Did anyone there catch his eye? Wasn't that the bigger question?

There was one man, sitting by himself at a table in the corner, smoking a cigarette. He seemed to be surveying the room as well. He occasionally put the cigarette in an ashtray and picked up a highball glass full of God knew what and took a slow sip. He was remarkably handsome, that was what Eddie noticed, with a shock of black hair on top of his head, dark eyes, and a shadow of stubble along his chin. He was athletic-looking, too; thin, but with broad shoulders. He had olive skin, like maybe he was Italian or Greek. He was a sheik, Eddie thought, like Valentino.

Eddie found himself drawn to this stranger for reasons he couldn't articulate beyond that he liked the man's face, liked his masculine carriage, liked the way everything around him seemed to spell *man*—and he wanted to keep looking at that face for a while, wanted to see what the man's hair would feel like under his fingers, wanted to know what it would be like to kiss and taste this man.

Which of course was impossible. Or was it? There was not a single woman in this club. Eddie suspected that if he hadn't known the password, he never would have been admitted. But *this* man was seated alone at a table. Maybe his date had gone to the men's room. Maybe he was only there to look.

The man looked up and made eye contact with Eddie. He crooked his finger. *Come here*, he beckoned.

So Eddie went.

The man kicked out the other chair at his table. "Have a seat," he said.

"Hello," said Eddie as he slowly sat.

The man took a drag on his cigarette and squinted at Eddie. "Do I know you from somewhere?"

Eddie considered asking if the man had ever been to the Doozies, but then the man would know for sure who he was. And Eddie was certain he had not met this man face-to-face before. This was someone he would have remembered. "I don't think so."

The man put his cigarette on the ashtray and took a sip of his drink. "You look a little lost."

"I'm not."

"You were looking at me." The man picked the cigarette back up and took a long drag. The action drew a lot of attention to the man's mouth, his thin but soft-looking lips, and Eddie couldn't stop himself from continuing to look.

He blinked. He couldn't figure this man out. Was he dressing down Eddie? Did he really recognize him? Was he a mobster who would take offense at Eddie looking? "You're nice to look at," he said with no small measure of defiance in his voice.

He braced himself for the impact of the man's retaliation—for Eddie then recognized the small circular pin on the man's lapel as marking him as a member of some kind of Mob organization—but the man laughed. "Well, thank you," he said, still chuckling. "Are you sure we've never met? You look terribly familiar."

"I'm sure."

The man smothered the stub of his cigarette in the ashtray. He extracted a slim silver case from his pocket, opened it, and displayed a neat row of cigarettes. "You want?"

Eddie shook his head.

The man shrugged and selected one. He slid the case back into his pocket and picked up a matchbook from the table. He looked right at Eddie as he lit the cigarette. Then, as casually as Eddie had seen anyone do anything, he shook the flame off the match and said, "We don't get many celebrities in here, Mr. Cotton." He took a drag on the new cigarette. "I suppose it's early days yet, but—"

"You recognized me this whole time."

The man shrugged again. "Took me a moment, I admit. I've seen your show a time or two. Last year's Doozies. You do that husband-and-wife act with Marian France."

Eddie nodded. "Yes. But we're not actually—"

"Sure, sure."

Eddie grunted. He didn't like the man's dismissive tone. "Marian and I are close friends, but we're not married. I know a great many queer men step out on their wives in order to come to places like this, but that's not me."

"Why *did* you come here?" The smoke from the man's cigarette wafted over his face, obscuring the handsome features that were already half hidden in shadow.

Eddie wondered briefly if all the dim lighting was to fool potential raiders. If you didn't look too closely, the individual in the sparkling champagne-colored gown dancing with the man in the gray suit might have been a woman. Eddie knew it wasn't. He looked back at his table mate, who was still smoking with an amused expression on his face. "I . . ." Eddie started to say.

"Do the ladies here interest you?"

"No, not at all." That, at least, was honest.

The man nodded. "Tell me what interests you."

Eddie scanned the room briefly. He made eye contact with a few of the men, but most of them were either flamboyantly dressed or there to look at the flamboyantly dressed. Eddie looked back at the man at his table, still smoking, still smirking, and came to realize that this was the most attractive man in the club. The man's gaze met Eddie's. Some silent understanding seemed to pass between them.

"Ah," the man said. He looked down and smiled.

"Who are you?" Eddie asked.

The man put down his cigarette and offered his hand. "Lane Carillo," he said. "I run this joint."

Eddie shook his hand but felt some measure of dismay. If Carillo ran this club, that meant he worked for David Epstein, and no matter how badly Eddie wanted this man, he did not want any part of Epstein.

"Can I buy you a drink?" Carillo asked.

Eddie's first instinct was to refuse him. He didn't like the push-pull his mind was going through, and everything was becoming muddled and confusing. Eddie wanted sex. He wanted to have sex with this man in particular. Carillo seemed interesting. But he ran a disreputable club and he worked for the Mob. His name might as well have been "Bad News."

"See here, Mr. Carillo—"

"Call me Lane."

Something about that completely disarmed Eddie. That Carillo—Lane—could so calmly offer his first name.

Before Eddie could speak again, a couple of fellas with their arms linked together stumbled into the table. Lane's glass was jostled, but he simply moved it out of the way.

"Hey now," one of the men said. Then he and his companion walked away, still engaged in conversation. They laughed, and one of them said, "You see the one in blue? What a dumb Dora!"

Lane put out his second cigarette. Eddie waited for him to reach for another, but he didn't, just picked up his glass and let it dangle from his fingers. Very long, elegant fingers, it didn't escape Eddie's notice. Lane had big, strong-looking hands, but those fingers belonged on a piano player, not a mobster.

The band started playing, "A Pretty Girl Is Like a Melody." The singer changed all instances of "girl" to "boy" as he blundered through the song.

Eddie sighed. "This place is something else."

Lane laughed. "I'll tell you a secret."

"All right."

Lane waved his hand, gesturing toward the room. "This place was my boss's idea. He seemed to think that the pansy clubs downtown were not properly filling this particular niche. Times Square is where everything is happening right now. Or so my boss says. I just ran with it. If he is letting me run this place, I will make it as outlandish as I can."

"You're not worried about getting raided?"

Lane raised his hand and snapped his fingers. He made some complicated gestures with his hands, and then pointed at Eddie. Eddie turned to look and saw a man in a black suit nod and vanish into a back room. "I'm going to get raided either way. I figure I'll have some fun before I do."

"This is your idea of fun? Men in dresses?"

Lane smiled and drank the rest of his drink. The man in the black suit appeared again, this time with two highball glasses on a small tray. He handed one of those drinks to Eddie.

"Don't be such a wet blanket," said Lane as the man walked away. He took a sip of his drink. "I do like the boys to have a good time."

Eddie turned and watched a group of men dancing and singing together near where the band played. It was hard to deny that they were enjoying themselves. He turned back to Lane, who was looking at him intently.

"Why did you invite me over to your table?" Eddie asked. "Just because you recognized me?"

Lane pursed his lips and looked into his drink. "No, not at first. That is, I didn't recognize you at first, I just thought you were a good-looking fella and you looked like maybe you'd walked into the wrong joint. I couldn't imagine how that was possible if you knew the password, so then I thought you might . . . interest me. But then I realized who you were, and well, that's pretty interesting, too."

"I interest you?"

"Yes. You do."

Eddie looked at Lane's hands again. Well, that was just swell. Eddie was completely in Lane's thrall. Mob or not, he was too intrigued to walk away.

Lane leaned forward. He looked up and Eddie met his gaze. It was like a bolt of lightning, the connection they seemed to have after just meeting, by chance, in a bar for queers. Here was a handsome man, and Eddie found he couldn't look away.

Until it became clear that Lane was about to kiss him. That just wouldn't do. He leaned back and looked down.

"Oh," said Lane. He moved back to his side of the table.

Eddie looked up and the disappointment on Lane's face was like a punch to the gut. That was not what Eddie wanted. He just didn't want to kiss. He didn't kiss, as a general rule; he didn't care for it, for starters, and thought it implied more intimacy than was usually involved in his encounters with men. Lane was giving him lust-filled glances now, but that's all it was: lust. They were men, weren't they? Eddie had no need for such womanly things as cuddles and chocolate and love.

So Eddie said, "Is there somewhere we can go?"

Lane's eyes widened in surprise, but then he smirked. "Well, old boy, the shady areas here are mostly taken up with my special elixir. Which, by the way, I've noticed you haven't touched."

Eddie looked at his glass. It looked and smelled like whiskey. He picked it up and raised the glass to his lips slowly before taking a small sip. Hot damn, it *was* whiskey. He took a bigger sip. "Where did you get this?"

"Canada. Or, I should say, that's Kentucky's finest bourbon, by way of Canada. Interesting legal loophole there." Lane smiled. "Anyway, as I was saying, there's no room at the inn here, but I suppose we could go to my place. It's downtown a ways, but . . ."

Too much bother, Eddie decided. "I have a room at the Knickerbocker."

Lane guffawed. "Well, why didn't you say so?"

"When can you leave?"

"For you? Anytime."

It was a line and Eddie knew it was a line. He suspected that, as manager of this establishment, Lane wasn't actually required to be there. "Are you sure?"

"Yes. I'll put Raul in charge and then we can go."

Which was how Eddie found himself walking side by side with a mobster on a breezy spring night. As they walked down Broadway, the blinking bulbs of the signs shone on them like spotlights. There weren't many people about, which was a blessing.

It was hard not to get caught up in the fever of the night, in the way the lights bounced off the glass of the buildings, off each other, in the way the very street seemed to glow. He glanced at Lane, who was looking at the sidewalk, though it didn't escape Eddie's notice that a smile played on Lane's lips. Eddie felt like he should say something, but there didn't seem to be anything to say.

Chapter 4

"Makin' Whoopee"

Lane was a little disappointed that the rooms of a Broadway star were not more lavish. The place was nicely decorated, but mostly plain, and clearly had been occupied for a while. There were costumes and makeup scattered over the desk in the corner and a lot of clothing hanging in the closet, from what Lane could see through the open door. The bed was unmade.

He didn't know what to do with the fact that Eddie Cotton had come into the Marigold that night. *Eddie Cotton*, of all people. Lane had seen the Doozies a half dozen times in the last two years and was quite familiar with Eddie's act. He'd assumed he and Marian France were married, in fact. Lane had considered that a shame, given how breathtakingly handsome Eddie was. The man had light brown hair cut very short, which showed off a strong face with large eyes and a wide mouth. Eddie was thin, but he had a dancer's grace and delicate step. Lane enjoyed watching him move around the room, shoving clothes in drawers and picking up his clutter. It was like watching him dance.

And as Lane had contemplated what would motivate a man like Eddie Cotton to come into a club like the Marigold, he'd noticed the profound sadness in the man's dark eyes.

Lane wondered what that could be attributed to. Shame? Loneliness?

"Sorry, sorry," Eddie was saying as he continued to pick up his room. "It's a mess. I have no excuse."

"It's fine. I like it, actually. The room looks lived in."

Eddie stopped what he was doing and turned to look at Lane. As had happened in the Marigold, Lane felt a jolt when their eyes met. Lust uncoiled in his gut. He wanted this to happen, but Eddie didn't seem quite ready yet.

Lane looked at the bed, considered the rumpled sheets, and then he looked back at Eddie, who stood there with some scrap of clothing in his hand.

"I don't know what to do," Eddie said.

Lane wondered if that wasn't the first really honest thing he'd said all night. "Do you need me to explain it? I realize your father probably didn't include much about relations between men when he explained the birds and the bees, but—"

"No, not that." Eddie tossed the bit of clothing he'd been holding on the floor. "I know how sex works. I mean I don't usually meet men this way."

Lane took a step closer to Eddie. He was close enough to touch the other man, but he didn't. "How do you usually meet men?"

"The sort I want to have sex with?" Eddie asked in a whisper. Lane nodded. Eddie sighed. "I . . . don't."

Lane suspected there was something Eddie wasn't telling him. "Get out. Handsome fella like you? Who works in the theater? I find that hard to believe."

Eddie grunted. "That's not really what I meant. I can meet men, obviously. It's just that it's . . . difficult for me to just go after . . . and I can't always tell . . . well, you must know how it is. So sometimes I . . ."

Eddie didn't continue, but Lane understood what he was saying. "Right," he said.

Eddie frowned. "So I don't know what I'm doing here. Not that this situation is wholly unfamiliar, it's just . . ."

Lane took another step forward. He reached over and ran a hand down the side of Eddie's face. Eddie flinched but didn't move away from Lane's touch. Lane raised an eyebrow. "When was the last time you had sex without paying for it?"

Eddie bristled, but he didn't put much effort into being offended. He opened his mouth, but then he shrugged. "I don't know," he whispered.

"I'm not judging you. It doesn't bother me. I only wish you would calm down. I'm not here to hurt you or take your money. I just saw you tonight and thought you were handsome and interesting. And I think you saw something of that in me, too. So think of this as just a meeting between two men who have a mutual interest in each other."

Eddie nodded. Then he laughed nervously. "This is . . . not what I do. But . . . I like you."

Lane nodded. "I like you, too."

He moved in for a kiss and was rebuffed again. At the club, he'd assumed it was because Eddie wasn't comfortable kissing in public, the nature of that "public" notwithstanding, but now, when they were alone, Lane moved to kiss him and Eddie turned his head away so that Lane's lips collided with his jaw. He was close enough now to smell Eddie, though, and he smelled whiskey and cigarette smoke from the club and something minty, and he also smelled sweat and man. Tentatively, Lane pressed his lips into the stubble on the edge of Eddie's face and liked the rough texture. Then he kissed and licked and tasted and enjoyed the salty tang of Eddie's sweat. Well, he thought, if Eddie wouldn't let him taste his lips, there was plenty of other skin to sample.

Eddie moaned softly and thrust his hips forward. Lane took the opportunity to help him out of his jacket, sliding it off his shoulders and tossing it on the floor. Then Eddie's hands were on him, pulling at his tie and starting to work on the buttons of his shirt. Lane carefully divested himself of his shoulder holster and slid it into the sleeve of his jacket as he took it off, hoping Eddie wouldn't notice the gun. He didn't seem to. They helped each other out of the rest of their clothes until they were down to undergarments. Lane was aware of the man before him, sweaty and hard, and a wave of desire rushed over him, so strong he thought he'd fall over with it. He pulled Eddie toward the bed.

When Eddie stood stubbornly at the edge of the mattress, Lane rolled his eyes and pulled his undershirt off. He lay down on the bed and ran a hand over the dark hair on his chest, hoping to entice Eddie enough that he'd forget about whatever problem was making him hesitate. Eddie's eyes widened and his nostrils flared—Lane knew he had Eddie's full attention—but still he stood there. Lane's gaze traveled south and he saw the way Eddie's hard cock jutted out against the confines of his white cotton underwear.

Lane sighed. "Come here."

"How are we . . . I mean, which one of us is the . . . ?"

Lane fought not to roll his eyes again. He didn't want it to seem like he was making fun of Eddie, but he was getting frustrated. He ran a hand to his own groin and cupped his hard cock in his hand. It didn't escape his notice that Eddie looked.

"It doesn't matter," Lane said. "Come here."

"But . . ."

"Come. Here."

Eddie finally relented and crawled onto the bed. Stiffly, he lay down next to Lane. Lane moved to kiss him again, and was again rebuffed, but Eddie offered his neck. He reached over and ran his palm down Lane's chest. Lane felt Eddie's breath catch in his throat. Eddie's cock brushed against his thigh. He shuddered suddenly, his wanting Eddie slowly consuming him. He reached his hands under the stretchy fabric of Eddie's shirt and pressed his fingers against the smooth skin there. Then he tugged on the shirt and Eddie let him pull it off over his head. Eddie lay back on the bed and slid his fingers into the waistband of his undershorts. He pulled them off in one smooth movement then lay there on the bed, looking open and vulnerable and like he wanted Lane's approval.

Eddie wasn't especially hairy, but he did have lovely smooth skin and strong legs and the tight musculature of a dancer. His cock was red and hard and lay against his abdomen. Lane took the opportunity to look over every inch of Eddie and liked what he saw immensely. For his part, his own cock was starting to cry out for release, and he couldn't think of a time he'd wanted someone so badly.

"Eddie, baby," he murmured. "I don't think there has ever been anyone like you."

Eddie choked on his laughter. He rolled into Lane, who caught him and pulled him into his arms. Lane wasn't entirely sure what to expect now, but then he felt a mouth against his shoulder. Eddie took tiny nips and bites in a line across his collarbone. He lifted his chin to give Eddie better access and was rewarded with a grunt and a groan and Eddie's hungry mouth moving across his skin. Then Eddie's hands slid into Lane's underwear and grabbed at his ass, his fingers sinking into the flesh there.

"Off," Eddie grunted.

Lane was happy enough to comply, shucking his skivvies and then lying naked and pressed against Eddie's long, graceful body. Eddie took a moment to look Lane over and sighed, seemingly content with what he saw. Eddie's hands were then everywhere, sliding over Lane's torso, along the line of his hips, and between his legs to cup his balls.

Eddie's hands and fingers were magic, making Lane's skin tingle. Lane moved forward and licked along the side of Eddie's face, and then pulled his earlobe between his teeth and sucked. Eddie moaned. Yeah, that was the spot. He kept his tongue on Eddie's ear, and slid his hands over all that skin, slick now with sweat. Eddie bucked against him, and Lane found his own hips getting in on the action of their own volition, his cock pressing against Eddie's hip. Then Lane moved slightly and pulled Eddie on top of him. He opened up his legs and Eddie settled between them. He shifted his hips and *there it was.* Their cocks pressed together, and Lane loved the feeling of that smooth flesh pressed against his own. He groaned and thrust against Eddie, who grunted himself before sinking his teeth into Lane's shoulder and pumping his hips. Close, far, moving together and it felt so amazing. It was like a shock through Lane's system, all sensation concentrated where their bodies met, Eddie's body sliding against his, their cocks sliding together, their balls colliding, their skin pressed on each other.

Eddie's body started to curl in on itself, his back arching. Lane reached up and pressed his hands into Eddie's back to keep him near, feeling surrounded by smell and taste and sensation. Eddie kept thrusting, and Lane thrust back, creating a delicious friction, and he felt his release growing and mounting. He was getting closer and closer . . .

"Fuck," Eddie grunted. "Fuck, *fuck* . . ."

Eddie's prick seemed to vibrate between them and then Lane felt Eddie's hot release on his belly and he groaned. Eddie cried out and clawed at Lane, and then Lane tripped and fell right over the edge, digging his nails into Eddie's back as the climax clobbered him and he let go between them, his release mixing with Eddie's, hot and sticky, like glue on their skin.

Lane regained the ability to think and noticed that Eddie had collapsed on top of him and was panting. He propped himself up with his hands pressed into the mattress and looked down at Lane, a small smile on his face.

Lane really wanted to kiss those pink lips of Eddie's. He wanted to taste Eddie, to suck that lower lip between his teeth. He lifted his head and moved to do so, but Eddie turned his head.

"I don't like kissing," he said.

Lane sighed and let his head drop back on the pillow. "I noticed."

"I mean no offense. I just don't kiss."

"Swell."

Eddie coughed and rolled off Lane.

"What does it matter?" Eddie asked. "You got what you wanted."

Lane wondered if he really did. He felt like he'd only just gotten a small taste of Eddie, hardly the whole entrée. Not that this encounter had not been thoroughly satisfying. "Sure, I got what I came for. But I've changed my mind. I want more."

Eddie pulled the sheet up so it covered his lower half. Lane glanced over and could see the residue of their coupling drying on Eddie's belly. Eddie said, "More what? I have nothing more to give you."

Lane didn't think that was true, but he didn't argue.

"Unless you want . . ." Eddie gestured toward his backside.

"No, that's not what I meant. Forget I said anything." Frustrated, Lane rolled onto his side. "Do you mind if I stay here tonight? I'll go if you really want, but it's already pretty late." That was a neat bit of subterfuge. Lane wasn't actually much concerned with whatever rougher element came out at this time of night—he could take care of himself. Hell, he *was* the rougher element, as the gun now wedged in the sleeve of his jacket could attest. But he wanted a second chance to break through Eddie's defenses, to see if maybe there was something more here than a quick rub against each other. Eddie intrigued him as few men ever had.

Eddie sighed. "Yes, you can stay."

"I'll be out in the morning, I promise."

"It's fine."

Lane looked over at Eddie, who was frowning. "Are you all right?" he asked.

"Everything is copacetic," said Eddie.

Eddie woke up in the night and found himself drenched in sweat. He was covered by the down comforter but something else was generating heat. Then he remembered: Lane.

Lane was still fast asleep. Eddie looked him over. His mouth was agape and a fringe of dark hair fell over his forehead. Flashes of memory from the night spent together paraded through his mind. He felt himself blushing as he remembered what this man—this breathtakingly handsome, somewhat hairy, and completely masculine man—had done to him in this bed.

And he remembered the look of disappointment on Lane's face when Eddie had explained about the kissing.

Well, he thought, getting out of bed. *Nothing gold can stay.*

He went to the bathroom. He ran a cold cloth over his sticky skin, and then he washed his face.

What was it about this man? He thought of Lane sitting in the Marigold smoking, how the cigarette had just hung from his fingers. He thought of that mouth, of the places it had traveled on his body. It had been such a long time since he'd had a partner whom he hadn't sought out and paid, though he supposed there had been times, before he had made it big on Broadway, that he'd been able to meet men with potential. He hadn't really expected to again, and yet, here was Lane, with his dark good looks and his voice like velvet and his hands and his mouth and everything.

Eddie rinsed the cloth and glanced out the window, where the sun was rising over the tall buildings in the distance. He had rehearsal time booked at the theater first thing in the morning, but part of him wanted to linger in bed with Lane, to see what, if anything, might happen between them. Lane had wanted more, wasn't that what he'd said the night before? Eddie didn't have much to give, but he was finding himself feeling strangely optimistic. Maybe it was worth giving it a shot.

He tossed the washcloth over a towel rack then returned to his bedroom. At first all he saw was the rumpled bedding. He smiled to himself as he thought about sinking into that soft bed and into Lane's strong arms.

But then he noticed: Lane was gone.

Eddie considered calling out for him. Maybe he'd disappeared into some corner of the room Eddie couldn't see. But Eddie noticed his clothes were gone, too, and he knew, deep down, that Lane had slipped through his fingers.

Too good to be true, he thought, sitting on the edge of the bed. Or else he'd dreamed it. He leaned forward and rested his head in his hands.

Chapter 5

"Without a Song"

Marian walked to the stoop of Jimmy Blanchard's five-story house on 26th Street. It was a little warm for the fur coat she'd donned before leaving her apartment, but she was determined to look stylish for her meeting with Jimmy.

Clyde, Jimmy's secretary, let her in and led her to the third floor before depositing her near a sofa and leaving again. Through the whole transaction, Clyde didn't say a word. Marian sighed and waited near the sofa, mildly concerned that Jimmy wasn't even home. It would be just like Clyde to just leave her there for an hour.

She slid her fur coat off and draped it over the arm of the sofa. She crossed her arms and waited.

Jimmy walked in a few minutes later. Marian was struck at first the way she always was by his handsomeness. He had curly dark-blond hair washed with gray that he kept cut short, a rectangular face, and a lean body that he often kept covered up with one of the many neatly tailored dark suits he owned. Today was no exception; he wore a gray suit with a red tie and he looked every inch the slick professional that he was. He smiled at her as he entered the room.

"Hello, my dear," he said. "How are you?"

"I'm just lovely." She uncrossed her arms and ran a hand down the front of the red day dress she'd put on that morning. She'd had the dress made for her, modeled after a design by Coco Chanel that she'd seen in a magazine. It had been an extravagant purchase, but she liked how it skimmed her body. Marian considered 1927 a good time for fashion; it was so much more accommodating of her boyish figure than the previous decade had been.

Jimmy stepped forward and took her hand. He raised it to his lips and lightly kissed her knuckles. "You are lovely," he said.

Marian wondered at the protocol. Would it be appropriate to jump into his arms? Should she make polite conversation? "Is anyone else here?" she asked. Jimmy did a lot of business at the house on Saturday mornings.

"I just had a meeting with Walter Rhodes, but he left a few minutes before you arrived. He's a composer. You'd like him. He's writing a few songs for next year's *Le Tumulte*, real showstoppers." Jimmy grinned. "I asked him to write a song for you."

"For me?"

"Yes, dear. You do that clown act with Cotton very well, but I think it's time for you to shine on your own."

Marian laughed in disbelief. "That's ridiculous. Eddie and I have a good act going. I've never had a solo before. What's all this?"

Jimmy stepped away and started to pace. "You fashion yourself a comedienne, I realize, like that Fanny Brice. But you have something Fanny Brice doesn't have."

"What's that?"

"You, Marian dear, are beautiful. Brice is a hag. Plus, you do that honking thing in your act with Cotton, but I know that you're capable of so much more than that. You have a silvery voice under all that nonsense. Rhodes is a genius with lyrics. He'll write some very clever things for you. I think a ballad. Something that shows off how talented you are."

Marian shook her head. "Forget it. I do the act with Eddie."

Jimmy rolled his eyes. "Eddie Cotton is a sideshow. He can dance, sure, and he has great comic timing, but that man is not destined for greatness, not the way you are. Why, you could go to Hollywood! They're making motion pictures with sound now. You would look so marvelous, up on the big screen, where everyone could see your gorgeous face."

"Jimmy, that's crazy. I don't have any business in Hollywood."

"Forget Hollywood, then. You could be the star of *Le Tumulte*. You, Marian dear. You are my muse! Yours and Eddie's act is everyone's favorite part of the show, and you know why? It has nothing to do with Eddie Cotton, I'll tell you that."

"You flatter me." Marian felt heat flood to her face. Jimmy exaggerated, but she didn't mind him buttering her up.

"It's the truth. You can do great things." Jimmy stopped pacing and turned to face Marian. "Just humor me, all right? I'll get a few songs from Rhodes, you can take a look at them, and then we'll decide."

Marian sighed. "Yes. Whatever you say, Jimmy."

"I know you like Cotton . . ."

Marian walked over to the couch and sat down. She was aware that Jimmy had a bizarre jealous streak where Eddie was concerned, and she didn't know how to assure him that nothing would ever happen on that score. Marian had known for a long time that Eddie's preference lay with men, though that hadn't stopped her from developing a bit of a crush on him shortly after they'd met. Once it became clear that there were no sparks between them, they'd settled into an easy friendship that translated pretty well into their act, where they often played a long-suffering married couple who sang ridiculous songs about the particulars of a long relationship. Marian often took the part of the nagging wife who wanted her hard-drinking husband to just wash the darn dishes.

"Things with me and Eddie—"

Jimmy waved his hand. "It doesn't matter. You can continue your act with Cotton, no one said you couldn't, I just thought, maybe what you need is a signature song. That would be good, right?"

"Sure, Jimmy."

Satisfied, Jimmy walked over to the couch and sat beside her. "I'm glad you came by the other night. Even if you did go out with Eddie first."

"We agreed that it would be good for the show if Eddie and I were seen in public together. It added to the act, or made it more convincing. No?"

"You're right, of course you are, dear, but, well, you know."

"You have no reason to be jealous of Eddie Cotton. You know that."

Jimmy draped an arm around Marian. "Thank you, dear. It soothes my old bones to know that a woman as delightful as you can still find someone such as myself attractive."

Marian sighed and sank into Jimmy's side. "You know I do."

"Would you like to go out for dinner tonight? They just opened a new place down the block."

"Can we just sit here for a few minutes? I feel like I need the world to stop turning for just a moment."

Jimmy chuckled. Marian felt it vibrating through his chest. "That we most certainly can do, my dear. That we can do."

Eddie was on the stage of the James Theater at three in the afternoon. He moved through some new steps for the act again. Forward, forward, back, back, to the left. He thought that if Marian mimicked his movements and held her hands out just so, that could look pretty good. To the right, to the left, turn, turn. He'd hold out his cane here and lift his hat there. He pictured the whole act, how Marian would look dancing beside him, how the audience would gasp when he tried this new move, how they would stand and applaud when they finished. He was so absorbed in the routine that he didn't notice he wasn't alone until he heard a man clear his throat.

Eddie stopped abruptly and turned to see who had interrupted. It was Jimmy Blanchard. He was dressed in a slightly out-of-fashion gray suit, but his shoes were shined to perfection and there was not a hair out of place on his head.

"Sorry to barge in, Cotton." Blanchard didn't look sorry at all.

A man with brown hair and a greasy mustache walked up behind Blanchard. He also cleared his throat.

Blanchard led the man onto the stage. "Eddie, this is Walter Rhodes. He's a songwriter."

Eddie shook the new man's hand. He was familiar with Rhodes. Between Doozies seasons, Eddie always took it upon himself to walk through Tin Pan Alley, talking to songwriters and musicians to get ideas for his act for the next season. Although Blanchard had ultimate creative control, Eddie found it greased the wheels a bit if he presented a lot of ideas first and then let Blanchard decide what he liked best. Plus, Eddie just liked Tin Pan Alley, liked listening to the various musicians pound out songs on old pianos or sing little melodies as inspiration struck. Eddie had met George Gershwin that way, in fact, a few years before when he'd been trying out some new songs, hoping to sell a few to one of the revues on Broadway. Eddie had heard that Gershwin was writing opera these days, which Eddie thought a damn shame. Opera was on its way out, he would have argued. Popular music and jazz, that's where the future was headed.

Rhodes was a composer in the same mold as a younger Gershwin. He was ambitious and creative, and Eddie knew a few of his songs had become big hits. He was surprised to find him talking to Blanchard, actually, because surely Rhodes could have sold songs to better producers.

"Nice to see you again," Eddie said to Rhodes.

"Likewise," Rhodes said, shaking Eddie's hand enthusiastically. "I've enjoyed your act this season. You're an Oliver Twist, moving the way you do on that stage. Marian France is a hot dancer, too."

"Yes, Marian is great," Eddie said. "To what do I owe the pleasure?"

Blanchard grinned and slapped Eddie on the back. "That's what I like about you, Eddie. You never beat your gums. You're direct but always polite." Blanchard laughed. "I've asked Walter here to come up with a couple of songs for next season, although I've told him that if he comes up with something really swell, we'll let him try it out later this season. In fact, I, uh . . ." He glanced at Rhodes, and then looked back at Eddie. "I've asked him to write a song for Marian."

"All right," Eddie said. That struck him as odd, but he was willing to entertain the possibility. Marian had a lovely voice when she wasn't honking like a goose.

"A ballad," Rhodes said. "I want to write the song for Marian that is like 'My Man' was for Fanny Brice."

That confused Eddie. "You mean a ballad *just* for Marian? Not part of the act?"

Blanchard threw an arm around Eddie. "Now, Ed, please don't misunderstand. I'm not breaking up your act. You and Marian still have one of the most popular bits in the show. I just thought we might try something different. Show off Marian's singing chops. What do you think?"

Eddie knew he didn't actually have a say, so he shrugged. "I guess that would be all right. What about me?"

The smug expression on Blanchard's face lasted a mere moment, but it told Eddie all he needed to know. Blanchard had little interest in Eddie besides as a means to make money, but Marian was the pretty girl, the ingénue. Eddie sighed. He let Blanchard offer him some platitudes, but knew not much would come of it.

"I don't have quite the song yet," Rhodes said, "but I have some ideas, if you would care to hear them?"

"Surprise me when it's done," Eddie said.

As Rhodes and Blanchard retreated, Eddie glanced at his watch, and then surveyed the theater. He'd have to clear out and get changed soon. For show, he tried a few more steps, did a turn, and then sauntered off the stage. A wave of exhaustion hit him as he walked toward his dressing room.

He wondered when it would be his time. When he'd shine like an Eddie Cantor or a George M. Cohan. Not that he begrudged Marian her success—she was obviously talented and he loved her like a sister—but he was getting a little tired of playing the fool on stage every night, and besides, he knew if he were just given the right opportunity, he could rule Broadway.

If, that was, anyone was willing to take a chance on him, which he suspected they'd be less inclined to do if they knew who he really was, the queer Jew dancer from the Lower East Side, whose immigrant parents hadn't approved of a life in the theater and so had pretty much given up on him when he'd started taking dancing lessons. Thus he'd reinvented himself, no longer Elijah Cohen but Eddie Cotton, with feet as free as Fred Astaire's and comic timing like Charlie Chaplin's, if only someone would give him enough space to move.

He sat down on the old wooden chair he kept in his dressing room and wondered for a brief moment if he was destined to remain an also-ran. The odds of him actually finding the success he craved were slim. It was, as were most things Eddie most greatly desired, just out of his reach.

Lane stood in the kitchen at the Marigold, watching his men carry in a dozen or so large wooden crates. They stacked them near the oven. Lane looked at Mook, who had been the one to show up with this delivery. Mook was a chubby man of vague ethnicity, and no one knew what his name was aside from "Mook," which Lane was pretty sure was a nickname some girl had given him. Lane found Mook extremely unpleasant and untrustworthy, but the man had connections to hooch deliveries that Lane couldn't get to otherwise. That, and Epstein's connection had gotten himself arrested the week before, and this was what Lane could get on short notice.

He grabbed a crowbar and walked over to one of the crates. "You got the real stuff this time, right? I'm not going to open one of these cases and find out that you've brought me bottles of sacramental wine some rabbi in Brooklyn made in his bathtub."

"Gen-yoo-wine article," Mook said, gesturing to the crates. "Got a shipment from Canada. Rum and gin. It ain't the greatest, but it's real. And I'm givin' you a deal, Carillo, because I like you so much."

"How much?"

Mook quoted him a figure that was about twice what Lane really wanted to pay.

"That's not what we talked about," said Lane.

Mook walked over to one of the crates and ran his hand over the top of it. "I ran into a little extra trouble with this shipment," he said. "I got some applesauce about unauthorized boats at the docks." He shrugged.

"You didn't have this delivered directly to the city, did you?"

"No, New Jersey. You think I'm stupid?"

Lane did think Mook was stupid, but he held his tongue. He named a compromise figure. "And that's assuming I can sell this to my customers at a decent mark-up. No one's gonna pay for bad moonshine."

"Aw, come on, Carillo. I worked hard for this. I got kids to feed."

"Not my problem. You want the money or not?" For show, Lane put a hand on his hip, whipping his jacket back enough to give Mook a flash of his shoulder holster.

"Fine. Deal," said Mook. They shook on it.

Lane moved toward one of the cases. He used the crowbar to pry the top off. There were a dozen bottles in the case, lined up and cushioned with shredded newspaper. He pulled one of the unlabeled bottles out and held it up to the light. It was clear, so that was something. He motioned to one of the men and a highball glass was placed on the counter. Lane poured a finger into the glass.

"If I die, you ain't getting paid," Lane said.

"It's good, Mr. Carillo," said Mook, all seriousness now, which didn't make Lane any more confident that he wasn't about to poison himself. It wouldn't have been the first time someone died from drinking formaldehyde or some other chemical in bad hooch.

Lane placed the bottle on the counter and picked up the glass, saluting Mook. "Bottoms up."

He took a sip. Much to his surprise, it was gin, real gin, not the hooey some of Mook's cronies were making in basement distilleries, if you could call a couple of barrels and a big tub a distillery. Lane drank the rest of the gin in the glass. "Fine," he said. "We have a deal."

Mook laughed. "I love doing business with you, Carillo."

Lane paid him in cash and ushered him out the back door. When he came back into the kitchen, he spent a couple of minutes trying to figure out where he'd hide twelve cases of alcohol. As he was mentally calculating where he had space, Callahan came in through the back.

"Hello," said Callahan, his eyes wide as he took in what he saw.

"Hi, Nick." Lane handed the crowbar to one of the associates and said, "All right, men, I need you to find places to stash all this. Start with the oven over there. It ain't like we ever use it."

That was enough to get everyone in the room moving. Callahan watched for a moment, and then walked over and shook Lane's hand. "How's business?" he asked.

"Not bad," said Lane with a grin.

Etta, whose real name was John O'Leary, hurried into the kitchen then, wearing his street clothes. "So sorry I'm late, Lane," he said. Then he glanced at Callahan. A smile spread across his face. "Hello, handsome."

Which made sense; Lane had always thought Callahan to be a fine-looking fellow, with longish blond hair and a broad body. Callahan definitely liked women, though. "Barking up the wrong tree there, Etta," said Lane.

Etta crossed his arms over his chest. "What's all this?" he asked, looking around the kitchen.

"What do you think it is?"

Etta laughed. "Well. I hope you sell a lot of this horse liniment."

"I hope so, too," Lane said. "And it's your job to help me sell it. We open in an hour."

"Yes, yes. I'll go powder my nose, dear. See you later. Save a dance for me, blondie." Etta blew Callahan a kiss and flounced off.

Callahan shook his head. "I don't know how you put up with fellas like that."

Lane shrugged. "I don't mind them. Etta adds color to this place. The customers like her."

"What was Epstein thinking, opening up a joint like this? Ain't no way it'll stay open. Cops'll be crawling all over this place once they catch wind of where Mook's latest imports landed, and they *will* find out."

"So we pay them to look the other way. I've got Hardy set up—"

"Not just Hardy, Lane. I mean, yes, you fix Hardy, that's half the battle, but he's one man. The precinct catches on you've got a club open for . . . for fairies, well, that ain't gonna end well."

"Wouldn't be the first time I've slept in a jail cell for a few nights," Lane said.

Callahan laughed. "I think sometimes that you've got a death wish."

Lane sighed and started unpacking one of the crates. "Look. I thought this was a crazy idea at first, too, when Epstein first brought it up. But you know as well as I do that I couldn't turn him down. I figure I'll make the most of it. Now that I'm here, I think he was right. Business has been good. There's a certain class of men in this city that go for this kind of . . . entertainment."

"Fellas like Etta," Callahan said, gesturing toward the door through which Etta had left. "Customers pay him for sex?"

"None of my business if they do."

Callahan raised an eyebrow. "Do you pay for sex?"

Lane smiled, but he didn't find the question that humorous. "Do I look like a man who needs to pay for sex?"

Callahan shrugged. "What you do in the privacy of your own bedroom ain't none of my business. Sorry for asking. Guess I was curious. Epstein told me he put you in charge because he knows you got some queer ways of thinking about sex."

"Don't we all? You like sex, Nick?"

"Sure I do."

"So do I. I just prefer to have it with men. If that's queer, so be it."

Callahan, who knew all this about Lane already but stubbornly refused to believe it, just stood there shaking his head. "Well, anyway. I just came by because I got a couple of tickets to see a show tonight, but my sister's flig of a husband is causing trouble again and I gotta go take care of it. I thought you might be interested in the tickets. That is if you ain't too busy here."

"I can put Raul in charge, maybe. What's the show?"

"The Doozies. I ain't been yet this season, but that Marian France sure is a choice bit of calico."

Which, of course, made Lane think of Eddie Cotton. It wasn't worth mentioning to Callahan that he'd spent the night in Eddie's bed not a week before. "Sure, I'll take the tickets."

Callahan reached into his pocket and produced them. "No charge, Lane, if you hook me up with a bottle of that hooch you just got in."

It seemed the least he could do for the chance to see Eddie again, even if it would only be from a distance. He recognized that as being a little bit insane as he handed the bottle over to Callahan. And, really, what was all that about? He hadn't been this hung up on a man since . . . well, since Scott.

Callahan tucked the bottle into his coat and exited through the back door. Lane turned back to the task at hand. Theater tickets or not, he had a club to run.

Chapter 6

"Ain't Misbehavin'"

Lane put Raul, his most trusted assistant, in charge of the Marigold for the night. Epstein's *modus operandi* had always been to open a club and then abandon it, holding court at Lenny's or one of the other Times Square restaurants while his underlings made the operation work. Lane preferred a more hands-on approach, so he spent most nights at the Marigold, but tonight, the theater called.

He called his friend Clarence, another refugee from the Midwest whom he had befriended shortly after landing in New York, and they met in front of the James Theater. Clarence, who was a bit of an Anglophile, was wearing an English driving cap with what looked like the Union Jack knit onto the top. He brandished the cap when he saw Lane. When they shook hands, Clarence leaned over and kissed Lane's cheek. "Hello, dearest. I was so happy you called me."

"Did you have an overwhelming desire to see the Doozies?"

Clarence laughed. "No, doll, I missed you. I've hardly seen you at all since Mr. Epstein put you in charge of that club." He pulled his hat off as they went into the theater. "We are going to drop by the club later, right? I very much would like to see it."

And, because it was the sort of place right up Clarence's alley, Lane said, "Yes. If you like, we can go after the show."

Their seats were surprisingly good, about eight rows back in the orchestra, although off to the side. Still, close enough to see the faces of the performers.

Lane had already seen the Doozies that year, but Clarence hadn't been to a Broadway show in a very long time. "Tell me about *Le Tu-*

multe," he said, settling into his seat. He over-pronounced the French words, which made the title of the show sound that much more ridiculous.

"Well, it's not as good as the *Follies*," Lane said. "If you want a spectacle, that's what you should go to see. The performers are better, the costumes are better, and there's a lot of sparkle and razzle-dazzle. But this show has some things to recommend it, too. Personally, I think the comedians are better."

"Yes. When you called me, I asked George what he thought, and he told me to watch out for Cotton and France."

Lane nodded but thought maybe it was smarter not to react to that.

The show got underway, opening with a lively dance routine, and as the revue progressed, Lane kept thinking what he suspected everyone in the audience was thinking: *That's good, but it's not as good as the* Follies.

And then Cotton and France took the stage.

For a few minutes, all Lane could see was Eddie. He wore a finely cut black tuxedo with tails, and he looked so incredibly handsome. He danced onto the stage, his feet moving quickly and his whole body looking lighter than air. But it was Marian France who caught the rest of the audience's attention. She twirled and leaped and the light caught the beads on her costume so that every part of her seemed to sparkle.

They danced together, their bodies flying, their feet moving, and everything looked like the epitome of beauty and grace. Lane knew that Marian was a gifted dancer and could appreciate the way her body moved, the way her costume moved, but he couldn't take his eyes off Eddie.

The dance finished and the curtain rose up behind the stars to reveal a set painted to look like a fancy restaurant. And then Eddie started to sing.

He had a nice tenor voice, soft and quiet at first but gaining strength as the song progressed. It was a love song, Lane realized, except it was sort of a bawdy one, because, though it started off sweet, the first verse ended with a line about taking the lady home. Marian, for her part, made a good show of being offended, and then belted out a verse about how she knew she was lovely, and didn't they make a handsome pair, but she sounded like a bleating goat. The audience roared with laughter. They finished the song, and immediately launched into a joke routine. All the words were exaggerated and overemphasized in order to be heard throughout the theater. It was strange to hear Eddie's voice that way when he'd heard it in more intimate settings, when he'd had whole conversations, when he'd heard Eddie moaning in bed as he . . .

The audience laughed, so Lane refocused his attention on the stage.

"My brother killed over a hundred men in the war!" Eddie said.

"Oh?" said Marian. "Was he a gunner?"

"No, he was a cook!"

Rimshot.

It was an old joke, and plenty of people in the audience groaned, but it was hard not to laugh at Eddie's enthusiasm.

They finished the act with Eddie offering his hand to Marian. "Marian, my dear, may I have this dance?"

It occurred to Lane that their talents might have been wasted on a comedy act, that they both could probably act better than they did, that Marian could probably sing without sounding like a dying animal, but then they were twirling around the stage and Lane again couldn't look away.

When they danced off the stage, Clarence whistled through his teeth. "That was great!" he whisper-shouted. "And, golly, Eddie Cotton is amazing. So handsome."

To put it mildly, Lane thought.

He sat back in his chair and contemplated the stage that Eddie Cotton had just vacated. There was no denying it, he really wanted to be with Eddie again. He wanted to watch Eddie's body move, he wanted to be held in those arms, he wanted to dance with him. Not that Lane could even really do more than shuffle his feet around the dance floor, but something about that man, from the moment he'd first walked into the Marigold, had snared Lane's attention.

"Lane?" Clarence whispered.

The next act, a line of chorines in sparkly costumes, came out and started some kind of kicky dance routine. They existed more to tempt the men—well, *most* of the men—in the audience. These were the girls who got bouquets of roses sent to their dressing rooms, lines of admirers after the show, chocolates and jewelry. Lane wondered if Eddie ever garnered that kind of attention. If he wanted to.

"Lane, are you all right?"

Lane turned and looked at Clarence. "Yes, I'm swell. Why?"

"You sort of disappeared there."

"Sorry." He glanced at Clarence and then at the stage. He suspected his poker face had deserted him.

Clarence laughed under his breath. "That Mr. Cotton sure did a number on you. Can't say I don't understand. He is pretty easy on the eyes. Of course, I have George at home, and I would never want to be one of those fligs waiting around near the dressing rooms of the performers."

Lane crossed his arms over his chest.

"Unless . . ." Then Clarence, who knew his old friend well, gasped. He coughed to cover it, and there was some grumbling from the audience members around them. Clarence leaned close to Lane and hissed in his ear, "You know something about our Mr. Cotton that I don't! Isn't that true? Has he been to your club?"

Lane shrugged him off. He didn't want to admit as much. "I've seen him around. And that's all I will say."

Clarence nodded. "Sure, doll."

They watched the rest of the show, which included some kind of minstrel act with a couple of white actors in blackface that Lane thought was completely devoid of humor; a ventriloquist act that was mildly entertaining; several singers who belted out songs or soft-shoed across the stage.

Finally, the house lights came back on. Lane stood up with a sigh, glancing at Clarence. "Did you like the show?"

"Yes, I found it highly entertaining. Thank you for bringing me."

"I'm glad."

Lane realized then that one of his reasons for bringing Clarence along was so that Lane wouldn't do what he was very tempted to do, which was go to the stage door to try to see Eddie. He was sure he could fake his reasons for being there, could say he wanted to meet Marian France. He couldn't really pull that off with someone like Clarence in tow, however, and besides, he was pretty sure Clarence would ask at any minute if they could go to the Marigold.

Indeed, Clarence hung on Lane's arm a little as they maneuvered through the crowd in the lobby. When they arrived outside, Clarence said, "Take me to your little bar."

The Marigold was a seven-block walk up Broadway from the James Theater. Clarence beat his gums the whole way, chatting about nothing in particular. When they got to the Marigold, Etta greeted them enthusiastically at the door. Then they were inside the club and it was all to Lane's specifications, everything dark and hot, mysterious unless you knew what you were looking at.

Clarence squealed with delight when he saw the place. "Lane, this is wonderful! Oh, please say you will dance with me."

Lane laughed. "Okay, sure."

Clarence beamed and led Lane right to the dance floor. It was awkward at first; Lane rarely danced and in this situation, he wasn't sure if he should lead or follow. Clarence did a few improvised steps that were a variation on the Charleston, flying around the floor. Then he put his hands on Lane's shoulders. There wasn't anything particularly intimate about it—Lane wasn't interested in Clarence as a sexual partner, and besides, Clarence had his George at home—but there was something triumphant about it, about two men dancing together as if no one was watching, in plain sight of a club full of people.

So Lane abandoned his inhibitions and threw his elbows in the air and threw out his feet. He clutched Clarence's shoulders, his hips, and once got a feel of his ass, which made Clarence squeal with delight again.

They danced until they were sweaty, until they were tired, until they were free. The bandleader changed the song to something a little softer, so Lane led Clarence over to his private table in the corner. Lane thought it interesting that most of the people in the club had figured out which was the boss's table and so left it alone, which meant that maybe they had enough regulars now that word got around even when Lane wasn't there.

Raul appeared with Lane's highball and asked Clarence politely if he wanted something to drink. Clarence nodded, so Raul was off again. Lane considered the shipment they got in earlier that day and started working through numbers in his head: how much business they could expect to get, how long this shipment of hooch would last. If word got out that the Marigold had good hooch, they might attract a bigger crowd . . .

Clarence beamed as he looked around the space. "This is amazing, Lane, I've never seen anything like it. How did you pull this off?"

"It was my boss's idea."

Clarence laughed. "Epstein, that old dog. He's got a man on the side, eh?"

"No, actually. Quite the contrary. This is purely a business venture, intended to fill a niche market. A smart move, as it turns out. Business has been good."

"That's wonderful."

Raul appeared with Clarence's drink then. Clarence took a sip and smiled. "Ah, the real stuff, too. I went to this speakeasy last week with George that I think was serving us bleach. It was horrific."

"I'm sure."

"But this place. I can't wait to bring George! Is it always like this?"

Lane took a moment to survey his kingdom. He'd pulled off a good thing, he tried to tell himself, a club where men of his inclinations could come and meet and find each other and dance and just be who they were without all the nonsense and subterfuge of everyday life. Lane was tired of pretending to be something he wasn't in public sometimes.

Which made him think of Eddie and his husband-and-wife act with Marian France. Lane wondered how many people knew about the true nature of their relationship, if Marian even knew that Eddie wasn't interested in women, if Eddie was stringing her along.

"I'm considering doing some kind of show," Lane said. "Maybe on Thursdays. Etta, that's the female impersonator at the door, she has some friends who want to do some kind of act, I think with singing and dancing. And I met this trumpet player a few days ago. He's a Negro, but, good God, he can wail on that trumpet. It's really something to hear. I want him here."

"Where does he play now?"

"Harlem, mostly. Late nights, though. He's young, not established enough to get regular gigs. But he's a prodigy."

Clarence nodded. "George and I went up to Harlem last week. We saw the show at the Cotton Club, and then we wound up at this other place. George knows the owner. Doll, you ain't seen nothing like it. A club like this, with dancing and men, and the music was wild. You can't even imagine."

"You'll have to take me sometime."

Clarence fingered the fabric of the dark tablecloth draped over the table. "Sure, I'll talk to George. He knows some fellas up in Harlem who know which clubs will take customers like us. George also knows some writers. There are a whole lot of them up there. Really interesting, creative people. There's a whole world up there nobody really knows about, except now that the white people are starting to go to the clubs to hear the music. And the music . . . Lane, the music! It's like nothing you've ever heard! Much better than this band. Loud and fast and bright. It's amazing."

"I want to see it sometime."

"Or get your trumpet player here. Bring a little bit of Harlem to Times Square. Use it as a selling point. I think you've got a good thing going here."

Lane agreed, but, ever pragmatic, he said, "Until we get raided."

Clarence shrugged. "Sure, until you get raided. Or you pay off your raiding party, right?"

Lane sighed. "My luck, I get the one enforcement officer who definitely doesn't like queers."

Clarence waved his hand. "You pay him enough and it won't matter. Besides, half the force is queer."

"That's not true."

"Maybe not half. There are a lot of queer cops, though."

"Well, I've decided to enjoy all this while it lasts." Lane took a sip of his drink. He let the burn of the liquor pass through his system, felt the alcohol warm his blood. He sighed. "I'm pretty sure this is going to end in disaster."

Clarence clapped him on the back. "Well, like you said, it'll be fun until it ends, eh?"

Julian placed himself under the flickering bulb of his regular Bryant Park streetlamp and lit a cigarette. He took a long drag, letting his lips linger over the tip of it to easily tempt anyone watching from the shadows.

Unfortunately, the only one watching was a working boy who called himself Horatio. The kid was seventeen if he was a day, and he wore such ridiculously flamboyant clothes that he was practically a walking advertisement. Tonight he was dressed like a parody of a golfer, his bright red sweater tucked into a pair of baggy golf knickers, and a tweed cap atop his head, perched at a jaunty angle.

"You heard about the cop who patrols this precinct?" Horatio asked.

"Which one?"

Horatio stepped into the light and smiled conspiratorially. "He calls himself Captain Hudson."

"If that's his real name, I'm Mayor Walker," said Julian.

"Doesn't matter, does it?"

"I suppose not."

"What matters is that he won't arrest you if you give him a little attention. I heard last night that he burst into the men's room and threatened to arrest everyone there unless one of the boys took care of him. Two practically fought each other to do it."

Julian thought the story unlikely. The cops he knew who patrolled the park were more subtle than that. But he said, "As long as no one spent the night in jail."

"Might be a blessing." Horatio grunted. "I ain't had a decent place to sleep in a week. I was rooming with Sam at a place over on Fifty-seventh, but the landlord kicked us out when he found out how we was paying the rent."

"Go talk to Mrs. Bloom. She owns a building downtown. She'll take care of you, darling." Julian rattled off the address of a friendly brothel madam he knew. He'd stayed at Mrs. Bloom's in the past, though lately he'd been bouncing around the apartments of men he knew around Times Square. Business had been slow lately and he didn't have quite enough to rent a place regularly, so he was relying on the kindness of friends until he could put enough money together to get his own place. Maybe then he wouldn't have to suck strangers' cocks to survive.

"Thanks," said Horatio. "I'll keep that in mind."

There was some activity over near the restroom building, a quick shout and then nothing. "This cop," Julian said. "You've seen him?"

"Sure did. Serviced him myself three nights ago. Small cock, but—"

"What does he look like?"

Horatio shrugged, which Julian found unnerving. "He's a big fella. Tall with big shoulders, I mean. He ain't fat, though. And black hair, but he's a mick for sure. Bet his real name is O'Neil or something."

Julian agreed this was probably true, but he didn't want to dwell. He promised to keep an eye out and then told Horatio to beat it so he didn't scare off any potential customers.

When Horatio was gone, Julian adjusted the scarf at his neck. He put out his cigarette and lit a new one. He slid the matchbook pack into his pocket and glanced around the park.

Then everything went to hell.

The noise from the restroom building became a cacophony of shouting, and then a half dozen men paraded out, followed by a man in a suit—he was also shouting, but Julian couldn't make out the words from across the park—and a pair of uniformed police officers. It took Julian longer than he should have to work out that the park was being raided.

He ducked out of the light from the streetlamp and hightailed it over to Sixth Avenue, where he could hide in the shadows cast by the elevated trains and survey what was happening from a distance. Everyone in the park was getting rounded up, all right, including a rowdy Horatio, who was twisting in the arms of one of the uniforms now, clearly resisting arrest.

"We're shutting this place down!" the man in the suit cried.

Julian ran to the stairs and ran up to the train platform. He hadn't been spotted, at least, but another minute spent trying to pick up a client would have gotten him arrested for certain. As a train rumbled into the station, Julian wasn't sure where he'd go—or if he was on the uptown or downtown track—but he got on it and got away from the park.

…orate melodies. That's what …

…y song about the way the sing…

…at of her lover, how she thought of …

…owers even when it was the coldest day of wi…

Really, it was lovely, and it was the sort o…

listener long for a love like that in his life…

Rhodes played the melody a few ti…

feel for it. Then he played the accom…

self. Rhodes's voice was thin and …

Marian jumped in and sang the…

up as she sang, which Eddi…

bell.

"Marvelous," Jimm…

this is the song, Mari…

"It's good," M…

"It sounds l…

completely c…

"Eddie…

ion."

V

ump

E

rand

ing up

into th

what w

waited while Di…

Marian watched Rhodes, looking…
both been telling her for a week that this song was a g…
it was the next logical step in her career, but she hardly ever sang in
her real voice, and Eddie knew she worried that it wasn't strong
enough. They'd been thinking about ways to integrate Eddie into a
love ballad, but as it wasn't a duet, it meant that for about two and a
half minutes, all eyes would be on Marian, and Marian kept saying
she didn't want that kind of undiluted attention.

But Jimmy was excited. Now Marian looked over the sheet music
while Rhodes and Jimmy talked it up. Rhodes played the melody, and
even Eddie had to admit it was a good song. It suited Marian's
strengths pretty well, too, which surprised him because he couldn't
imagine how Rhodes would have picked up on them from her regular
routine. Eddie had heard her natural singing voice dozens of times,
but she rarely used it in their routines. The Doozies act didn't call for

his song was,
er's heart soared
warm weather and
ter.

love song that made the
A dream, in other words.
es so that Marian could get a
paniment and sang the song him-
eedy, not up to the task of the song.
last verse with him. Jimmy's face lit
understood; her voice rang clear as a

said, clapping. "That was just lovely. I think
an. I really do."
rian agreed. "What do you think, Eddie?"
vely," he said, not wanting to give away that he wasn't
omfortable with this song's introduction to their routine.
, please tell me what you think. I want your honest opin-

e sighed and stood up. "It's a good song, Marian, and your voice
unds marvelous. I had quite forgotten how well you can sing.
You'll really wow the crowd next season."

Marian opened her mouth as if she were about to say something, but she didn't get the opportunity.

"I was thinking," Jimmy said, walking over to stand next to Marian, "that we might try the song out later this month. See how the audience reacts to it."

That caught Eddie's attention. He turned toward Jimmy, trying to decide if he had the audacity—or the desire to risk his job—to protest.

"You would change the show in the middle of the season?" Marian asked.

"Just a small change," Jimmy said. "You still do your act, but I was thinking that instead of 'Turkey in the Park,' you sing this song. Sing it to Eddie, since he's supposed to be your husband. Then the two of you dance off the stage together. What do you think?"

Eddie nodded, but he kept his face neutral. "So I would just sit there while she sings?"

"It's just one measly number, Cotton," said Jimmy.

Eddie didn't like it. He turned to Marian to see what she thought.

"We could just try it, Eddie," she said. "A couple of performances. If it bombs, we go back to the old routine. Yeah?" She looked around to see if anyone else agreed.

Jimmy nodded enthusiastically. Eddie wanted to make Marian happy, but he couldn't help but think that he was being pushed out of the act. Jimmy threw an arm around Eddie and escorted him out of the room.

Eddie hated Jimmy's proximity; the man smelled of sour sweat and cigar smoke, not the most pleasant combination. But Eddie went with him into the hallway, where Jimmy said, "Look, Cotton, you know I love your act. You and Marian are one of the most popular acts I got. But if you don't change, you get stale."

"I understand, sir."

"This number is going to make your act, you got that? And let's keep the lady happy, eh? She wants this, Cotton, but she won't say yes unless you do."

Eddie glanced back into the room, where Marian was talking excitedly with Walter Rhodes. She did look happy.

"All right. We'll do it."

Jimmy clapped Eddie on the back. "That's a good fella. I'll let her know. Now scram for a bit so I can talk to Marian."

Eddie was frustrated that he was getting kicked out of his practice room, but he nodded and said, "I'll just be down the hall."

Jimmy nodded and turned to go back in the room. Eddie lingered in the hall for a moment to eavesdrop. Jimmy said to Marian and Rhodes, "Cotton wants us to do the song, so we'll add it to the program." He tilted his head as if he were considering that. "Yes, this will be good. I think next month. Cotton is changing the dance routine anyway, right? So, keep doing the act the way you have been. Then in July, we'll introduce the new numbers. We'll bill it as a new Cotton and France act. That is guaranteed to put a lot of people in those seats." Jimmy nodded to himself. "Yes. *Yes*. This will be spectacular. What do you think, my dear?"

"Let's give it a try," said Marian.

Jimmy whooped. He made a show of showering Rhodes with compliments before escorting him out of the room. Eddie ducked into an office to escape being seen. Jimmy saw Rhodes down the hall and then returned to Marian alone and all smiles. "This will be wonderful, Marian."

Eddie walked back into the hall and stood near the door to the practice room.

"You're sure I am ready for this?" Marian asked.

"You're the real star of the show. Everyone knows that. One of these days, you will outgrow Eddie Cotton. I hate to say it, but he's at the pinnacle of his career right now. He will never get any better. But you, Marian, you could be a real star. And I want to help you become that star."

Eddie bit his lip to keep from yelling. Blanchard's opinion wasn't a surprise but it still hurt like a knife to the chest.

"You really think so?" asked Marian.

"Of course. Trust me, Marian."

"I want to," she said. "I will. It's just that Eddie and I do the act together. We have for nearly a decade. We're good together. I don't want to work without him. He makes me better. Can you understand that?"

Eddie let out a breath of relief. Marian, at least, still wanted him. Maybe he wouldn't be tossed aside just yet.

"Certainly, love," said Jimmy. "Don't worry about it. You know my main goal is to make my show the most spectacular revue on Broadway."

"Okay. Let's just not be hasty, okay?"

"I am never hasty."

Eddie ducked away from the door as Jimmy and Marian turned to head his way. He jogged down the hall to the other dance studio, but not before he heard Jimmy and Marian talking as they walked down the hall.

Jimmy said, "Let's blow off rehearsal for the rest of the afternoon so I can take my ingénue to lunch."

"I promised Eddie I'd work with him on the new dance steps."

"Tomorrow, then. We'll go to Keens, have a real fancy lunch."

"Tomorrow. Let me check with Eddie, but yes, tomorrow should be fine."

"I look forward to it. Now, let me tell you about a few other things I have in mind for *Le Tumulte*."

Eddie closed himself in the studio as they walked off, presumably toward Jimmy's office. Eddie tried to concentrate, putting himself back through the basic paces of a warm-up, trying to let the rhythm of his regular dance routine distract him from his frustration over the changes to the act. After ten minutes of that, he started practicing the new routine he'd devised.

He kept flubbing the steps. He let out a breath, recited the steps in his head—forward, back, pivot, spin, kick out, left, left, right—but then when he tried out the routine, he tripped. Frustrated, he hopped up and down a few times and tried to shake it out. He tried again and missed a step again.

He knew he had to focus. It wasn't just that Walter Rhodes had shown up with Marian's new signature song, and it wasn't just the probability that Blanchard was sidelining Eddie next season, although both were bothering him a great deal. On top of that, he felt like an ass for not responding more enthusiastically when Marian was telling him about her new song, because it really was a good opportunity for her and the act. Jimmy was right; a new addition to the act would put butts in those seats. Eddie planned to apologize to Marian later.

But, actually, the thing that nagged at his mind more was that he was pretty sure he'd seen Lane Carillo from the Marigold in the audience the previous night, which brought about an unhappy thought: it was among his most fervent desires to see Lane again.

That was what was really making him lose his steps. He cried out in frustration, and tried again. Forward, back, pivot, kick out. He got it that time. So he tried again. And again. When Marian walked into the room, he danced right over to her, grabbed her hand, and pulled her into the dance. He led her across the floor and, because she had also been doing this for years, she got right into it with him, following his lead, falling into the steps. She laughed when he spun her.

"This is great, Eddie," she said when he stopped.

"I found a tune," he said. "A little ditty by a composer nobody's heard of, but it's catchy. Here." He grabbed the sheet music from where he'd left it on a chair in the corner. He stood next to Marian as she looked it over, and he hummed a few bars so she'd get the melody. It was a little-known fact that Marian struggled to read music, but she had a prodigy's talent of being able to sing or play anything after she'd heard it once.

"Oh, I like it," she said.

"It goes like this," Eddie said. He stepped away from Marian and did the steps he'd planned out. He breathlessly hummed the tune and hissed and clicked his tongue where appropriate to approximate the percussion, and then he stepped out and held up his hands. "What do you think?"

"It looks great, Eddie."

"Thanks." He took a deep breath. "So. You're going to do the song. 'My Heart Is Full'?"

She nodded. "Well, Jimmy wants me to. But you're my partner, Eddie. If you say no, that's it. I'll tell Jimmy no."

Eddie didn't want to put her in the position of having to be the one to tell Jimmy Blanchard she wasn't going to be a part of his vision for the show. And, besides that, it was clear that Marian wanted to do the song. "Sing it," he said.

She clapped her hands together. "It'll be great! You get the orchestra to play that little song of yours, do that dance routine. You'll knock the socks off the audience. Then I'll come out and sing this song, and everyone will be so surprised because it's so different from what I've done before. I think this is really the next step for us. This is the future of our show."

Eddie smiled because it was hard not to get caught up in Marian's enthusiasm. "Yes. It'll be great. I'm sorry for being a sap earlier. The change in plans just took me off guard."

Marian grinned. "It's all right. I'm just glad you're agreeing to the change. I really think this will be great for the act."

"I agree."

"Good. I'll let Jimmy know."

He walked over and gave her a kiss on the cheek. "Please do. But first, try these steps with me."

After the show that night, Eddie walked out of the theater and found that his feet just took him up Broadway to 48th Street. He wanted to see Lane, he admitted to himself. Why, he wasn't exactly sure. Well, he wanted to have sex again, but there was more to it than that. He wanted to sit in the club and talk to Lane again, too. He wanted to find out what Lane had been doing in the audience at the Doozies.

When he rounded the corner onto 48th Street, he was so startled to see a man walk out of the Marigold that he ducked back around the corner. He peeked, and felt ridiculous for doing so, but saw that the man was, in fact, Lane Carillo. He was dressed expensively in what looked like a black suit with white pinstripes, wide-legged trousers, and a black bow tie. His shoes were so shiny they reflected the light from the street lamps. He pulled the silver cigarette case from his jacket pocket, extracted a cigarette, and then went about lighting it and taking a long drag. He looked so cool, Eddie thought, so in command of his domain, and so impossibly sexy.

Which Eddie thought was a problem. He panicked briefly. What if his advances were unwanted? What if it wasn't Lane in the audience? What if it was?

No sense going home, though, he thought. He'd made it this far.

He took a deep breath and rounded the corner. He stepped on a twig, and the sound caught Lane's attention. There was surprise on his face at first, but it eased into a smile.

"Well, shit," Lane said. "I never thought I'd see you again."

Eddie laughed nervously.

Lane dropped his cigarette and put it out with his heel. "You're, uh, just in the neighborhood, right?"

Eddie figured he wasn't kidding anybody. "Actually, I came to see you."

Lane bit his lip, but not before Eddie saw him smile a little. Something about that little look that Lane gave him for the briefest of seconds eased his worry.

Eddie added, "You came to the show last night."

Lane's eyes widened in surprise, but then he laughed. "I'm surprised you recognized me. But yes. An associate of mine had tickets he couldn't use and offered them to me."

"Oh." Eddie wasn't sure why he found that disappointing, but at least he hadn't been mistaken.

Lane took a step closer to where Eddie stood on the sidewalk. Forty-eighth Street was mostly deserted, but, either way, they were partially hidden by the awning on the shop next door to the Marigold, a rundown storefront that, from the looks of it, sold sewing machine supplies.

Eddie blinked and Lane was standing right in front of him.

"Why did you come to see me tonight?" Lane asked.

"I'm not sure, exactly," said Eddie, which was mostly true. "I, um, saw you last night. In the audience. And I . . ." He shook his head, not wanting to admit to anything.

"What?" Lane stepped into the space around Eddie. Then he reached over and tucked a loose lock of Eddie's hair away from his face and into his hat. That little touch was like a jolt through Eddie's whole system.

"I saw you last night and I haven't been able to stop thinking about you since."

One of those suppressed smiles flashed on Lane's face again. He shook his head. "I just came out for some fresh air. Do you want to come back in with me and have a drink? The band is in rare form tonight."

"All right," said Eddie. "Yes, let's go in."

Over cups of ice and the very excellent whiskey Mook had managed to procure, they sat at Lane's corner table and chatted.

"Do you go to theater often?" Eddie asked.

Lane shrugged. "Sure. I try to see the big shows every year. When I was a kid in Illinois, my mother got one of the New York newspapers delivered, and it always had theater reviews. I used to read them and imagine myself in the audience. We went to see theater sometimes in Chicago, though. Florenz Ziegfeld did a revue there when I was a teenager, maybe in 1911. Eugen Sandow was his headliner. Did you ever see him?"

Eddie smiled. "I met him once, actually. I was really young, fifteen or sixteen, and I was doing stupid little routines on the boardwalk in Coney Island for pocket change. He held an exhibition there for bodybuilders, and I snuck into it. After the show, I was feeling particularly brave, so I walked up to him when he was signing autographs and introduced myself." He laughed and shook his head. "I was so young."

"He was a fine specimen of a man, though, wasn't he?"

Eddie laughed again. "Oh, lord. That man was something else."

"Seeing him on a stage did some strange things to me." Lane shook his head at the memory, recalling that seeing a scantily clad man flexing his muscles had been about the most arousing thing his teenage self had ever seen. The memory brought with it some nostalgia, but horror, too, as it had been one of the first times Lane had realized he was different from the other boys. "Strange things," he whispered.

"I'll bet." Eddie winked.

Raul walked over and told Lane he had a phone call. Lane nodded and excused himself. Eddie tipped his hat as Lane left the table. He walked to his office, in the back of the building, off the kitchen. And, somewhat to his chagrin, he found it was David Epstein on the phone.

"How's business?" Epstein asked, his customary greeting.

"Good, good. Full house tonight."

"Excellent. I understand Mook got you a shipment of whiskey from Canada."

"Yes. It's very good."

"I've got a guy who can get you rum from the Caribbean. Knows the runners in the boats off the coast."

"Thank you, sir, but I promised Mook—"

"I'm not actually giving you a choice in the matter. I spent a lot of dough on this deal. Expect a shipment on Thursday."

Lane sighed. He didn't like doing business with unknown parties, but he didn't want to anger Epstein. Sometimes staying alive required being threatening, but sometimes it required going along. "Of course, sir."

He endured a long lecture from Epstein about loyalty. Epstein offered him a pair of Yankees tickets, which Lane thanked him for but declined as politely as he could. He liked baseball all right, and there were remarkable things happening at Yankee Stadium that season if the sports pages were to be believed, but he didn't have time to waste in the Bronx just then. After a few minutes, he finally managed to get off the phone. He walked back out to the floor.

Lane liked the look of Eddie sitting at his table with a drink in his hand and a dazed expression on his face as he took it all in. He bobbed his head slightly in time with the music.

The band was good. It was made up of musicians who had been exiled from other bands. Legs Aurelio had some contacts at other clubs and had helped Lane find them and get them to play together. Something about their shared status as outcasts had made the musicians come together in a spectacular way. Tonight, their playing just worked and nearly everyone in the place was competing for space on the dance floor.

Lane wanted to be one of those men competing for space.

He walked over to the table and smiled at Eddie. "Would you care to dance?"

"With you?"

Lane bit back a laugh. "That is what I was implying, yes."

Eddie eyed the dance floor warily. "I don't know . . ."

"Please don't tell me you don't know how to dance."

Eddie looked up at Lane, a blank expression on his face. Then, finally, he cracked and started to laugh. "Oh, sure, I'm hot on a stage, but here?"

Lane walked over to where Eddie sat and offered his hand. "One dance."

Eddie stared at Lane's hand. "What if . . . ?"

Lane understood then that Eddie's reluctance was due in fact to a fear that someone would recognize him. "Wear your hat."

Eddie fingered the edge of the fedora that sat on the table. He looked like he was still deciding until the band kicked it up a notch, playing a lively tune that Lane didn't recognize, though Eddie seemed to know it. He picked up the fedora, put it on his head, and stood up next to Lane. Very softly, so that only Lane could hear, he sang a few bars of the song. His voice was smooth and rang out, even through all the noise in the club. It was a strong reminder that this man was, in fact, a gifted performer, the same man he'd seen and been enchanted by on the stage the night before. And yet, he was also just Eddie.

"Let's dance," Eddie said.

Before Eddie could change his mind, Lane grabbed his hand and dragged him over to the floor. "I'll warn you that I am, in fact, a completely terrible dancer."

Eddie took a moment to listen to the tune. Then he said, "Try this." He took a few steps. Lane tried to mimic them. Then Eddie tried something a little more complicated, and Lane tripped when trying to copy the moves. Eddie laughed. He reached over and put a hand on Lane's shoulder. "You really do have two left feet."

"I think I have five."

"Here, watch me."

Eddie pushed gently away from Lane, and then he was off, his feet moving impossibly fast as he stepped to the music, and it was impressive enough that the other men on the dance floor started to notice. Eddie, granted, had his hat pulled low on his face and was wearing street clothes, so it was probably not obvious to anyone but Lane who he really was, but it was clear he was a professional dancer. Some of the other men hooted and whistled when Eddie really got going. Then he stopped suddenly and held his hand out toward Lane.

Lane took it reluctantly and immediately found himself in Eddie's arms as they did some kind of improvised close dancing that felt ridiculous and amazing all at once. "There's no way I can keep up with you."

Eddie laughed. He had a great laugh. Lane was amazed that the otherwise morose Eddie seemed most happy when he was dancing. "Oh, I'm just showing off. Ignore me."

"I couldn't ignore you if I tried."

Lane put his hand on Eddie's waist and looked around as they danced. There were other men on the dance floor showing off for each other, throwing their feet around or trying out wild steps. There were a few smudgers, too, men dancing close together. There was even a couple kissing in the corner. Lane turned back to Eddie, who was grinning and trying to lead Lane in some kind of dance. Lane really wanted to kiss him.

When Lane leaned in, Eddie turned his head, so Lane contented himself with kissing his cheek. He resolved, though, that if they were going to keep seeing each other, Eddie was going to relent and let himself be kissed one of these days.

But for now, they danced closely. They danced until the band took a break. Sometimes Eddie would stop to teach Lane something. Sometimes they would both just make up steps. Sometimes they danced so close that Lane could feel the whole length of Eddie's body pressing against his.

The band stopped playing, and a very sweaty Eddie laughed as he pulled away from Lane gently. "This is fun," he said. "I've never danced with a man before."

"Really?" Lane couldn't imagine how that could be possible, except that he could. There weren't many opportunities for men to dance together like this, at least not in public.

"Really," Eddie said. "I appreciate that you let me lead. I probably could have figured out the follower's part, but—"

"I'm happy to have you lead me. I've never danced much at all."

Eddie smiled. "You'd be just fine with a little practice."

Lane put his hand on the small of Eddie's back and started to steer him back toward his table. Eddie stopped suddenly and turned around. He grabbed the lapels of Lane's jacket and leaned in close, his lips grazing the edge of Lane's jaw. "You want to go to my place?" Eddie asked.

Lane laughed. "Like you wouldn't believe."

Chapter 8

"Ain't We Got Fun?"

There was a jumbled dream about horse racing and losing a bet and drinking too much, and then Eddie eased awake and found himself naked in bed with a hand not his own pressed to his belly.

He thought that an interesting development. He shifted slightly so that he could see where the hand went, how it was connected to a long arm decorated with dark hair, how the arm curved, how the biceps and shoulder muscles stood out prominently, how the collarbone led to the beautiful face of Lane, whose eyes were closed and mouth agape as he slept.

Eddie sighed happily, remembering how they got to this point. His movement caused Lane to stir, but he didn't wake up, and instead snuggled closer to Eddie. Eddie had a vision of what life could be like: instead of hiding behind the heavy curtains of his room at the Knickerbocker, they were in an open, sunny bedroom, lingering in bed in the morning, maybe reading the paper, maybe eating breakfast, maybe just talking about nothing. It was a nice image, but, Eddie reminded himself, it was not a world they were a part of, and that's not what this was.

Lane mumbled something and then came awake slowly. He blinked a few times, and then saw Eddie and smiled. He leaned over and kissed Eddie's cheek. "Hello," he said.

"Hi."

Lane yawned. "What time is it?"

Eddie looked over at the bedside clock. "A little after five."

"Plenty of time, then."

"For what?"

Lane reached under the sheet. His hand moved around Eddie's lower body until it settled on what it was looking for and gave a gentle squeeze. Eddie grunted and shifted his body a little closer to Lane's.

Lane smiled at him and smoothed Eddie's hair out of his face. "You know," Lane said, "we could make this a regular thing."

"We could." Eddie couldn't think of a reason not to.

"It makes sense, right? We make some arrangement to meet regularly like this. This is a good thing, what we have here. Right?"

"Sure. Yes." It was good. Eddie allowed himself to hope for a moment that this regular thing could continue to be good, though he knew moments like this were fleeting.

Lane shifted and moved his legs so that they were layered with Eddie's. He sighed sleepily and then drifted off before Eddie could say anything more.

Lane woke up in an empty bed. He sat up and looked around. Eddie was seated in a chair at his desk, hunched over what looked like a notebook, staring intently at the page. Feeling inspired, Lane very quietly got out of bed. He walked up behind Eddie and slowly snaked his arms around him. Eddie instantly stiffened, but didn't otherwise move away. Lane felt him sigh.

"Are you all right?" Lane asked.

"Just looking at some music," Eddie said, gesturing to a page of notes in front of him. The title on top of the page read, "My Heart Is Full."

"Are you singing this song?" Lane asked. The notes on the page might as well have been a foreign language for all the sense they made to Lane.

"No. Marian is."

Eddie's tone was so neutral that Lane found it alarming. There was no emotion at all. Lane looked at the page and wished he could read it, wished he could see what Eddie saw there. It all looked like a jumble of lines and dots and symbols. "Do you like the song?"

"Sure, it's pretty. Not the kind of thing Marian usually sings."

"How did she—"

Eddie cut him off. "It's not important."

Lane held up his hands and backed away.

Eddie turned around in the chair. He frowned. "I'm sorry for snapping. But we're not . . . you and I are not friends."

"We could be."

Eddie gestured at the space between them. "See, this is why I pay for sex. At the end of the night, the other fella leaves. There's no bull."

"There's no feeling."

"Maybe I like it that way." Eddie turned back around to his music.

Lane was surprised by how hurt he felt by that. He tried to come up with a joke to cover it, but his mouth stubbornly asked, "So this regular thing we decided to have is just sex. I come here and we fuck and that's it."

"That's what I said." Eddie didn't turn around. He kept his head down, looking at the music. After a long pause, he added, "Look, that's all I have to offer you, okay? I can't have some happy little romance. That's not how this works."

Lane sighed, not sure that he could come up with a convincing counter-argument. Eddie's attitude was one Lane had encountered before. He had a number of friends in the New York queer community, and plenty of them felt strongly that long-lasting relationships between men were an impossibility, that all that there could ever be was sex but not love. Sometimes Lane believed that. But what about Clarence and his George? What about Scott?

More to the point, Lane thought as he stared at Eddie's back hunched over that desk, there was a lot more here than just sex. It wasn't a mere transaction. There was also conversation and affection and, yes, maybe even the beginning of friendship. Maybe it wasn't a romance, but it was a lot more than sex.

Which was why Lane didn't run out of the room then. He wasn't sure what made Eddie so stubborn, if it was some past experience or else just a delusion that queer men were not capable of anything more than fucking, but something in Lane wanted to stick around and get to the bottom of it. So he said, "All right. I'm not proposing we get all sweet. I'm not going to bring you flowers or try to talk you into necking in the back of a taxi. All I was trying to do was say that I like you, which I thought would be evident anyway since I've now spent the night with you twice."

Eddie dropped his head back and looked at the ceiling. He didn't say anything.

So Lane started to get dressed. "Not that I think friendship is such a bad thing. Seems to me, you could use a friend."

Eddie didn't say anything, but Lane saw him close his eyes.

"Worth thinking about, at any rate," Lane said, pulling on his shirt. "Look, anytime you want me, come by the Marigold."

Eddie stood up and nodded. Then he really surprised Lane by shooting him a wounded look. Yes, this man was hurting on the inside. Lane knew he should probably give up on Eddie, that even regular sex with Eddie would probably be more trouble than it was worth, that he didn't need any more stubborn people in his life. But something about that look had him wanting to stay, wanting to figure out how to heal it. Eddie, Lane decided, needed him.

Then Eddie said, "You could, uh, come by the theater. After the last curtain. I usually leave around eleven. Stage door, the one that exits onto Forty-first Street."

It wasn't an admission of anything, but it sure was a hell of an invitation. "All right," Lane said. "Maybe I'll stop by sometime."

Chapter 9

"I'm Just Wild About Harry"

A tall man with greasy hair stood in the Marigold's kitchen, sneer-
ing at his surroundings. Lane knew this was Epstein's rum runner, the guy whose hooch he had been ordered to buy, but Lane didn't
want to do business.

"I heard about you, Carillo," the man said.

"I'll just assume it's good things. I have a club to open, so let's get
to business."

The man flicked his wrist. A couple of men in rough clothes
strolled in carrying wooden boxes. One of them had a pin on his collar
advertising a construction workers' union. That was just great, Lane
thought. This guy had probably infiltrated a local union and was not
only skimming off the top but also getting his legitimate workers to
help him with his illegitimate activities. Lane knew he couldn't judge
too much, but it was one thing to put members of your own organization in harm's way to make a buck; it was another to exploit honest
working men.

The men put the boxes on the floor. Lane moved to open the case,
but the man pulled a gun. "Explain to me why I should sell my wares
to a two-bit faggot such as yourself."

Lane blinked to keep the panic that had bubbled up off his face.
"My money's the same color as everyone else's," he said. "Also, I
shot the last guy who asked me that question."

Lane pulled his gun as he walked over to the crates. He raised his
hand and Raul appeared with a knife, which he used to pry open the
first box. Everything looked like the real McCoy—the bottles were

sealed and their labels indicated they had come from a distillery in Jamaica that Lane was familiar with.

Lane held the gun such that the man in his kitchen could definitely see it, but he didn't point it, not yet. "Explain to me why I should believe there is rum in these bottles and not water."

"You think I would swindle you?"

"I don't know you." Lane lifted the gun, transferred it between his hands to show how good his reflexes were, but he still didn't point it at the man. "Look, I have regular people who keep this place wet. I am buying this shipment as a favor to our mutual friend. But I certainly don't need this, and if there turns out to be anything but actual rum in those bottles, I *will* shoot you. Do we understand each other?"

The man didn't move or speak.

Lane rolled his eyes and pointed the gun at the man. "Raul," he said.

Raul went to the case and pulled out one of the bottles. He looked the bottle over. "Label's fake, boss," he said in his lilting Spanish accent.

"Of course it is," said Lane. "Why give the faggot *capo* real alcohol?" He fired a warning shot that whizzed by the man's head, splintering the wood in the doorway behind him. Lane had missed deliberately, not wanting to harm the guy but to get him to rethink his strategy. "Look what you made me do."

"Jesus Christ, Carillo. You could have shot my ear off."

"Indeed. I won't miss next time. Now where's the rum that Epstein asked you for?"

The man raised his gun.

Lane's reflexes were faster.

The man missed, but Lane didn't. The bullet from the stranger's gun went into a cabinet behind Lane's head, the impact sending bits of wood and dust flying back at Lane. But it didn't matter, because Lane had already put his bullet in the space between the man's eyes.

"What a mess," Lane said, reholstering his gun. He felt angry and frustrated and resentful that not only would he have to clean this up, but he was out a case of liquor. "What's in the bottles, Raul?"

"It's rum, but it's watered down. Maybe one part rum to three parts water."

"Useless, in other words."

Raul nodded.

Lane rubbed his forehead, a headache blooming behind his eyes. "Call Callahan and Legs Aurelio and clean this up. Then I'll call Epstein and figure this out."

"Yes, sir."

A half hour later, Lane walked into Lenny's, so angry he practically vibrated with it. Epstein was, thankfully, at a table alone.

"Sir," Lane said.

"Did you get your shipment?"

"Well, if by 'get my shipment' you mean 'get watered-down rum from a man who tried to kill me,' then yes, I certainly did."

Epstein frowned. "He was legit. Your own cousin Tony swore by him. He's been making deliveries to clubs in Times Square for five years."

Lane crossed his arms. He had to put the lid on his anger before he said something to Epstein that he regretted. "He pulled a gun on me."

"I presume he is no longer among the living."

"What was I supposed to do?"

Epstein sat back and looked surprised. "Well, this is interesting. I've never seen you fume like this."

Lane let his hands fall to his sides. "He didn't want to do business with me because apparently my reputation precedes me."

Epstein tilted his head, the question left unasked.

"I'm a faggot," Lane said through his teeth. "So he tried to sell me watered-down liquor like I'm some kind of dumbbell."

"And that angers you."

Lane sighed. "Bottom line is we make money. If he's selling something to the family, why should it matter if he sells it to me or cousin Tony? It's all the same."

Epstein nodded thoughtfully. "I agree."

"So." Lane put his hands on the table, thinking it was a good time to leave.

"Keep your anger in check, Carillo. It won't do for you to lose your cool demeanor."

"I need to get back."

"Of course. You've got a cleaning crew?"

"The runner has a date with a rock at the bottom of the East River."

"I do like you." Epstein shifted his tremendous weight in his chair and leaned forward. "I'm on your side. You believe that, don't you?"

"Yes, sir."

"Good. Get out of here and make me some money."

On the walk back to the Marigold, Lane thought about what Epstein had said. Lane couldn't remember being so angry. What was the cause? Long hours, not enough sleep, enough frustration each week to last a lifetime? There was alcohol to smuggle into New York and there were cops to pay off and he lived every day wondering if this was the moment just before everything crashed down around him.

And then, of course, there was Eddie. Each night spent with Eddie was like an ice pick to Lane's frozen heart, to the part of himself he'd let go numb after Scott's death. One had to be numb to pull the trigger, to end the life of a fellow human. Lane spared a moment of regret for the life he'd taken, though he knew that if he hadn't fired, he'd have been the one lying dead on the cold tile floor of the kitchen of the Marigold.

Funny to realize he didn't want to die. There had been a long period—years, even—when he hadn't much cared if he saw tomorrow. Lately, however, his life had taken on a purpose it hadn't had before, a reason to keep on. The club was a big part of it, his own slice of real estate in the bustling city, the one place on earth where men like him could be themselves without fear of violence or reprisal. And if that weren't enough, he had a dancer with hot feet whose bed he'd begun to grace with some regularity.

It wasn't a life he'd ever envisioned for himself, but it wasn't half bad. And if things kept on going the way they were, maybe he'd have something worth killing for.

Eddie pulled the brim of his fedora over his eyes as he strolled into the bar at the Hotel Astor. It was crowded and noisy, which kept attention from coming his way—and he'd dressed as inconspicuously as possible in a gray suit, no bright colors or identifying markers anywhere. He made his way toward the oval-shaped bar, where a man was slinging drinks—"coffee," presumably—and a small group of men had gathered in their designated area off to the left.

A man in a threadbare brown suit and an old bowler hat caught Eddie's eye. He was putting on airs, clearly, a big brawny man out of his element and trying to make new friends at the bar.

Eddie paused a fair distance away to take in the scene. The thing was, he knew he could have Lane anytime he wanted now. They'd been seeing each other regularly for a couple of weeks. With every new encounter, Lane seemed eager, seemed to want more of Eddie's time. He played it off nonchalantly, but Eddie was on to him. Too bad this was not meant to be; maybe two men could shack up and share a house and pretend everything was hunky-dory, but it was an illusion, and one that couldn't possibly last.

And here Eddie was, proving it. He'd overheard one of the stage-hands at the James Theater saying that Bryant Park had been cleared out a few weeks before; so he'd come here instead, although now he regretted it. Yes, that man by the bar was intriguing, but did he want cheap sex just to prove something to Lane? To prove something to himself? And what, exactly, was he proving, aside from the fact that he was utterly pathetic?

He felt ridiculous and exposed suddenly, and his pulse kicked up a notch as he thought about what he'd been about to do. Lane hadn't asked him for anything other than regular companionship. Eddie liked Lane a great deal and could have gone to him tonight. So why had he come here to try to pick up a stranger?

He was a fool.

Once he was back in the lobby, he felt like he needed to regroup. He dodged around columns and people milling about and made his way toward the men's room. Once there, he splashed water on his face and tried to pull himself together.

The Astor, at least, was still considered a respectable establish-ment, perhaps because the queer men who congregated in the bar kept to their own section and remained the portrait of discretion. Eddie had always appreciated the bar for that reason; he could ex-plain away his presence if caught there. So, if he should slip back through the well-lit lobby and run into someone he knew, there was no reason to think he couldn't simply say he had an engagement of some sort at the hotel. No matter that it was now after midnight. So that's what he'd do; he'd slip out and go home and maybe he'd go to see Lane or maybe he wouldn't, but either way, the answer to his cur-rent state of befuddlement would not be found in the Hotel Astor bar.

He heard a groan come from behind him. At first, he thought he might have walked in on an assignation—it wouldn't have been the first time—but then there was a second groan, one that sounded more like pain than pleasure.

"Hello?" Eddie asked the room.

He got a pained grunt in response. Alarmed, Eddie turned around and walked to the back of the room, where he saw a man huddled. He considered just backing away and leaving the man there, until he grunted again and Eddie noticed the blood pooling on the floor tile.

Eddie cursed in surprise and then said, "Can I . . ." before realizing how silly it sounded. Careful not to step in the blood, he knelt next to the man. There was something familiar about that exact shade of blond hair, though the man's face was swollen and distorted. Blood ran from his nose.

Then the man looked up and their eyes met. And Eddie knew those eyes intimately.

"Julian."

"Leave me," Julian whispered.

So he was conscious, at least. "Who did this to you?"

Julian just shook his head.

"Should I take you to a hospital?"

Julian's eyes went wide and he shook his head vehemently. "Arrest," he whispered.

But Julian didn't look good. Eddie could see the familiar features through the swelling, but his shirt was stained with blood and there was an unhealthy amount on the floor. All Eddie really knew was that he had to get Julian out of this bathroom, and he had to do it without drawing any attention to himself.

He went back to the sink. There was a stack of bright white towels piled on the counter. Eddie hated to soil one, but he didn't have a lot of options. He soaked it and walked back to Julian. He used the towel to wash the blood off his face—the nose bleed seemed to have stopped—while he considered the options. He didn't have many; Julian lost consciousness, his head lolling back on his shoulders.

Eddie quickly turned over several ideas for where to take Julian. The Knickerbocker was a few blocks south. Eddie considered getting a room at the Astor, but he didn't think he had enough money on him.

Then it occurred to him: the Marigold was close. Just on the other side of Times Square. All Eddie really had to do was get Julian across the street and up a couple of blocks.

He pressed the cool towel against Julian's face. Julian stirred.

"I need to get you out of here," Eddie said. "Can you walk?"

"I can't . . ."

Eddie ran back to the sink and grabbed one of the other towels. He used it to soak up the blood on the floor and then stuffed it into a trash receptacle under the sink. Once he got Julian as clean as he'd get, he pulled Julian's jacket closed to hide the red stains on his shirt. Then he hooked an arm around Julian's torso.

"I need you to stand," Eddie said. "I'll get you help."

Julian let out an almighty moan as Eddie lifted him off the floor. Panicked, Eddie waited for a moment to see if anyone would barge through the door to see what was happening. When no one came, Eddie pulled himself and Julian upright.

"Put your arms around my neck," he told Julian, a bit concerned about propriety. But Julian needing attention immediately was the larger concern.

Julian put his hands limply on Eddie's shoulder. Eddie squeezed him a little, which caused Julian to let out a wheezy breath.

Then Julian started crying.

Eddie more or less dragged Julian out of the bathroom. He moved as fast as he could across the lobby. When Julian passed out again, his head rolling across Eddie's shoulder, Eddie held him up. To a man looking on curiously, Eddie simply said, "My pal had too much to drink. Gotta get him home before his old lady finds out!"

Eddie felt safer out on the street. He was less exposed and better able to keep to the shadows. He managed to get a very limp Julian to the corner, but then he gave up and scooped the man into his arms. Julian sighed and put his head against Eddie's shoulder. Eddie carried him across Broadway as if he were a recently rescued damsel in distress.

When he got to the Marigold, Eddie kicked the door. Etta opened it and gave Eddie a sardonic look. "I appreciate the gesture, dearest, but you didn't have to bring me a man to be let in to the club."

"I need Mr. Carillo right away. Is he here?"

Etta seemed to notice then that Julian was bruised and unconscious. She gasped. "I know this one. He works in Bryant Park."

Eddie nodded. "I found him beat all to hell in the men's room at the Astor."

"Christ. Come inside, come inside. Raul! Get Lane!"

Lane appeared a moment later. "Eddie, what are you . . . what happened to him?"

"I found him this way. Can you help?"

"Of course. Let's get him into the kitchen. The lighting is better there."

Lane helped Eddie carry Julian through the club and into the kitchen. They lay Julian on the counter—not ideal, but it looked clean. Julian moaned again.

"He seems to be coming around," Lane said.

"Can you help him? Is he going to die?"

"I know a little first aid, but . . . let me make a phone call." Lane stepped away and started to head toward the hall. "I assume there's a reason you brought him here and not to the hospital."

"He's a prostitute. He'd get arrested." Eddie tried to convey the urgency of the situation with his gaze, but Lane stood there, his expression blank. "And he's one of us," Eddie added.

Lane pursed his lips and nodded. "Stay here." Then he was gone.

Julian was coming around. He moaned softly and shifted his weight on the counter. The split on his lip was slowly trickling blood and his left eye was swollen shut, but he was moving. He was still alive.

Lane came back a moment later, carrying a blanket and a towel. He folded the towel and put it under Julian's head before he draped the blanket over Julian's body. Then he went to the icebox and took out a block of ice. He pulled a handkerchief from his pocket and wrapped it around the ice. He handed it to Eddie.

"Eddie, hold this to his eye. It will bring the swelling down."

"What, um. What do we do?"

"You're in luck. This is not the first time I've had to help out someone beaten within an inch of his life who can't risk getting arrested." Lane smiled ruefully. "I assume that's why you brought him here?"

"I didn't mean to bring you any trouble. It's just that you were the closest, so I—"

"It's fine. I understand. What's his name?"

"Julian."

"Which you know from a previous acquaintance. Because he's not speaking much."

"Yes."

Julian raised his arms. He clasped onto Eddie's hand.

"Julian?" Lane said. "You awake?"

Julian nodded.

"I'm Lane. Eddie brought you to me for help. I won't hurt you and you won't be arrested. Do you understand?"

Julian nodded again.

Just then there was a knock on the back door. Lane went to open it. "That was fast," he said to the man on the other side of the door. The man was short and rotund with a graying bristle-broom mustache. He carried a large black leather case. He had a pin on his lapel that was similar to the one Lane wore, so Eddie concluded this guy was also Mafia.

"This is Uncle Vito," Lane said. "He's a doctor."

Uncle Vito looked nothing like Lane except for the fact that they had the same Mediterranean complexion. That didn't necessarily exclude some kind of blood connection, but Eddie suspected Vito was an uncle to Lane by association only. Eddie stepped away from Julian, deciding to trust Uncle Vito if Lane did. If he was Mob-involved, he wouldn't give Julian to the cops. Hopefully.

Eddie trusted Lane deep in his gut, so he allowed things to proceed.

Vito examined Julian, peering at his swollen face, peeling off his clothes to check for cuts and bruises, and pressing into Julian's side with his fingers until Julian grunted in pain.

"The good news," Vito said at last, "is that most of the injuries are superficial. I'd say that nose is broken, and he's got a couple of bruised or broken ribs, too, but those aren't life threatening if we set them properly. We do need to clean up some of these bad cuts to avoid infection, and we need to bandage him up so he doesn't lose any more blood. This cut on his chest needs stitches." He mulled over Julian's prone form. "Laney, you have any whiskey?"

"You're going to have a drink now?" Eddie asked.

"No. It's for the patient. To help with the pain."

Five minutes later, Lane and Eddie were assisting as Vito cleaned, closed, and bandaged Julian's wounds. By then, Julian had passed out again, but Eddie hoped it was just as well; he wasn't conscious of the pain, at least.

Eddie was relieved to see with his own eyes that Julian was going to be all right, although those bruises would linger for some time, most likely.

Vito pulled a fresh block of ice from the icebox and handed it to Eddie. "Keep this on his face. The swelling is already going down, but he looks like he could use more help with that."

Lane pulled Vito into a corner where they had a hushed conversation. Then Lane shook Vito's hand; the gesture was so smooth that Eddie wondered if money was being exchanged. Perhaps Lane was paying Vito not to mention that he'd come to the Marigold to patch up a flamboyant man who had clearly met the wrong end of some rough's fist. Eddie wondered, too, if it would be obvious to Vito that Julian was a working boy, but he supposed there was nothing in Julian's dress that would give that away.

Vito left, and Julian was now asleep, breathing softly, his chest rising and falling. The counter couldn't have been comfortable. Eddie picked up the blanket and draped it over Julian again.

"I knew you weren't a heartless bastard," said Lane.

"All right."

Lane stepped closer. Eddie looked down at Julian, concentrating on holding that ice to his face.

Lane said, "You put up this façade. You don't care about anyone. You're only out for your own interests. But deep down, you *do* care about other people. You care about this Julian."

Eddie shrugged.

"I suppose," Lane continued, "I can only hope that if you should find me near death in a hotel men's room that you'd rescue me."

"Lane, I—"

Eddie stopped talking and closed his eyes when Lane gently ran a hand down the back of his head.

"I understand you trying to protect your heart," Lane said. "It's a tough world out there. But you don't have to pretend with me."

"I'm not . . ." But what was he really doing? Eddie wasn't quite sure. He and Lane had been meeting regularly for a couple of weeks, yes, and often they did more than just fuck. They'd talk or sleep or dance at the Marigold. Eddie often looked forward to the next time they would meet. And wasn't that the whole reason Eddie had gone to the Astor tonight? He was getting too close. His emotions were tangled in a way he had never experienced, the nights with Lane giving him brief peeks at joy at the expense of his old, closed-off ways, and frankly, he found that terrifying. But if he'd spent the night with another man, well, wouldn't that prove he didn't need Lane? Because he didn't. He just liked the man.

"You're the only man I've been with in quite some time." Lane spoke so quietly, Eddie thought at first he'd misheard. But he leaned slightly into Lane's hand.

"You, too," Eddie said quietly after a moment, almost reflexively. He didn't need Lane, he repeated to himself, but there was no need to lie. "I mean, since I met you, I haven't been with anyone else. Not even Julian. That was . . . that was the past."

Lane nodded. "So this has to be worth something, right?"

Eddie nodded. "But this is not like a man courting a woman. We don't go on dates. There won't be some flowery ceremony down the road, or a house we live in together, or kids and a dog."

"I know that," Lane said. "Believe me, I do. Especially not for a man like me. Not for one like you, either, but the way things are with my job, and Epstein, and the club and everything, I learned a long time ago not even to hope for . . . Well."

Lane looked at Eddie warily, but then something came over his face and his whole demeanor changed. His guard went back up, that was the only way Eddie could think of to describe it. Like he'd let the walls of his outer fort go down long enough for Eddie to get a good look at him and see that there was a lot of complexity, a lot of pain, under his mostly happy outside. He sighed. "I'm not saying you should get on your knees and swear your unending devotion to me." Lane glanced at Julian. "He's your past, as you said. All the things you did before you met me, the men you knew, the moments you're less proud of, all of that is in the past. Consider letting me be your future. That's all I'm asking."

Eddie looked up at Lane, really looked at him, and realized he'd already considered. Whatever he'd been out to prove that night hadn't come to anything, had it? What had he been out to prove? That he didn't need Lane? That whatever had happened between himself and Lane hadn't changed his life? Whether or not those statements were true seemed beside the point now as Lane stared at him. He'd come here tonight because he needed a safe place to get help for Julian, but he was drawn here, too, he was drawn to this man who stood before him who had no expectations beyond that he wanted to simply be with Eddie. And that was what Eddie wanted, too.

He'd come here tonight because he felt safe at the Marigold. He felt safe with Lane. And that was more than he could say for any other man he'd known in years.

"He needed my help," was all Eddie said.

Lane nodded. "I hope that whatever is between us is mutual. That you spend as much time thinking about me as I spend thinking about you."

Eddie's breath hitched in his throat and his heart sped up. Hell, he came here tonight because Lane had been on his mind, because Lane was always on his mind. "Maybe I do."

"Good." Lane offered up a small smile. "I don't want a promise. I just want to spend more time with you."

"All right. That we can do." Eddie felt like they'd just agreed to something, though he'd be damned if he knew exactly what it was. He looked back down. The ice was melting into his hand. "Now what do we do about Julian?"

"Wait for him to wake up."

Lane shut down the Marigold for the night while he waited for Julian to come around. Eddie kept vigil. Concentrating on Julian was certainly easier than worrying about Lane and the ambiguity of the conversation they'd had an hour before. Sometime after two A.M., Julian finally stirred, looked up at Eddie and Lane, and sighed heavily.

"Edward, darling," he whispered. "My hero."

"Can you tell me what happened?" asked Eddie.

Julian coughed. "What do you think happened? A client used me and then beat the stuffing out of me."

"Did you get a good look at him?" Lane asked.

"Yes, but . . . who are you?"

"I'm Lane. I'm a friend." To explain, Lane threw his arm around Eddie's shoulder. "I'm with Eddie now."

"Oh?" Julian asked. He rubbed his eyes and lifted his torso off the counter. He grunted, clearly in pain. He sighed and rested back on the counter. When he spoke again, it was quietly, but with more strength than before. "I've never seen you around before. Where did he pick you up?"

Eddie suddenly panicked. How could he explain this to Julian? How could he really explain Julian to Lane? Lane thought he knew what had gone on between Eddie and Julian, but did he really? Eddie squirmed away from Lane. "I have to go. I need to go outside. Get some air."

"As it happens," Lane said casually, "I'm not a prostitute." He hooked his arm around Eddie's, preventing Eddie from getting away. "No offense intended."

Julian coughed. "Well, darling. Aren't we all prostitutes?"

Seeing that he couldn't escape, Eddie said, "Julian, what the hell happened?"

Julian turned toward Eddie as Lane backed away slightly. "I was at the Astor. I, um . . ." His brow furrowed. He lifted a hand and rubbed his right temple. "I can't recall exactly. There was a man who called himself Harry. I met him outside. Had a conversation about baseball or something. He had a room, so he took me there. After we . . ." Julian held up his hands and made an obscene gesture. "Well, after that, he, uh, took out his aggressions on me, I suppose. Called me a fucking faggot fairy and . . ." Julian gestured toward his bruises.

Eddie closed his eyes, absorbing that. "He beat the stuffing out you, you mean."

"I've never seen hatred like that," Julian said, looking off in the distance. His flat tone was alarming. Eddie had never seen him this way, without the airs and affectations. It was like a light had been put out. "He hated himself. He hated me."

Lane came around and curled his hand around Eddie's elbow again. "How do you feel now?" Lane asked.

"Sore." Julian looked around. "How did I get here? Where am I?" Raw fear flashed across Julian's face.

"You're at my place," Lane said.

"You can trust him," said Eddie. "He called a doctor who came and bandaged you up. The doctor can also be trusted to be discreet."

Julian didn't seem convinced.

Eddie said, "I found you in the first-floor men's room at the Astor, bleeding all over the floor."

"How did I get there?"

"I was hoping you could tell us."

Julian let out a breath and rubbed his eyes. "I haven't the foggiest."

"Do you know anything about the man?" Lane asked. "His name, where he works?"

"No, nothing. Just the name Harry, probably not even his real name."

"Do you have a place to stay tonight?" asked Eddie.

Julian shook his head. "I had been hoping to . . ." He sighed. "My stuff is at a friend's place, but he's always three days from getting evicted, so I don't know. I pay him what I can, but . . ." He let out a breath. "God, what my face must look like. It hurts like hell. I can't imagine I'll get much work all banged up."

They were all silent for a few moments while Eddie gathered his thoughts. His head was swimming, it seemed like.

Julian let out a breath and seemed to deflate on the counter. He grabbed the edge of the blanket and pulled it up to his chin.

Lane tilted his head back and forth a few times, considering Julian, and then said, "You need a job?"

This clearly shocked Julian as much as it did Eddie, because Julian's whole body tensed, though he recovered quickly. "Sorry, darling, I don't do multiples. Not unless you're willing to pay triple."

Something in his old manner came back, which was a relief to Eddie.

"No, not that," Lane said. "Do you want to know where you are? You're in the kitchen of the Marigold. Have you heard of it?"

"Heard of it?" Julian's eyes went wide. He looked around as if he was noticing his surroundings for the first time. "It's the talk of the town, darling! How slick of you to make a club for fairies and queers and keep it open this long. Except of course you didn't. Everyone knows it's owned by the Mob."

Lane raised an eyebrow.

That mostly served to remind Eddie that he had been having sex with a gangster. Not that he hadn't known that, but suddenly everything seemed more dangerous.

"Well, Edward!" said Julian, his old self trickling back in with every word. "I never pictured you as the type to get a *mafioso* sugar daddy!"

"What? No. Hey, no. He's not my—"

But Julian waved his hand. "What sort of job are we talking?"

Lane grinned. "I was thinking we could use a few pretty boys to walk around the floor. It's a waiter job, basically, except more than that, too. You'd bring customers drinks but also keep them happy, make jokes, encourage them to dance, that sort of thing."

"Interesting," Julian said, looking around again.

"I assure you that the club itself is far more glamorous than the kitchen. And there's a steady paycheck in this, obviously."

"Mob money," Julian said.

"No. I pay my employees with money earned at the club," Lane said, though Eddie doubted this was completely true. "Besides, I hardly think you're the type to wonder where a dollar came from."

Julian laughed softly. Then he winced in pain. "Well. You've got me pegged, darling."

Lane held out a hand. "Do we have a deal? You can start as soon as you like. After you recover, obviously."

Julian hesitated, but then reached out and took Lane's hand. They shook on it. Lane rattled off some of the particulars, while Julian nodded.

"And you can sleep here tonight if you need to. I've got an office. There's not a lot of space, but the carpeted floor will be softer than this counter."

Still worried about Julian's welfare, Eddie said, "Or you can come back to my place."

Julian shook his head. "I'm sure that I don't want to be the extra wheel in whatever you've got going with the *bel homme*. I'll manage here on the floor. Thank you for the offer, though, darling. I do appreciate it. If nothing else, you've always been good to me." His smile was a little strained, but Eddie felt like there might be some real affection there.

"Will you be all right here by yourself if I leave to get a few hours of shut-eye?" Lane asked. "Everyone is gone for the night. Only me and my assistant Raul have keys to this place."

"I can take care of myself."

Eddie and Lane worked together to help Julian off the counter—it was a struggle, and Julian groaned in pain—and into the office. Lane rummaged around and produced another blanket. He put the blankets together on the floor and pulled a pillow off his desk chair. "It's not great," Lane said, "but it's the best we can do."

"It's just one night. And I'm so very tired, darling. I'll be all right here for a few hours."

"We probably shouldn't leave him alone," Eddie said. "What if he has a more serious injury? A concussion or some bleeding the doctor missed?"

"All right. We can all bunk here if you want to."

Eddie did. He fretted suddenly that Julian was more seriously injured than the doctor could see. That happened all the time, didn't it? Some boxer got hit in the head and seemed fine, but then six hours later, he was dead as a doornail. Come to think of it, maybe Julian shouldn't sleep if he had a concussion.

"Calm down, Eddie," Lane said softly, running a hand down Eddie's back. "It will be all right. We'll stay here with Julian and keep an eye on him."

"Okay."

Lane turned to Julian. "I'll get you squared away with the job tomorrow."

Julian nodded and settled into his spot on the floor.

A half hour later, Eddie and Lane stood outside the office. Julian seemed to be dozing and so far had not shown any further evidence that his injuries were severe.

"You didn't have to do that," Eddie said. "Help out Julian, I mean."

Lane shrugged. "It was the right thing to do. He needed our help, and I was in a unique position to help him. Besides, he's a handsome fella. I think he'd fit right in at the Marigold. Don't you?"

"Well, sure, but—"

"I understand, Eddie. I know what went on here, what Julian was to you. Consider this an unrelated business transaction."

Eddie frowned.

"Besides, this is what you want, right? You're worried about him. I can tell you are. So I'm setting him up. I'm giving him a way out of a bad situation. It's a step toward legitimacy and away from the violence he saw today. That's good."

Eddie stared at Lane. He was still reeling from this night and everything that had happened, what he'd seen, what he'd done. He wasn't sure what to make of any of it, but it felt like he'd turned a corner, that they'd turned a corner together.

Lane reached over and smoothed the hair away from Eddie's face. "I wish that I had the foggiest notion of what goes on in that head of yours."

"Was offering the job about making me happy or doing something for Julian?" asked Eddie.

Lane shrugged. "Maybe a little of both. Call me crazy, but I want to do things that make you happy."

Eddie gave Lane a hard look.

"I'll go out on a limb," Lane went on, "and wager that you would do the same for me, even if you don't want me to think so."

Eddie let out a huff but, when he thought about it, couldn't deny it.

"Thank you," Eddie said softly.

Lane smiled. "Come on, I've got a few more blankets in the closet. Let's camp out here and get a few hours of shut-eye together before we have to face the world again."

Chapter 10

"My Man"

Eddie stood in the middle of Times Square. He liked the chaos of it sometimes, of the flashing lights and the people skittering by. It was an especially busy afternoon for no discernible reason, people everywhere moving like bees.

He stood near the *Times* building, and looked up at the news ticker. *Lindbergh Lands in Paris!* the ticker announced. Eddie laughed and considered how absurd that seemed. He'd seen photos in the paper of *The Spirit of St. Louis* and thought now how bizarre a quest it was for a man to pilot a rickety little plane like that across the ocean.

He shook his head and considered whether he should walk to the Marigold and see if Lane was there or just go to the theater. Eddie wasn't sure he had any business dropping in on Lane at his place of business in the middle of the day, but on the other hand, a tiny part of Eddie just wanted to see him.

He laughed and shook his head. It was a strange turn his life had taken. He opted to walk to the theater to get some extra practice in, reasoning that Lane was probably not even at the Marigold this early in the day. Still, thoughts of Lane brought a smile to his face, enough so that he didn't mind so much when a group of drunk carousers collided with him, or when a busker started belting out "Swanee" badly, or when a newsboy practically assaulted him while trying to sell him a paper. No, none of it mattered, because Lane had put a swing in his step, so he walked to the theater in a celebratory mood.

It didn't last.

* * *

Blanchard had decided to change the show much earlier than expected. As soon as Marian was able to sing the song, he ordered Cotton and France to add it to their act over Eddie's protests that they weren't quite ready. Still, toward the end of May, they debuted "My Heart Is Full" at *Le Tumulte de Broadway* to a packed house.

Eddie and Marian did their usual routine, dancing, joking, singing a few bawdier numbers. Then Eddie pulled out a chair from stage left and sat in it while Marian stepped forward. She was ostensibly singing the song to him, her stage-husband, but she faced the audience as she sang. All of her usual tricks were gone. She wasn't brash. She didn't honk like a goose. Marian sang the way that few knew she could sing, plaintive and rich and lovely, her voice soaring over the orchestra, over the audience. She nailed the song, infusing it with longing and emotion, as if she were singing to a man she loved dearly.

It brought the house down.

Eddie had never seen anything like it. Marian sang the song, and before Eddie even stood to dance her off the stage, the audience was on its feet, cheering and hooting.

After their act, they rushed backstage together. They stood in the hallway that led to the dressing rooms for a moment, catching their breath. Marian laughed. "Wow!" she said. "I didn't think I could do it. That was amazing. Have you ever seen anything like that?"

Eddie laughed with her. "No, I was just thinking the same thing. That was incredible. You were incredible. But I knew you had it in you."

"Thank you, Eddie." She jumped up on her toes and gave him a hug. "Thank you for everything. The act is great, isn't it? We've really arrived now."

Eddie found it hard not to get caught up in Marian's enthusiasm, but at the same time, something nagged him at the back of his mind. Had anything really changed? Blanchard hadn't let Eddie add his new dance. The routine was good, probably one of the best Eddie had ever choreographed, but Blanchard had flatly refused. Cotton and France were doing the same routine they'd done all season except they'd swapped out a comedic number for the new song for Marian, with nothing new for Eddie. Marian was getting all the attention, and Eddie felt pushed into being her sidekick. But he wasn't supposed to be the sidekick, he was supposed to be her equal. Her partner. Not second banana.

But he congratulated Marian and hugged her. Then Blanchard appeared. He walked over to them. He shook Eddie's hand and then gave Marian a rather tender kiss. That surprised Eddie. He'd had his suspicions for a long time that Blanchard was sweet on Marian, but he hadn't known their relationship had progressed to the point where they would kiss like this.

Suddenly the whole situation became a lot clearer.

"You were wonderful, my dear," said Blanchard. "That was fantastic. This will really bring 'em to the theater. We'll fill this place up every night!" He laughed.

Eddie's good mood soured. The show, his future, was playing out in front of him in a way he hadn't expected. Marian was having an affair with Blanchard—something she hadn't told him even though they were supposedly friends—and Blanchard had chosen a song for her as a tribute. Probably so that he could continue a good thing. Eddie would have blamed Marian, but he knew Blanchard wasn't so much interested in her as he was interested in making his show a huge hit. He wanted to overtake George White, he wanted to overtake Flo Ziegfeld, and Eddie knew perfectly well that Blanchard didn't have the talent or vision to make either of those things happen. He had put together a perfectly respectable vaudeville revue, but it wasn't as flashy as the *Scandals* or as over-the-top as the *Follies*. Regardless, though, the song was really just a ploy to put more people in those seats in the theater. Which meant, ultimately, that Blanchard would get his small victory, at the cost of Marian's heart.

And where did that leave Eddie?

He excused himself and went to his dressing room. He sat at his dressing table for a long time, staring at the mirror, looking at the way his makeup had smeared after he'd sweated while dancing under the stage lights. He sighed and grabbed a cloth and started to wipe it off. And as he cleaned the makeup away, his panic mounted. Something about this situation had suddenly, irrevocably turned, and not for the good.

He cleaned his face and changed into his street clothes. He was trying to decide what to do with the rest of the evening—did he want to just go back to his room and wallow, did he want to try to find Lane?—when there was a soft knock at the door.

Eddie answered it. Marian stood there, still in her costume, still all smiles. "Mr. Blanchard wants to take everyone out tonight to celebrate. Maybe to the Waldorf. What do you think?"

"Sounds nice."

"Come with us, Eddie. This is as much your show as it is mine."

He loved Marian, he did. He reached over and pulled her into his arms and gave her a tight hug. He thought about things he'd overheard while eavesdropping. He knew she really believed what she said, that she hadn't figured out yet that this was all part of Blanchard's scheme. She was too naïve to see how Blanchard was manipulating her. And who knew, maybe things would work out for her and he was being unduly cynical. In the end, he didn't blame her for his new plight. But that didn't make him feel any better about his fate.

"I'm not feeling that well," he said.

"Oh, Eddie, come on. You can have a drink with us, a nice meal, celebrate the show! For me?"

"I . . . Is the kitchen there even still open?"

She gave him the pouty face that she knew perfectly well was Eddie's downfall.

"All right," he said. "I'll go for a little while."

She cheered. "Thanks, Eddie! I'll just change. Meet me and Jimmy by the stage door in ten minutes."

Eddie went back to the mirror after she disappeared and stared at himself some more. He looked tired, he thought.

He wondered—and he didn't like this line of thinking but he let it run rampant anyway—what Lane saw in him. Did Lane think him handsome, or did he keep coming back because Eddie was easy sex? Not that the sex wasn't good, at least from Eddie's perspective. Lane attracted him, that was for sure, and surprised him and made him laugh. It was Lane whom Eddie's thoughts turned toward lately more often than not, Lane whom he thought of when he was having a rough day, Lane whom he thought of now that everything was going wrong.

Well, not explicitly so. But Eddie felt uneasy just the same.

He adjusted his tie and found his lucky fedora. He walked out of the dressing room and toward the stage door. A half dozen people stood there, among them a few of the other dancers, one of the chorus girls, Walter Rhodes, and Blanchard. Marian came bustling over a moment later, and everyone applauded her. There were murmurs of "Great!" and "Brava!" Marian smiled and bowed.

"Thank you all so much," she said. "It really means a lot to me."

"It's a great song," Eddie said.

Marian grinned. Eddie held his arm out for her. She tucked her hand into his elbow. Blanchard shot Eddie a disapproving glare, but Eddie didn't care. He wanted some of Marian's giddiness to infect him. He wanted to feel something other than the distress he'd felt back in his dressing room. He wanted to feel for just a few minutes like this might really work out, like everything might really be okay.

Apparently a fancy late-night dinner at the Waldorf was not to be. Instead, they wound up at Lenny's, a restaurant that was only one step up from the Automat or a cafeteria, but Eddie knew Blanchard couldn't really afford to feed all these people at a more expensive joint. Still, the food was good. Eddie and Marian split a steak and a number of buttery side dishes while Blanchard regaled the assembled crowd with tales of the theater, most of which seemed too embellished to be true. It didn't escape Eddie's notice that there was also a small group of men in dark suits sitting in another corner. He overheard one of the stagehands say that the large man at the corner table was David Epstein.

That, of course, made Eddie think of Lane. He wondered if Lane was required to put in an appearance at Lenny's on nights when Epstein was holding court. He'd heard that the Mafia bosses had regularly scheduled meetings in this place, though it had never occurred to him to pay attention until he'd met Lane. Suddenly, the Mob had become real in a way it had never been before.

And then, as if he'd been summoned, Lane himself waltzed in through the door.

Eddie put some effort into ignoring him. He tried to pay attention to the conversation around him. Blanchard was going on about something, probably raving about Marian's performance some more. Lane looked over and made eye contact, but he did not otherwise acknowledge Eddie. Instead, he slid into the chair across from Epstein. Eddie tried not to look, but it didn't escape his notice that Lane and Epstein were huddled close together.

The evening became impossible. He drifted in and out of the conversation with Marian and Blanchard and he kept an eye on Lane. Marian kept having to repeat things she said.

"I'm sorry," Eddie said, finally. "I guess my mind is elsewhere."

Marian smiled at him.

Blanchard said, "You got a sweetheart, Eddie? I know what puts a look like that in a man's eye."

Eddie couldn't help but laugh. Marian looked at him askance.

"No, sir," Eddie said. "No sweetheart. Just a little distracted. Thinking about the show."

"Of course. You agree that Marian's performance was spectacular, don't you?"

"Yes, of course." Eddie gave Marian a little nudge with his elbow. "She was great."

And Eddie felt awful.

Dinner wrapped up much faster than Eddie expected, which was all to the good because he wasn't sure how much more he could take. Marian and Blanchard left together—Eddie supposed they no longer felt the need to keep their affair a secret, although he wondered now how long that had been going on—and then everyone else wandered away. Eddie lingered near the front entrance, and then he went outside for some air. It was a nice night, it was hard to deny that, warm and smelling of summer.

Lane walked outside a few minutes later. "Hello," he said.

Eddie felt like he might collapse suddenly. "I'm a terrible person."

Lane smirked. "I disagree, but I'm curious about why you think so."

Eddie pointed down Broadway, toward the Knickerbocker. Lane nodded and fell into step with him. Eddie explained about the new act, and then said, "You know, Marian and I have known each other for years. She's probably one of the closest friends I've ever had. I wish all the best for her. Really, I do."

Lane nodded. "But?"

"I think the producer is playing her, first of all, and I don't know how to tell her. But more than that, I feel pushed aside. Shouldn't I be happy for her? Shouldn't I want her to do well?"

"Sure, but Eddie, you're half of the best act of that whole production. You're hardly being pushed aside."

Eddie appreciated that Lane was trying to console him, but he knew better. "I don't have the right parts to hold Blanchard's attention. Blanchard's the producer."

"Ah," said Lane.

Eddie shook his head. "I'm being ridiculous."

Lane slung an arm around Eddie's shoulders. "Come on, I'll help you take your mind off things."

*   *   *

Lane watched Eddie while he paced the room. He sat on the bed, figuring he'd wait out Eddie's fit, that he'd make a move when Eddie calmed down.

The cause of Eddie's distress was becoming increasingly clear as he ranted and paced. Lane wished he could do something, but he wasn't sure of the best way to go about it. Would he piss Eddie off? Would he offer comfort? Did Eddie want Lane's comfort?

"You're worried about losing your job," Lane ventured.

Eddie stopped pacing and stared at Lane. "Well, of course! Lane, this is my whole life. Do you know how long I've been dancing? Performing? I spent years getting to this place, and now I might lose it all because Blanchard has decided Marian is his muse. It's like I'm not even there. It's like . . ."

And here was where Eddie finally lost it. His whole face crumpled. Lane worried briefly that he might cry, but instead, he rubbed his face and sat on the bed.

"It might be nothing," Lane said, putting his arms around Eddie. "Maybe Marian's song will bring more attention to your act. You guys really are the best part of the Doozies. Everyone knows that. Your producer can't fire you. He'd lose half his audience."

Eddie leaned into Lane. "I know, I know." He sighed. "I'm probably being irrational, but I can't help but think I'm being pushed out."

"You can cross that bridge when you get to it. No sense worrying yourself, especially since there's not much you can do about it now."

Eddie took a deep breath. "You're right, of course."

"I am sometimes."

"Well, thank you for letting me lose my mind."

"Anytime."

They were quiet together for a long time, just leaning against each other, Lane's arms wrapped around Eddie. Lane leaned his cheek against Eddie's hair. He liked the way Eddie smelled, the way Eddie's body felt against his. "For what it's worth, I'm sorry you're going through all this," he said softly.

"I'm overreacting," Eddie said, burrowing his face into Lane's neck. "You're right, it's probably going to be fine."

"You want someone to lean on, someone to talk to about this, you can come to me. You want not to talk, if you want me to just make you forget, I can do that, too."

"Thank you."

Something warm spread through Lane's chest. It wasn't just that he was aroused, that he wanted Eddie, but he also wanted to make Eddie feel better, he wanted to hold Eddie, and he cared about what happened. He wondered briefly how that had happened, but then he realized that it had probably been that way all along.

And then he really wanted to kiss Eddie. And he wasn't willing to take no for an answer this time.

He eased away from Eddie slightly. He held Eddie's face in his hands, while Eddie's hands moved to his waist. Their eyes met and something intangible passed between them. So Lane moved in. Their faces were so close, and he looked at Eddie's eyes one more time to get permission. When Eddie didn't move away, Lane lunged forward and pressed his lips against Eddie's.

Eddie hardly reacted at first, so Lane moved in deeper, using his tongue to open Eddie's mouth, and then sucking Eddie's lower lip between his teeth. Eddie let out a strangled mumble but then seemed to relax, opening his mouth, kissing Lane. They got lost together as everything around them faded. It was just the two of them, their lips sliding together, a slow congress, a sweet meeting. It was better than Lane imagined, more intimate, more arousing, closer, warmer.

Eddie pulled away slightly, but kept on kissing Lane's face, nipping at his jaw. Lane sighed as Eddie's hands moved to his body and started loosening his clothes. Lane gave in to him, letting him touch anywhere he wanted. Eddie's fingers dug into Lane's flesh as he pulled off items of clothing. Lane gave it all back, pulling at Eddie's shirt, undoing buttons, moving his shirt off his shoulders.

And then everything was urgent. Fabric tore, buttons popped, and articles of clothing were tossed on the floor. Soon enough, they were naked, pressed together on the bed, all hands and fingers, arms and legs tangled, smooth skin, rough skin, hair, nails.

Lane moved to kiss Eddie again, but was refused this time, Eddie turning his face away. Lane rolled his eyes, but kissed Eddie's face, hoping to coax him back. He touched Eddie everywhere, sliding his hands over his skin, touching and feeling and getting lost in Eddie's flesh.

Eddie moaned. Their cocks thrust together, and Lane's hips seemed to move by their own power, pumping and pressing against Eddie, needing that friction. Eddie's hands pressed into his back, holding him close, and the crescendo began in Lane, warmth spreading through his body, tingles over his skin. Then Eddie's fingers found their way along the crack of Lane's ass. "I want . . ." Eddie whispered. ". . . to be inside you."

"Yes," said Lane.

In an instant, Lane found himself on his back. He spread his legs for Eddie and felt Eddie's cock pressing against him, and his body seemed to keen and yearn toward Eddie, everything in him screaming to be closer to Eddie, and then suddenly, Eddie was gone.

Lane's arms felt empty, his body cold, and he was surprised that being parted was such a shock to his system. He propped himself up on his elbows and watched Eddie lope across the room. He picked up a tub of Vaseline from the vanity table in the corner, and then walked back, a smile on his face.

Well, the smile was nice to see. It had been a real rarity lately. Lane opened his arms. "Come here. I want you."

Eddie dipped his head, but not before Lane saw him smile again. He walked over to the bed and fell into Lane's arms, and Lane wrapped himself around Eddie tightly. Eddie wriggled a hand between them and started to prepare Lane, sliding his fingers across Lane's entrance and gently probing. Lane widened his legs, wanting Eddie close to him, inside him, more than anything, wanting to grasp onto that closeness that had been growing between them. Eddie slipped a finger inside Lane and Lane groaned, not minding the invasion, wanting it. Eddie's Vaseline-covered fingers were slick and he was careful, stopping to ask if what he was doing was okay, slowly stretching and opening up Lane.

Then, when Lane couldn't take gentle and careful anymore, he said, "Now, Eddie. Please."

It happened so quickly, Lane almost didn't believe it, but suddenly, Eddie was poised to enter him. Lane pulled his legs up to his chest and felt Eddie's cock pressing gently against his opening. Lane shifted his hips to show Eddie he wanted it. Eddie pressed forward, holding his breath, then letting it go on a moan.

"You feel so good," Eddie murmured, thrusting inside slowly. "So good, baby."

Lane put his hands on Eddie's lower back to encourage him forward, because Eddie was filling him up and touching all the right places, finding that spot inside Lane that sent lightning flashes everywhere. Lane's cock was trapped between their stomachs, and all the texture and friction was driving him wild, making him sweat and tingle, and he wanted Eddie to keep pushing inside, to move, to thrust, to keep hitting that magic spot.

Eddie did. Eddie moved, at first at a steady pace and then erratically. For Lane, everything was feeling and sensation and it was overwhelming. He smelled Eddie, he was tangled up with him, and it pushed and pulled at Lane until he couldn't see or speak, couldn't do anything but feel. He looked at Eddie and their eyes met, and the look on Eddie's face was ecstatic. Eddie's cock rubbed against that spot inside Lane, and his hairy stomach pressed against Lane's cock, Lane felt himself topple right over, the orgasm reaching all corners of his body as he came between them.

Eddie hissed and sighed and moaned and kept on thrusting until he, too, seemed to get lost. He closed his eyes and shuddered and Lane held him as he rocked and came, and then they collapsed together on the bed, sweaty and sticky and satisfied.

Lane regained the capacity for rational thought a short time later, but found he liked being wrapped up in Eddie, comfortable in the bed. Eddie sighed so deeply his chest vibrated against Lane's.

"I've never . . . had an arrangement like this before," Eddie said.

"Do you like it?"

"I . . . yes. Very much."

"Good," said Lane. "I do, too. Let's keep it going, shall we?"

Eddie laid his head on Lane's chest and circled his arms around Lane's waist. It was a little awkward, but Lane felt warm and cared for, and that was what mattered. Eddie took a few deep breaths and then said so softly Lane barely heard, "Yes. I think I'll keep you."

Chapter 11

"Crazy Blues"

Jimmy Blanchard sent a stagehand to fetch Eddie, so Eddie dutifully appeared in Jimmy's office a few minutes later. "Did you want to see me, sir? Because I've also got some ideas for—"

Jimmy stood as Eddie walked into the room. He remained standing as Eddie approached the spare chair, leaving Eddie to wonder if he should sit or not.

"I'll be brief," Jimmy said. "You were spotted at the Marigold."

Eddie opted to sit in the chair, seeing as how his knees were about to give out. "I don't know what you're—"

"I don't care whether it was you or not. Rumor in the theater is that you're a goddamn faggot dancing pansy, and we all know rumor carries more weight than the truth."

"Jimmy, I—"

"Here's the situation. Marian is the crown jewel of this whole production. You are only still here because she insists that you stay, and far be it from me to deprive that girl of what she wants. But she doesn't have the final word. I do. So I'm putting you on notice. You do anything to embarrass this production—if you flub a number or if you are seen within a block of that club—that's it. You got that?"

"Yes, boss, I—"

"Good. We're finished here."

Eddie walked back to his dressing room in a daze. It felt a little futile to rehash his movements for the last few weeks, wondering when he'd been spotted. He did anyway. He'd known it was a possibility for one of the stagehands from the James Theater to have seen him at the Marigold, but he'd been banking on the threat of mutual incrimination to keep him safe, and besides, he hadn't recalled seeing anyone he knew at the club. On the other hand, there were so many times that he'd let his guard down, that he'd stopped being careful, and probably there were a dozen opportunities for him to have been seen. He had to be more careful if he was going to keep his job. Thus he resolved not to go back to the Marigold.

Then he thought: Lane.

He walked into his dressing room and thought about what was more important: Lane or his job. He figured it was only a matter of time before he'd have to choose. He reasoned also that he'd been working toward this dream of performing for two decades, but he'd only known Lane for a few months. If he kept this job, there would be other men.

Of course, none of them would be Lane.

He chastised himself for imagining this relationship with Lane was more than what it was. He'd begun to fancy that they might have some kind of partnership, something more sophisticated than a simple arrangement, but he saw the folly in that now. He took a few moments to mourn the loss of those late nights dancing at the Marigold. But he knew it would take more than a few moments to mourn Lane.

His heart ached as he got ready for that night's show. Maybe he could see Lane without going to the Marigold. That seemed like a good idea until he figured that it was also only a matter of time until some stagehand saw them out and put two and two together. No, better to sever all ties, to stick to the theater and what he'd wanted his whole life than to let himself succumb to the fantasy of a man in his life as great as Lane. There was no way that would ever work.

But, God, he would miss Lane so much.

Lane didn't know what to do with the fact that Officer Al Hardy was standing in the kitchen of the Marigold.

He ran a finger over the ridge of folded bills in his pocket. He hated to part with this much money, but he knew he had enough to keep Hardy from raiding for at least a little while longer.

Hardy looked around. "You serve a lot of food here?"

He sounded so skeptical that Lane decided honesty was the best approach. "No. Most of the appliances don't work."

"So what sort of establishment is this?"

"A social one." Lane tried to remember exactly how much cash was in his pocket. "A place to come to hear music."

Hardy raised an eyebrow. "I don't like what you're doing here, Carillo. I get reports about men dancing and cavorting together."

"Dancing is not illegal."

Hardy took a step toward Lane. "Lewd behavior in public is."

"Nothing lewd happens here. I have rules. Everyone here keeps their clothes on."

"Right." Hardy kept walking forward until he stood within a foot of Lane. "So let's discuss that man in a dress who guards your front door."

Lane rubbed his forehead. He'd sweet-talked Hardy into looking the other way during shipments at other clubs in the neighborhood at which he'd worked, but he worried now Hardy wouldn't be able to see past the nature of this club. He reminded himself that this was always the risk. Still, maybe money would be the deciding factor.

Hardy was already uncomfortably close, but Lane leaned forward and lowered his voice. "Etta is harmless. We're all law-abiding citizens here."

Hardy surprised the hell out of Lane by grabbing his tie. "What you are, Carillo, is filthy. I know what really goes on here." He yanked on the tie, pulling Lane forward until their bodies met. Lane tried to pull back, but Hardy more persistently pressed his hips against Lane's. Lane gasped.

Hardy was hard.

He let go of Lane's tie, dropping it like it had caught fire. Lane took a step back, trying to quickly regain his composure. As gracefully as he could, he palmed the cash from his pocket.

"I think perhaps we understand each other," Lane said. He held out a hand. "It was great to see you again, Officer."

Hardy shook Lane's hand and took the money. "Likewise. I want to believe you're a good man, Carillo." He glanced at the bills in his hand before shoving them in his pocket. "You've always known your way around the business."

"Thank you."

"Stay out of trouble. I better not find out you're bootlegging."

When Hardy left, Lane retreated to his office. He lit a cigarette and fretted about the situation he now found himself in. This meeting had been . . . revealing. Hardy's particular agenda was clear now to Lane, but Lane worried there wasn't a way out of this one besides to continue to pay the man off. Hardy was perhaps bitter or angry about his lot in life; he was a type Lane had met before, a man who might take out his aggressions on those living the life he felt he couldn't have. It took a particular sort of self-loathing to behave the way Hardy did. And that put Lane in a precarious position.

He considered breaking into his personal reserve of whiskey, but thought better of it. He needed something more powerful to calm his nerves. Like sex.

He thought of Eddie, which sometimes also made him think of Scott. The harder he fell for Eddie, the more guilt he felt over what happened to Scott. Lane sat at his desk and conjured up his memories, thinking fondly of his early days in New York with Scott at his side. He'd been deliriously in love, or thought he'd been, anyway, and he'd happily pledged his life to Scott. Scott had declared his love right back, and everything seemed too amazing to be true. Which, of course, it was. The image of Scott's bloated body being pulled from the river flashed back into his head.

He bent forward and rested his forehead against his desk. There were days he still missed Scott, missed how he smelled, missed his laugh, missed the way they could talk about anything for hours, missed how Scott had felt in his arms. He worried that his involvement with Eddie was a betrayal of Scott, but Scott was gone. Scott had forfeited the right to influence Lane's life the day he jumped off the Brooklyn Bridge.

Lane sat up suddenly, surprised by that last thought. It was Scott who'd given up, Scott who'd left, Scott who'd jumped. Lane had persevered without him. Now Scott was nowhere but Eddie was mere blocks away. It was Eddie who played on his mind during idle time, Eddie he'd held in the night most recently, Eddie who was slowly stealing his heart.

It occurred to him that he hadn't seen Eddie in a few days, which struck him as odd given that Eddie had spent nearly every night of the previous week at the Marigold.

And once that thought had popped into his head, Lane made the decision to head over to the theater that night. As the evening wore on, the idea seemed increasingly appealing, though it was also tinged with anxiety that something had happened.

He fretted that he didn't know Eddie well enough to tell what could have happened. Maybe Eddie had gotten hurt. Maybe something had gone wrong at the theater. Maybe he'd met someone else. He'd said he wanted to give them a chance, but what if . . .

It was a slow night, so Lane didn't feel guilty about ducking out of the club early. He walked over to the James Theater and leaned against the lamppost at which he often waited for Eddie. He pulled his hat low so that the brim hid his eyes and watched the various performers leave the theater. He recognized a few of the chorines who snuck out the back way that night, and then he saw Marian France leave the theater on the arm of an older gentleman. He wondered for a brief moment if Eddie had already left, but then, finally, the stage door opened and Eddie emerged.

Lane cleared his throat.

Eddie looked up. He took off his hat and pushed his hair out of his face. "Lane," he whispered.

"Haven't seen you in a few days."

"Yeah, I . . ." Eddie shook his head and stepped toward Lane. "I can't talk to you here." He lowered his voice and added, "Meet me at my room in ten minutes."

He was gone before Lane could ask what was going on. He finished his cigarette, keeping an eye on street traffic. He cooked up a few theories for what Eddie was up to as he walked and only became more puzzled as he made his way down the block. Did Eddie have another lover who might have caught them? Why the need for secrecy?

When he got to Eddie's room, he hesitated before knocking. When Eddie opened the door, he whispered, "Is anyone else in the hall? Did anyone see you come in here?"

"No one's here. I don't think anyone saw me."

Eddie nodded and then grabbed the front of Lane's shirt and hauled him into the room.

"What's going on?" Lane asked.

Eddie frowned. He pulled off his hat and jacket. "I can't come to the Marigold anymore. Someone saw me there and told my boss. If I'm seen there again, I'll get fired."

Lane gasped. That was not at all what he'd expected. "Shit. He can't do that, can he?"

"He told me as much four days ago."

Lane walked over to the bed and sat down. "Well, all right. We'll all miss you there, me most especially, but I'll still see you, right?"

"I don't know. I can't risk getting caught again, at least not for a while. I don't *want* to stop seeing you, but I don't know if—"

The end of Eddie's sentence was muffled against Lane's chest as Lane pulled him into a tight hug. Eddie let out a shaky breath and put his arms around Lane. He mumbled Lane's name a few times before resting his head on Lane's shoulder.

"God," Eddie said. "I don't know what to do. I've worked so hard. I can't lose this job. I was just going to . . . but then I saw you outside the theater and . . . I can't lose you, too."

Lane's breath got caught in his throat. They really were a pair, weren't they? He stroked Eddie's hair. "I understand about your job. We'll figure something out." Not in a million years would Lane let Eddie push him away. Not when Eddie held him this tightly, needed him this badly. They could still be together while Eddie danced at the Doozies. Lane knew all about discretion. "We'll find a way."

"But what if—"

Lane kept stroking Eddie's hair. "I don't know how, but we'll do this."

Eddie pulled away slightly and looked up at Lane. "My whole life, the stage was all I ever wanted. To sing and dance for people. Blanchard has been out for me for a long time, I think. He and Marian are an item, so he has no use for me. Marian is my friend and would stick her neck out for me, but Blanchard really only needs an excuse." Eddie's eyes looked wild, wide and staring unfocused, and he kept shaking his head. "If it gets out that I . . . that we . . . well, I'll never work again."

"That can't be true."

"Broadway is full of homosexual men, but no one wants to talk about it. And Marian, the act, that was propelling me to the top. I didn't expect for us to keep the act up forever, but I need this job, at least until the end of the season." Eddie sighed. "I *need* this. I can't let Blanchard take it away."

Lane held Eddie close, tried to comfort him by stroking his back, his arms. "You won't lose the job. You can't. You're Eddie Cotton."

"I don't know what I'll do if he fires me. I'm nothing without the act. Nothing."

"Eddie, come on, how can you say that? If he fires you, well, he's a damn fool, but you'll figure something out. You'll get another job. You can change your act, refine it, audition for a better producer. Hell, you could dance for Ziegfeld and become even better than you are now. I have faith in you."

"It's nice that one of us does."

Eddie sometimes thought that going out in public required more acting than being on stage.

Marian called it "an appearance." They'd been doing this since they'd created their act together; mostly it involved being seen at whichever club was the bee's knees that week. The point was to see and be seen, to remind people of what they represented, to do their couple act but out in the wild. So, on a warm spring night, at Marian's urging, they walked into the 300 Club, Texas Guinan's late-night hotspot. Eddie had to grease the palm of the bouncer, since apparently just knowing the speakeasy's password didn't guarantee admittance anymore.

"This place has gotten swanky," Marian commented as they did a lap around the room.

It had, that was true. Texas Guinan herself held court at a table toward the middle. Eddie had met her once, years before, and doubted he held the sort of clout that could keep her attention. She prided herself on catering to the rich and famous, neither of which really described Eddie, despite his best efforts.

Appearances like this were intended to put Eddie and Marian in the gossip pages. Eddie always thought seeing his name in print created an illusion of fame he wasn't quite sure he lived up to.

They checked their coats, which revealed that Marian had put on a long, slinky gown covered in tiny silver beads. It caught the light in a way that made Marian sparkle and she looked exceptional in it. He held out his elbow for her and she tucked her hand into it.

"You look lovely tonight, dearest," he said, loud enough for people around him to hear.

"Why, thank you, darling."

Eddie held out a chair for Marian at a table near the dance floor, ideal for being spotted at. She played along, demurely sitting and then gently caressing Eddie's shoulder as he sat. Eddie had to tip the waiter generously, too, in order to get a drink with some giggle water in it.

At the next table, there was a Jane hanging all over some fella in a pinstripe suit, both of them the picture of fashion and elegance. The woman looked like she was genuinely interested in the man—in a way that Eddie and Marian weren't interested in each other—but who knew? Here Eddie and Marian were drumming up attention for their husband-and-wife act, and yet they weren't really married and both were sleeping with other people.

Eddie had been wanting to confront Marian about Blanchard but didn't quite have the heart yet. This might be a good venue to at least mention that he knew what was going on, but then his attention got snagged by the couple at the next table.

"I'll level with ya, doll," the man said in a gravelly voice with a thick Brooklyn accent. "You got gams forever, but I can't get you a job at the Riviera. That's Epstein's joint."

Hearing the name Epstein made Eddie think of Lane, although it didn't take much to make him think of Lane lately. Suddenly, Eddie felt like a moll, a gangster's girl, and that was a strange position to find himself in. But that was the situation, wasn't it? He was Lane's. They belonged to each other. If Eddie couldn't bring himself to leave Lane even when the stakes were as high as they were, he was hooked. He realized, thinking about Epstein, that it was probably dangerous getting involved with a man like that; Lane's life seemed fairly free of trouble, but how well did they even really know each other? Lane was still part of the Mob. He was a club owner, a bootlegger, potentially a killer. It was easy to forget that when they were in bed or having a quiet drink at a bar. But that was the real truth at the end of the day.

"What's eating you, Eddie?" Marian asked.

"Ah, nothing. Just thinking about . . . things."

"Jimmy was right, wasn't he? You got someone you're stuck on."

Eddie shook his head. "I'm not stuck on anyone."

"That man who comes to the theater after the show. The fella with the expensive shoes who smokes near the lamppost. He's waiting for you often enough. I thought maybe you had something going with him."

That Marian knew about Lane was alarming. So much for discretion. "Who else has seen him?"

"No one, as far as I know. But I see him there all the time and figured he must be waiting for someone. I thought it was one of the chorus girls. Then, last week, I left just after you and saw you talking to him. I just wondered."

"It's nothing."

"It would be fine with me if it were. I understand about you, Eddie."

"No."

Marian sat back in her chair a little and shrugged. "All right."

"You and Jimmy Blanchard are an item."

Marian huffed. "That's hardly news."

"Well, then use your keen sense of sight to see what's right in front of you." Eddie took a deep breath and tried to calm down. He wasn't really angry at Marian and he didn't want to take his frustration out on her. She didn't deserve that. Quietly, he said, "Your Jimmy has been looking for an excuse to fire me. I know he has. You can't say anything about the man you've seen outside the club. Not a word. This would be Blanchard's excuse."

Marian frowned. "He doesn't want to fire you."

"He does. He wants you to be his star. And you deserve it, Marian, you really do. That new song, it's wonderful, and Blanchard probably doesn't think you need a ball and chain like me hanging around your ankle."

"That's not what you are. The act doesn't work without both of us."

"Blanchard doesn't see it that way. But I want this, Marian, I want our act to succeed. You know I love to dance. So you can't . . . you can't tell Blanchard you think I'm sweet on some fella because then that's it for me. He'll let me go."

Marian reached over and placed her hand over Eddie's. "I won't say anything. And for good measure, I will play the doting spouse right now to better convince all these people that we're an item. That's what Jimmy wants. For us to get people in those seats."

Eddie turned his hand over and squeezed hers. "Thanks, Marian."

But how sad was it that a lie was safer than the truth.

Chapter 12

"The Song Is Ended"

Julian came into work—and, he thought fondly, this was work, legitimate work, work he didn't have to spread his legs for—and took in the scene of the Marigold with sunlight streaming through the windows. The brightness made the place look dirtier and shabbier than it did at night when the lights were low. He caught sight of Lane speaking to someone in the corner and wondered about that, too, about how a man like Lane came to work in a place like this. Or, given what Julian knew of Lane's proclivities, perhaps the nature of the club was not so much of a surprise as its ownership.

Still, Julian liked Lane, and not only because he'd set Julian up with a job and a place to stay. Well, the boardinghouse on 16th Street left something to be desired, but it had a bed and it was clean and Julian didn't have to pay for it, either with money or his body. He suspected the boardinghouse was owned by the same people who owned the Marigold, and there were a number of shady characters occupying the other rooms, but what Julian appreciated was that his room had a door that closed, so he could shut out everyone else. It had been years since he'd had such a luxury.

So he was happy, if still a little sore. Makeup covered the bruises well enough and Lane let him hide out in the office when the pain from his injuries became overwhelming. But now Julian whistled a tune he thought might have been Gershwin—or a bastardization thereof—as he walked to the kitchen. He felt good today.

When he came through the door, he saw one of the other waiters sitting on a chair in the corner, flipping through the newspaper. "Oh, hey," the waiter said. "I think I seen this guy here before."

"Who?" Julian asked, walking over. He held out his hand. The waiter handed over the page he was reading. The paper—the *Evening Graphic*, Julian noted—was open to Walter Winchell's column, which decried the firing of the gentleman in a slightly grainy photo on the right side of the page: Eddie Cotton.

Too surprised to speak, Julian read the column. Apparently, Doozies producer Jimmy Blanchard had decided that Marian France was to become a star on her own, and that Cotton and France would no longer be a duo. Which meant that Jimmy Blanchard had no use for Eddie Cotton.

Julian ran back out into the club proper, paper still in hand. He hesitated when he saw that Lane was still speaking to the fellow he'd been talking to before, a greasy looking man in a dark suit. They appeared to come to some sort of understanding, both nodding their heads. They shook hands and the besuited man put his hat back on. Lane then turned his attention to Julian. "Did you need something?"

"You should see this," Julian said, handing the paper over to Lane.

Lane frowned, and then his face crumpled. "Oh, no," he said. "No, no, no. This is terrible. I . . . I have to find him."

Julian followed after Lane as he walked through the kitchen and to his office in the back. The first thing Lane did was pick up the phone. He tried to connect to several different people before he slammed the phone in its cradle and groaned in frustration. "Where could he be?" Lane asked.

Julian was surprised to see all that anguish on Lane's face, the way his eyebrows knit together with worry, the frown lines suddenly more prominent. Julian racked his brain. "I don't know," he said honestly. "It's not like we were friends. He used to come find me under the elevated tracks on Sixth Avenue, next to Bryant Park, or else sometimes we'd meet by the *Times* building, or at the Astor. Otherwise, I don't know where he goes when he's not at the theater."

"Train tracks?" Lane said, his eyes going wide. "No, not again. This can't happen again."

Julian wanted to ask what couldn't happen again, but Lane pushed him aside and half-ran out of the office. By the time Julian got outside, Lane was already at the corner. He turned around and shouted,

"Raul is in charge. You got that?" Then he turned onto Broadway and was gone.

It was like a slide show or a bad nickelodeon movie. Scott's face, smiling, the last night in Waukegan. Eddie dancing. The Brooklyn Bridge. The Sixth Avenue El. Eddie smiling but trying to hide it. Eddie's face when he was in Lane's arms. Eddie's sadness. Scott's body being pulled from the East River. Scott's face bloated. Eddie's face shining. Eddie dancing. Eddie singing. Eddie. Eddie.

Lane knew he could have been wrong. He was probably wrong. But something—instinct, intuition, fear, Lane didn't know—propelled him forward.

As a token, he tried the Hotel Astor first, and then the James Theater, and then he tried Eddie's room at the Knickerbocker, but he knew that Eddie would not be in any of those places. So he ran down 42nd Street to Bryant Park. He jogged a lap around the park, but didn't see anyone besides the usual transients loitering near benches and a few men that he was pretty sure would offer him sex if he stopped running. Instead he ran back to Sixth Avenue and looked up at the elevated tracks. He didn't see anyone up there, so he ran up the stairs to the platform. A few people stood, waiting for a train, but there was no sign of Eddie.

At a loss, Lane stood and stared. Why had he felt the conviction that this was where Eddie would come? He clearly wasn't here. And yet . . .

Lane ran back down the stairs to the street. He considered his options, whether to go north or south, and figured he'd start by going south. He'd keep running if it took him all afternoon to find Eddie, all night, all week. He could not lose Eddie, and he was sure beyond any doubt that Eddie meant to do himself harm. He remembered that look on Eddie's face when they'd talked the week before, when Eddie had assumed his days in the Doozies were numbered, how sad and desperate he had looked.

Lane took off down Sixth Avenue, moving swiftly but keeping his eyes open, looking everywhere for where Eddie might have gone. When he got to a station, he'd run up the stairs and check the platform, and when he didn't see Eddie, he'd run down the stairs again and keep running south.

He'd gone almost a full mile when he nearly collided with a newsboy who tried to sell him a copy of the *Post*. "Doozies fires Eddie Cotton!" the kid shouted. "Read all about it!"

Lane tossed the kid a few coins and took a paper. He scanned the story, still not seeing any rhyme or reason for Blanchard firing Eddie besides a quote near the bottom of the story: "Marian France is the biggest star on Broadway!" Blanchard had apparently told the reporter. "She'll be bigger than Fanny Brice! Bigger than Ethel Barrymore! Bigger than Sarah Bernhardt! She'll be a household name!"

Lane tucked the paper into his jacket then hurried up to the platform at 23rd Street. And there, at long last, was Eddie, standing at the edge of the platform, swaying on his feet.

Lane whispered his name. Worried about startling him and sending him falling onto the tracks, Lane approached slowly, murmuring "Eddie" and hoping to draw his attention. When he was within five feet, Eddie turned.

The utter devastation on his face was heartwrenching. His hair was mussed and his eyes were red and his forehead was creased with hurt and shame. "Good God," he said. "Lane. What are you doing here?"

"I heard about what happened. I've been trying for more than an hour to find you."

"Well, here I am!" Eddie said. He swayed on his feet, more with what Lane was realizing was serious drunkenness than with a lack of balance. As Lane got closer, he realized that Eddie reeked of alcohol, that he must have been very drunk.

Lane gently curled a hand around Eddie's arm and tugged him away from the edge of the platform. Eddie acquiesced easily enough. "Where did you find alcohol at this time of day?"

"Speakeasy on Twenty-fourth. They're open all day. The hooch was awful, tasted like cleanser, but it did the job, didn't it?"

"Certainly seems that way."

Eddie wriggled away from Lane and looked down. He reached into his pocket. "Why did you come to find me?"

"I couldn't let you—" Lane stopped abruptly. He considered how best to say what he wanted to say. "Someone at the Marigold had the paper. Walter Winchell wrote about you. He said in his column that he thought Blanchard was a fool for letting you go."

"That was nice of Wally."

"I thought so, too. But I saw the column and I thought about what you said last week about how important this job was to your life, and I wanted to stop you before you did something too foolish."

Eddie's facial expressions were all comically exaggerated, and Lane would have laughed if the situation hadn't been so troubling. His jaw dropped. "Why does it matter? It's not like anybody cares about me at all."

"That's not true."

"It is true." Eddie started walking back toward the tracks. "No one would notice. If I jumped on the tracks, if the next train ran right over me, it's not like anyone would notice I was gone."

"Plenty of people would notice."

Eddie shook his head. "You're a fool, Lane, to have come after me."

Lane took a step toward him, hoping to grab his arm again and pull him away from the tracks. Eddie seemed determined to teeter there right on the edge.

The platform started to vibrate, indicating a train was on its way. In horror, Lane watched Eddie stand there and lean over to peer down the platform. Lane could hear the train before he saw it, a great heavy thing, painted dark green, rumbling toward them. For a few seconds, Lane was completely convinced that Eddie would jump, and when he moved to grab Eddie and pull him away, Eddie shoved him so hard that Lane fell, landing on his ass. He scrambled to his feet again as the train moved through the station. Its brakes squealed as it came to a stop, and Lane noticed that Eddie just stood there, staring at it, as the doors rolled open.

The train was gone again before Lane had a good handle on what had happened, but he did know one thing: Eddie was still among the living, and he stood right there on the platform, watching the train leave the station with his jaw loose and his eyes open wide.

"You can't do it, can you?" Lane asked.

Eddie looked back at Lane. He didn't say anything, but something at his side caught Lane's attention, something that sparkled. Lane realized it was a gun, the slick metal of the barrel glittering in the sunlight.

"Eddie," said Lane.

"I'm a coward," Eddie said. "I can't jump. It takes too long to think about how to do it. But this." He raised the gun and pointed the barrel toward his temple. "This will be fast."

"Killing yourself is the coward's way out," Lane said.

Which got Eddie to falter enough that he pointed the gun away from his head.

"Eddie, please don't do this."

Eddie dropped his hand, still holding the gun. Lane saw that his finger was curled around the trigger. There was a brief awful moment where he thought Eddie might turn the gun on him, but it remained pointed toward the ground. "Blanchard thinks I'm useless and he's right. I'll never be good enough to be in a better production than the Doozies."

"What are you talking about?" Lane considered how to end this. Stalling Eddie meant that Eddie might sober up enough to realize what a ridiculous decision he was making. "You're great. You're so much better than Blanchard's production. You could audition for other shows. Walter Winchell—*Walter Winchell,* Eddie—said in his column today that Blanchard was a fool for firing you. Isn't that a hell of an endorsement?"

"Why does it matter? No one cares about me."

Well, now this was getting tiresome, but Eddie still had the gun. "I care about you," Lane said. He took a step away, trying to get a hold on his emotions. It wouldn't do for him to lose control when Eddie was so fragile. "The thing men never think about when they kill themselves is who they leave behind. If you do this, you won't just be hurting yourself. You'll hurt me, too. And Marian, and all of your friends, your family, everyone who cares about you."

"I don't have any family."

Lane grunted. "Don't do this. Please don't. Stay. Stay here. Stay with me."

Eddie stood very still for a long moment. He turned and looked back at the tracks, and then he looked at Lane. "I can't."

It wasn't clear what Eddie couldn't do, if he couldn't jump or if he couldn't stay. The platform started to vibrate again. As the train got nearer, Lane shouted, "Don't."

It was like a flash of lightning. One minute, Eddie was facing away from Lane, toward the platform, the gun clutched in his hand, and Lane imagined that gun blowing Eddie's brains out before Eddie toppled onto the tracks and was bowled over by the train. When Eddie's arm moved, Lane lurched forward and shouted, "No!" but was helpless to do anything but watch. Eddie tossed the gun and then it was flying through the air, creating the most beautiful arc through the sky, curving until it crashed onto the tracks, rattling against the rail and settling in the rail bed. The train plowed into the station and stopped. Passengers got out and pushed past Lane and Eddie as if they weren't there. When the train rumbled away, Eddie and Lane were left alone on the platform again. Eddie turned back to Lane, his face registering his distress, his features twisted in pain. Before Lane could catch him, Eddie collapsed on the platform, like his legs had just stopped working. Lane scrambled to his side, sitting on the hard, rough platform and pulling Eddie into his arms, not caring about who saw them or who cared.

He realized that Eddie was sobbing.

They sat there for a long time, though Lane wasn't sure how long; it could have been five minutes or it could have been an hour. The light in the sky started to change as the sun lowered. Eventually, Lane helped Eddie stand and said, "Come on, let's get away from trains."

Eddie let himself be hoisted up. "Where will we go?"

"My apartment is not far from here," Lane said.

Eddie nodded and let Lane help him down the stairs, back down to the street. He wiped his eyes and looked around. Lane was aware they were back in public, dozens of people moving about on the sidewalk. He handed Eddie his hat. Eddie took it and pulled it down low on his head, hiding his tired eyes from onlookers. "I've never been to your apartment," Eddie said, perfectly calm, as if he hadn't been about to kill himself, as if he hadn't been crying.

Lane didn't want to have to explain how deliberate that was, how he hadn't been willing to let Eddie into the space he'd shared with Scott. He still wasn't really happy about it, but he knew that letting Eddie—Eddie, who was still very much alive—into the space once occupied by a man who was dead was more important now. Lane said, "We usually don't leave Times Square."

Eddie seemed to be satisfied with this answer. He nodded. They walked a few steps and then Eddie stumbled, reminding Lane that he was probably still drunk.

Lane said, "Come, I'll put you to bed."

They started and stumbled, until suddenly Eddie doubled over. Sensing what was about to happen, Lane steered him toward a trash can on the street, at which point Eddie started groaning and retching and then, finally, vomiting.

When that seemed over, Lane led Eddie a few blocks uptown and then west on 26th Street to the apartment house he called home. When they were in the lobby, Lane slung an arm around Eddie and helped him up the stairs to Lane's third-floor apartment. Once they were in the apartment, Lane pointed Eddie at the bed—the bed Lane had once shared with Scott, he couldn't help but thinking. Eddie lay down and immediately curled up in a ball. Lane sat on the edge of the bed and helped him out of his shoes. Then he went into the kitchen and put some water on to boil, thinking he could make some tea.

Lane had to stop what he was doing and take a few deep breaths. He'd never let another man into the apartment, not since Scott's death. He'd been with a few men over the years, but none had gotten to him the way Eddie had. And now Eddie had almost taken himself away the same way Scott had done, and Lane felt the loss of that. He was glad, too, that he'd stopped history from repeating itself.

He kept a framed photograph on a side table near the sofa. It was a picture Clarence had taken of Lane and Scott shortly after they'd come to New York, and the smiles on their faces were happy and relieved, full of a sense of awe that they'd arrived in this city of endless possibilities. Scott would jump off the Brooklyn Bridge four months later, which had changed everything, made those possibilities seem like foolish dreams.

"I'm sorry," Lane said softly to the Scott in the photo. "I promised I would never let any man take your place in my heart, and no one ever will, but you're not here now, and it seems I've already given a part of my heart to him. I won't ever forget you. But he needs me right now."

The kettle whistled. Lane turned it off and made a cup of tea. When he carried it into the bedroom, he saw that Eddie had gone to sleep. He put the tea on the side table and sat next to Eddie. He smoothed Eddie's hair out of his face. "I hope your dreams are sweet," he said.

Eddie grunted and stirred in his sleep but didn't wake up. Lane lay down next to him, hoping that the mere fact of his proximity would be of some comfort to Eddie. He decided to drink the tea, so he scooted back to sit against the headboard, sipping tea and watching Eddie sleep.

Chapter 13

"There'll Be Some Changes Made"

Eddie came to in a bedroom he didn't recognize, but, funnily enough, it *smelled* familiar. It smelled like Lane.

Suddenly, the last day flashed through his mind, and he remembered horrific patches of what had happened: Blanchard telling him that he and Marian were no longer a duo, that Marian was his star, and that Eddie's song-and-dance skills would no longer be needed. He remembered leaving the theater and the emptiness he'd felt as he realized he was not only out of a job but that he was out of doing something he loved. He'd walked around downtown for a while until he'd found that speakeasy, the one he knew would be open in the middle of the afternoon, and he'd put all that completely awful juice into his body until the pain started to ease.

Exactly where the gun had come from, he couldn't quite remember. There was some business with a man in a threadbare suit at the speakeasy who said he had the easy solution for Eddie's problems. Eddie had forked over a hundred dollars, and twenty minutes later, he'd gotten the shiny gun out of the deal. The gun, he remembered now, that he hadn't fired, that now lay on an elevated train platform. It had been a sad waste of money, especially now that Eddie's source of income had dried up.

He wondered how he would pay for his room at the Knickerbocker, the place he'd been calling home for the last two years. Now that Blanchard had let him go, he knew he couldn't compete with the upper echelon of performers for space in the bigger productions, and he knew he couldn't stomach the embarrassment of auditioning for a lesser show. Sure, there were burlesques that might take a song-and-dance man, but Eddie would be competing with beautiful, scantily-clad women for the attention of the audience, and then he'd be back in the same situation. No, that would be unacceptable, too.

For a brief moment as he'd stumbled out of the speakeasy, it had seemed like a good idea to go see his father. Why this was the case, Eddie wasn't sure; he hadn't spoken to his father in more than a dozen years, not since the day Eddie had been thrown out of the house. Eddie had felt for years that he had no family, even though his blood relations were right there on the same island. He hadn't seen them since he'd left, though, and they hadn't come after him and had never attended his show, to his knowledge. He'd reasoned that if they couldn't support him doing something he loved, he had no need for them. But then he'd seen the Sixth Avenue El in the distance after he'd stumbled out of the speakeasy and he'd considered taking it downtown and going back home with his tail between his legs and telling his father that of course he was right, that Elijah Cohen had no business dancing on Broadway, and he'd of course die alone and destitute just as his father had predicted, because no one had any use for a queer performer.

And he'd ached, oh, how he'd ached, and he couldn't think of a way to make the ache stop except for the increasingly appealing idea of just lying down on the tracks and letting physics take over, but he couldn't quite bring himself to do it, some tiny part of him not quite ready to give up yet. And he stood on the platform and waited for a train, and when one pulled up, he couldn't make himself get on it, either, couldn't make himself go down to the Lower East Side and admit his defeat to his father. He'd let the train go by, stared at the tracks, and thought, well, there would be another.

But somehow, rather than sliced into pieces or stuffed into a tenement with his family, Eddie was in a bed, a very warm one with nice sheets and a down comforter, a bed that smelled like Lane.

Lane.

That's what had happened. Lane had appeared like he'd been conjured, and he'd stood there and he'd said, "I care about you. Stay with me," and that had seemed like an impossible thing to argue with. The part of Eddie that hadn't been quite ready to give up yet had won over the part that was, and he let himself be led to Lane's apartment. That was, apparently, where he was now.

His head hurt. That was the next thing he became aware of. Not just a dull ache, but full on acute pain, like someone had shoved a knife into his right eye. He rolled onto his back and grumbled and looked around the room. Somehow, it had become night. The light was on in the bedroom, but it was perfectly dark outside. He rolled over and looked around and saw that Lane was there, sitting propped against the headboard, his head bowed forward, asleep.

Eddie tried to ignore the pain in his head, although that was a futile activity if ever there was one. He needed . . . something. Food. Water. Lane. He reached over and ran a hand over Lane's knee, which pulled Lane out of sleep.

"Hello there," Lane said. "How do you feel?"

"Like I've been dragged through Hell on my head."

Lane smiled. "That good?" Then he lowered his voice. "Do you remember what happened?"

Eddie nodded, which hurt tremendously. He put a hand to his forehead and stifled a groan.

"I think I have some aspirin," Lane said, getting off the bed. He vanished through the bedroom door and came back a moment later holding a glass of water and a small brown bottle. He motioned for Eddie to sit up, which Eddie did with great effort, and then Lane handed over the glass of water. Eddie took a sip and watched Lane dump a couple of pills out of the bottle. He handed those to Eddie, too. "That should take care of your headache. As for the rest, well, I'll do what I can."

Eddie swallowed the pills and drank the rest of the water and then handed the glass back to Lane. He lay back down. "This is a nice apartment," he said. "How long have you been here?"

"Five years or so."

Eddie nodded. "How is it we've never been here together before? Even that time we went to the club on Fourteenth Street, we still wound up at the Knickerbocker."

Lane walked over to the bed and sat down. "Honestly? I didn't want you here."

Eddie felt shame wash over him. As if this day hadn't been bad enough. He lowered his head. "Oh."

"Not for why you think," Lane said. He shook his head. "Might as well tell you. I ran to New York from Illinois. With a man named Scott."

Eddie nodded. "Sure."

"We lived here together."

Eddie nodded, trying to figure out what Lane was telling him. Did Scott still live here? Would he cause trouble for Eddie?

"He, ah. He's dead."

"Oh. I'm sorry."

Lane smiled, but there was no oomph behind it. "He hated himself. Hated what he was, what we were together. And we . . . I was supposed to marry his sister. But I just couldn't. She was a nice girl, but we barely knew each other. Our mothers were great friends, though, so we planned this wedding. I thought I could do it, that I could just pretend, but I got one look at Scott and it was all over. He was what I wanted, not my fiancée. Scott came to me one night, snuck into my room at my parents' house, and said we should run away to New York. We hitchhiked to Chicago and caught the Twentieth Century Limited the next day. And everything with us was great, but as time went on, it wore away at Scott. He was miserable away from his family, and he was ashamed of his life with me, and we got harassed sometimes when we went out together. And he just . . . it ended one night. He went to the Brooklyn Bridge and jumped into the East River."

"Oh God," Eddie said, letting that sink in.

"So you can see why one lover bent on doing himself harm was quite enough."

Eddie could only imagine what must have gone through Lane's head. "Is that why you came after me today?"

"Well, in part."

Eddie grunted. "Couldn't have another suicide on your conscience, eh?"

Lane balked. "No, Eddie. I want you, I want to be *with you*, and I couldn't bear not to have you around anymore. I mean that honestly." Lane pressed a hand to his heart. "I will admit that I thought of Scott when I heard the news that you'd been let go from the Doozies and I worried that you might try to do something extreme, and I had to find you because I couldn't lose you the same way I lost Scott." He gave a tiny half smile. "It seems I've grown quite fond of you."

Eddie didn't know what to do with that. He couldn't fathom how this had happened, how he'd found himself in the apartment of a very nice—albeit Mob-tied—man who seemed to genuinely like him, how everything in his life had gone so horribly wrong in the space of a day, but yet here was this one beacon of hope.

When Eddie turned to Lane, he saw that Lane was looking at him intently.

"Here's the crazy part," Lane said. "I'm falling in love with you."

That really didn't make any sense to Eddie. They hadn't known each other that long, had they? Only six weeks, two months, something like that. Or three months, maybe; Eddie had lost track. Granted, they saw each other a few times a week, and sometimes the days blended together. Eddie liked Lane a great deal. And Lane had gone to all that trouble to talk him off the subway platform, hadn't he? And still . . . "This was an arrangement."

"It's not anymore," Lane said, leaning closer to Eddie. "At least, that's not all it is. Not to me."

Eddie wanted to protest but found the words died on his tongue. He was still too tied up with grief over everything to be able to sort through his feelings tangled in the gnarled branches that seemed to have taken root around his heart, and everything felt tainted and ruined. Everything was, of course, except Lane, sitting there next to him, looking so serious. Lane who was offering love and hope. Lane, who had kept him from making what was increasingly starting to feel like a terrible mistake.

But was it enough? Men didn't love each other, not the way men and women did, or that was what Eddie had always thought. And yet . . .

He reached over and took Lane's hand and threaded their fingers together. He realized that he wanted that love, he wanted it desperately, and he wanted to reciprocate it, though he wasn't sure how.

"I've never known anyone like you," Eddie said. "When I was young, I would fool around with the other boys I met, the ones who hung around Coney Island and later the ones who worked in the theater. There was one, his name was Bailey, he worked at the New Amsterdam for Mr. Ziegfeld as a stagehand." Eddie shook his head. "This was so long ago. We were so young. We were completely infatuated with each other. He wanted to be a dancer, too, but he could never get the rhythm quite right. He was always too awkward on his feet. Anyway, we used to meet at this cafeteria on Broadway. Do you remember it?"

Lane nodded. "Big Jasper Fish used to hang around there, right? The one near Forty-eighth Street? Closed last year?"

"Yes, that's it. Did you know Big Jasper?"

"No. Only by reputation"

Eddie sighed. "So Bailey and I would meet there every Tuesday. We'd use our piddling wages to buy dinner and then we'd find some place to go for the night, usually the room he had at a boardinghouse in the West Thirties. Then one Tuesday, he wasn't there anymore. Big Jasper himself told me he'd heard Bailey had taken up with some opera singer and moved downtown. Jasper told me that it wasn't worth it for me to give up my heart because queer men would never be to each other what men and women are."

"So you haven't. Given up your heart, I mean."

"No, not since then."

Lane reached over and traced a line along Eddie's jaw with his finger. "Jasper was wrong."

Eddie found himself hard pressed to disagree when he was this close to Lane. He leaned a little closer, hoping Lane would take him into his arms, but instead, Lane started to lean forward, his lips slightly parted, and Eddie knew what he wanted. Only Eddie wasn't sure he was ready to give it quite yet. He turned his head to the side and let Lane kiss his cheek.

"Bang it, Eddie. Let me kiss you."

Eddie couldn't explain why he was so reluctant to kiss Lane, not in a way that was rational or made any sense. The one time they'd kissed before had confirmed a lot of things for him, namely that he was falling for Lane, too, and that getting lost in those kisses was a surefire way to get his heart stomped on. Because while he believed that Lane meant every word he said now, there was still a niggling doubt in the back of his mind, a worry that it would all end as soon as Lane met someone better than Eddie. Which, as far as Eddie could tell, "someone better" could have been a great number of men.

Lane made a frustrated snarl at Eddie's hesitation. "When we kissed the last time, the world did not end. The stars kept shining, the earth kept turning."

"Why do you want to?"

"Why don't you?"

It felt like a dare. Eddie looked at Lane and saw his eyebrows furrowed in frustration, but he wondered if he didn't also see a little bit of sadness there, a little bit of pain. He wondered how much Lane's Scott had contributed to that pain and sadness, and how much Eddie himself contributed to it.

"I'm sorry, Lane, I—"

"Don't apologize. Kiss me."

And Eddie still hesitated, but the look on Lane's face was so earnest that it was hard to shy away from it. He swallowed his pride and moved forward. He gently pressed his lips against Lane's.

And then he was lost. The warmth of Lane's lips and his body under Eddie's hands went a long way toward soothing the turmoil inside him. Lane groaned softly as he lifted his hands and moved his fingers through Eddie's hair. He pressed his tongue forward and pried Eddie's lips open, so Eddie opened and let him in. They devoured each other and Eddie wondered briefly why he'd denied himself this pleasure, but of course, he knew: this was too good, too perfect. He pulled away slightly and sighed.

"See, that wasn't so bad," Lane said with a smile. He still had his hands in Eddie's hair, so he tugged a little, and then they were kissing again.

Eddie found he didn't really have the energy to do much more than that, but he liked the kissing, despite himself. Lane's lips were warm and tasted of something vaguely metallic and very masculine. And wasn't that the greater problem here? That Lane was so masculine, that he wasn't a woman, that everything about Eddie's life had taken this turn away from where he should have been? That instead of taking the opportunity of losing his theater job to go back to the straight and narrow and to do what his family wanted of him, he instead decided his life was over? What did that say about him?

He sighed and put his arms around Lane. He pressed his forehead to Lane's shoulder.

"What are you thinking about?" Lane asked.

"I can't believe that any of this has happened."

"Maybe you should sleep some more. I don't know. Do you feel better at all? How's your headache?"

Eddie's head didn't hurt much anymore, but he did feel suddenly tired. "I feel like I could sleep for a week."

Lane smiled. "You're safe here. Take all the time you need. You want to stay for a week? Stay for a week."

"Thank you, Lane." Eddie felt like he should thank Lane for everything. "Do you have to go to the club tonight?"

"Raul is in charge. I really don't have to be there very often, actually. I just go because I like to make sure things are running smoothly, I guess. It drives Epstein nuts that I have that much control, I think. If he had his way, there'd be more interference. But, really, don't you think I'm in a unique position to know what's best for my club?"

Thankful for the shift in conversation away from Eddie's problems, Eddie rested his head on Lane's shoulder and said, "How's Julian?"

"Great," Lane said. "You might be happy to know that my instincts were right. The customers love him."

"That's good."

"Eddie, rest. If you want to flap your lips about nothing, we can do that tomorrow, okay? Unless you need to go back home?"

Eddie knew that by "home" Lane was referring to his room at the Knickerbocker, where Eddie knew he'd have to return eventually, but the impulse to go see his father flashed through Eddie's mind again. He wondered if he'd be able to ever go back and face the man. He'd have to give up Lane to do it, that was for sure, but how could he do that when he and Lane had just found each other?

Lane eased Eddie down so that he was lying on the bed again. "You hungry at all? I think I have some things I can whip up into a decent supper. Maybe some soup I can heat up."

"No, I'm all right. Did you eat?"

"Yes, a little while ago."

Eddie felt himself sinking into the pillow. Tomorrow, he thought. He could deal with all the nonsense tomorrow.

Chapter 14

"What'll I Do?"

Marian woke up in Jimmy Blanchard's four-poster bed, and she took a moment to luxuriate in the satin sheets before she began to wonder where Jimmy had gone off to.

The performance the previous night had been strange. Without Eddie there, Marian had had to do something completely different. She hadn't had much time to prepare, and she resented Jimmy for pushing Eddie out so abruptly, but she'd been able to rally all of her theater training and put an act together on short notice. She'd improvised a little solo dance routine, she'd told a few of the jokes that worked without Eddie there to supply the punch line, and she'd sung a few of her comedic songs. She wrapped up the show with "My Heart Is Full," and again, she brought the house down. Or so Jimmy had said. Marian hadn't been able to hear anything over her own pounding heart.

Part of her knew the routine didn't work without Eddie, and she'd protested loudly when Jimmy told her he was letting Eddie go. "You're the star now," he'd insisted. "Eddie Cotton's time is over. He's too old to be a star and not good enough to be your partner anymore."

Marian didn't really think this was true. Her Eddie was younger than Eddie Cantor, who was headlining the Ziegfeld Follies that season. And, while she thought she did a good job with her new routine, not having Eddie by her side during the show was nerve-wracking. She hadn't truly appreciated how much he helped her calm down, nor how well their routine worked as a duo, until now. It wasn't just that the act wasn't as good; *she* wasn't as good without a partner to play off of.

But after the show, Jimmy had lavished her with praise, and she took all of it and held it close to her heart. He took her to the Waldorf after and they had an elaborate and expensive dinner before going back to Jimmy's apartment. And now she was in the marvelous bed and it was hard to remember what she'd been upset about.

Jimmy came into the room wearing a silk robe. There was a cigar dangling from his lips. He took a long drag from it before taking it away from his mouth. "Hello, dear," he said. "Good morning."

"Good morning," she said, smiling. She wanted to ask Jimmy again about whether firing Eddie was really very smart, but she didn't want to mar an otherwise lovely morning. She lifted the sheet so that Jimmy might be tempted to climb back into bed with her, because then, at least, she wouldn't have to think about the show anymore.

She hadn't even been able to say good-bye. That was what bothered her. She'd wanted to talk to Eddie, but Jimmy told her not to, and then he'd gone into Eddie's dressing room, broken the news, and then gotten a few security guards to escort Eddie outside.

"I know you're thinking about Eddie Cotton," Jimmy said, sitting on the bed next to her. "This was the right move, though. Because you, Marian dear, are the star of *Le Tumulte*. Don't let Cotton or anyone else tell you otherwise."

Actually, Eddie would probably have agreed with Jimmy's assessment. Marian was the one who wasn't sure it was true.

"It was a business decision, dear," Jimmy said, putting out his cigar in the ashtray on the bedside table. "This is good business."

"Of course," Marian said, though she felt sick to her stomach over it, now that she considered it.

"Look, Marian, there are things . . ." Then Jimmy shook his head. "Well, it's not proper for ears such as yours to hear them."

She rolled her eyes. "Not proper for my female ears to hear, you mean." She poked at Jimmy's side. "I've been working in theater for fifteen years, Jimmy. I'm not naïve. I've probably heard it all."

Jimmy gave her a long look. "Look, I found out a few days ago that Cotton has been regularly going to a club called the Marigold. Have you heard of it?"

Oh, Eddie, she thought. Her heart went out to him, wherever he was, but being seen there had been a stupid thing to do. "Yes, I've heard of it. On Forty-eighth Street, right?"

"Do you know the nature of the club? Have you ever been there?"

"No, I've never been there."

"Good. Because that really is no place for a woman. Before you get mad at me, I'm not being unfair to women. It's a club for fairies, Marian. Do you know what that means?"

She felt a little angry. "Yes, I know what that means. What's your point?"

"Eddie Cotton is one. He goes to this club and he dances with other men there."

Which Marian, of course, already knew, but she wasn't sure if it was prudent to tell Jimmy that. "Is that why you fired him?"

"I fired him," Jimmy said, sitting up regally, "because he's not good enough to be your partner, because it's good business to have Marian France as the headliner on my show instead of half of a duo, and because you, my dear, are the real star and Cotton's a nothing, a has-been. He's also a faggot, which, yes, contributed to my final decision, but honestly, I probably would have fired him anyway. Still, do you really want someone like that working with you? What he is, dear, it's unnatural."

Marian huffed. She'd tried to talk Eddie out of going to places like the Marigold but he was, of course, his own man and made his own decisions. She wondered, sometimes, if her life would have been different if he'd consented to marry her when she'd first asked him all those years ago. Because *she* had asked *him*, because she thought he was being thick-headed, and then he'd broken the news to her that he wouldn't be getting married, probably ever.

"Very well," she said.

"Don't be mad, Marian. It doesn't become you. I need your more pleasant disposition. You're always so full of sunshine."

Marian wanted to huff and make a scene and get angry, but when Jimmy smiled at her like that, with his perfectly straight teeth shining, it was hard for her to remain angry. "I just am not sure about . . . well, it doesn't matter now, I suppose."

"You'll be marvelous, darling. I'll get Walter to write some more songs for you. You'll light up all of Broadway."

She nodded and sighed. She leaned into Jimmy and lay her head on his shoulder. "Thanks," she said.

"Aren't I good to you?" he asked.

"Of course, Jimmy. Of course."

Eddie had more or less emerged from his quasi-coma a couple of days later and told Lane that he wanted to go downtown.

"What on earth for?" Lane asked.

"Do you have to be at the club today?"

Lane hadn't been to the club since he'd taken Eddie to his apartment, and while it was true that it was starting to drive him nuts that he couldn't be there, Eddie was more important. But there was a shipment due in that afternoon, so he thought he should at least drop by. "Not until later today."

Eddie looked in the mirror and adjusted his tie. "I need to do this thing. I think I need you with me."

"What are we doing?"

But Eddie shook his head.

They walked out onto 26th Street. Eddie hesitated at the curb. "Ah. The IRT?"

"That way." Lane pointed east toward the subway entrance. "There's a station on Twenty-third Street and Fourth Avenue."

They walked together in companionable silence, Lane wondering the whole way what they were doing.

When they got to the subway station, Eddie led the way down the stairs. He dropped a nickel into the turnstile and plowed through, so Lane did the same. They waited for the train, and as they waited, Eddie grew increasingly agitated.

"Are you all right?" Lane asked.

"Maybe this was a mistake."

Lane glanced around the platform. There was a woman in an outdated black frock a few feet away, and a couple of men lingering but not paying attention to Lane or Eddie. "I might feel better able to judge that if I knew what we were doing."

"I just have to see."

Lane put his hands on his hips and frowned. "Are you going to give me a clue at least?"

The train rumbled into the station before Eddie could answer that. Lane sighed.

They rode the train down to Canal Street. When they emerged from the station, there were pushcarts everywhere and lots of people moving around. Eddie started walking north, so Lane followed. Then, suddenly, Eddie stopped walking.

"That," he said, pointing to a sign taped on a lamppost.

Confused, Lane walked over to the sign. It had been printed professionally, probably by someone with access to either a printing press or a lot of money, because there was a photo on it and fine print. The top half of the sign was in English, and the bottom was in strange letters that Lane thought might have been Hebrew. The photo was of a man with a huge light-colored beard. The caption under it read, RABBI ISRAEL COHEN.

"I don't understand," Lane said. "Did you want to go to the synagogue? It's not a holiday. Or is there some holiday I don't know about? I didn't even know you were Jewish."

Eddie sighed. "Would it change your opinion of me if I told you I was?"

"Of course not." Lane put his hands on his hips and looked at Eddie, still baffled. Was Eddie Jewish? "What position am I in to judge another man? I don't care if you're Jewish. Are you Jewish?"

"Nominally," Eddie said. He pointed to the sign again, right at the photo of Rabbi Israel Cohen. "That's my father."

The surprise of that was like a punch in the gut. "You're pulling my leg."

"I wish that I were."

Lane looked around and realized that the black garb most of the people on the streets wore—and the signage on the stores, which was in English, Hebrew, and a German-like language that Lane assumed was Yiddish—had indicated that they'd walked onto a Jewish pocket of the Lower East Side. "Cotton is not your real name, then."

"Does anyone in the theater perform under their real name?" Eddie grunted.

"Are we going to see your father?"

"I don't know."

This was frustrating. Lane pointed at the sign. "Did we come down here just to look at signs?"

"I don't know what I thought would happen," Eddie said.

Eddie's confusion was something of a balm to Lane's frustration. Lane took a deep breath and watched for a moment as Eddie struggled, and his heart went out to Eddie because he looked so lost. Eddie pulled his hat off his head and ran a hand through his hair—dark blond normally, but the gray streaks were apparent in the midday sun—then he sighed.

"I came down here because my life ended three days ago, or my career did. I don't know. Something felt final when Jimmy Blanchard told me I was done at the Doozies. And I guess I thought that seeing my family would change something, but now that we're here, I'm not sure what seeing him would accomplish. I haven't seen him in so long. Twenty years, maybe."

"That long? Really?"

"I left home when I was fourteen. Or my father kicked me out, more accurately. I told him that I wanted to be a great actor, and he told me that acting was not a respectable career for a Jew. I knew some other things by then, too, not just that I wanted to act and dance and sing and perform. Those were my passions. I also knew that I was queer, and that my father would never find that acceptable, and I never intended to tell him, but he caught me with another boy from the neighborhood, and . . ." He trailed off and shook his head. "It doesn't matter. It was ridiculous. And then Father told me that it was all right, if I really felt that I needed to perform, I could go to that Yiddish theater on the Bowery, do some productions with other Jews, but that's not what I wanted, not that nonsense. I wanted to do vaudeville. I wanted to be in the *Follies*! But, of course, that wasn't meant to be."

"Your father kicked you out because you wanted to be an actor? Where did you go?"

"Not far. I went to Coney Island for a few years, performed for pennies on the boardwalk, taught myself to dance. And I never came back. I never wanted to. Not until the other day, when everything ended, and I thought, well, maybe I can go back now. Maybe I can see my father and tell him what happened and he'll welcome me back. Except, now that I'm here, I think that was a foolish whim, because why would he do that? Why would he accept me now? He'd just make me marry a woman or go to rabbinical school or get whatever he considers to be a respectable job. And then I'd . . ." He shook his head. "Then I'd have to give up you."

"Eddie."

"They named me Elijah when I was born. I think now, though, that Elijah died twenty years ago."

Lane wanted to do something, wanted to comfort Eddie in some way. His pain and distress were plain on his face. But there was little they could do with so many people around.

Eddie stared at the poster. "I had to see. I don't know. This is all making me feel crazy."

"How can your career be over? You're too good. Forget the Doozies. Go try out for a different show. Go try out for Ziegfeld. Why do you feel you have to torture yourself like this?" Lane couldn't fathom how the thought process in Eddie's head worked, although a lot of other things were starting to become more clear. "Look, I'm yours if you want me. So don't worry about that."

Eddie continued to stare at the poster, now with his brow furrowed.

Lane pointed to the photo. "This man? He may be your blood, but he stopped being your family when he threw you out twenty years ago. What he wants for you doesn't matter. The important thing is what you want for yourself. And you, Eddie Cotton, are a great performer. One of the best I've ever seen. He can't take that from you." Lane took a deep breath and briefly touched Eddie's arm before withdrawing his hand. "I ran away from my family, too, and you know what I've learned? That you have to make your own family. Your friends, the people you choose to surround yourself with, those people are your real family. Me, Eddie. *I'm* your family."

The look on Eddie's face was astonishing. His eyes were damp and his lip trembled, and though he didn't look happy as such, he did look a little surprised.

"Let's get the hell out of here," Eddie said.

Which was easy enough. Lane didn't need a response; he just needed Eddie to know he'd be there no matter what. They were together now. He led Eddie back down to Canal Street, and just crossing the street and getting out of the neighborhood that Eddie must have grown up in made him noticeably calmer. That reinforced for Lane that he was right to get Eddie out of there, that he was right about who Eddie's real family was, who it should have been.

"Let's get a cab, huh?" Lane said.

Eddie nodded.

Chapter 15

"Ain't Nobody's Business If I Do"

Eddie wanted to send a love letter to Walter Winchell, because the newspaper columnist had managed to drum up enough outrage about Eddie's getting canned that he was able to get an audition for Florenz Ziegfeld with a couple of well-placed phone calls. He wondered if it would have been so easy without that. Maybe things were looking up, he considered as he left his room at the Knickerbocker one night. Maybe Jimmy Blanchard had done him a favor.

It was a hot July night, the air humid and heavy. Eddie walked up Broadway without a jacket, his shirtsleeves rolled up to the elbow. He considered how unfashionable and uncouth this probably was for the crowd assembled around Times Square, headed for the theater, but he didn't care.

He walked to the Marigold and was greeted amiably by Etta when he came through the door. "Hullo, Mr. Cotton," Etta said with a wide grin. "Your table is waiting for you."

Lane was seated at his usual table, a highball glass in his hand as always. He picked a cigarette up from the ashtray in front of him and took a long drag before he noticed Eddie there. Eddie knew the moment Lane realized he was there because his whole demeanor changed, from hardened gangster to something kinder and gentler. Eddie stood at the table and crossed his arms over his chest. "Guess who landed an audition with Flo Ziegfeld!"

Lane made a complete transition away from gangster to something else entirely when he whooped and jumped out of his chair. He threw his arms around Eddie. "Eddie! That's amazing! Congratulations!"

"It's just an audition," Eddie said. "I'm not actually in the show yet."

"No, but come on. You'll be great, I just know it. Then I'll have to come to the *Follies* to see you." Lane pulled Eddie tight against him. Eddie realized from the vibrations rumbling through Lane's chest that he was laughing. "Oh, Eddie. I'm so happy for you."

Eddie looked up and saw that Lane was looking at him with an inscrutable expression. Eddie wondered briefly if Lane would kiss him. Eddie had told Lane the previous week that he was okay with kissing behind closed doors but definitely not in public. He'd tried to explain about how he didn't like kissing that much, but Lane hadn't bought it. And the truth, anyway, was that he liked kissing Lane. Just not where other people could see.

"Be happier for me when I'm actually in the show," Eddie said.

Lane backed away, but he still smiled. "All right. Well, let me get you a drink so you can celebrate. Sit, sit. I'll go find Julian."

So Eddie sat, feeling content and a little smug. He was already mentally rehearsing the routine he'd do for Mr. Ziegfeld, a modification of the routine he'd been working on before he got fired from the Doozies, only with slightly more complicated steps, something designed to impress the man that Eddie had always dreamed of working for.

Julian appeared. He was dressed nicely. Or, he was dressed as all of the rest of the staff was, in a crisp white shirt and black trousers, but he looked a lot more elegant than usual. Eddie didn't mind Julian's flamboyance, but it hadn't escaped his notice that most of Julian's wardrobe was threadbare and patched together. He almost looked like a new man in the new clothes.

"Edward, darling," Julian said, bustling over. "Mr. Carillo did not even need to tell me you were here. He's been in a foul mood all afternoon, and then suddenly he wasn't. I figured you must have come by."

"Why was in he in a foul mood?"

Julian shrugged. "Who knows about these things? Can I get you a drink?"

"Yes, that would be wonderful."

Julian reached over and pinched Eddie's cheek before he walked away. Eddie rubbed the spot, but even Julian's antics couldn't have bothered him that night.

Lane came back a moment later. He sat at the table and shot Eddie a grin. "Hello."

"Julian said you weren't in the greatest of moods. Is anything wrong?"

Lane shrugged. "Just business. You don't care."

Eddie reached under the table and rubbed Lane's knee. "You listen to me prattle about shows and dancing all the time. Talk to me about your business." He smiled, but then realized that Lane's business was probably not fit for public discussion. It was so hard to remember that a man as friendly as Lane could be a member of the Mob, that a man in command of everything he came in contact with was beholden to a boss who controlled so many aspects of life in New York. "I mean, tell me if you can. You don't have to."

Lane smiled and reached over to gently slide a finger along Eddie's chin. "Let's just say it takes a lot to keep a place like this open. And now Epstein wants me to promote prostitution."

"What?"

Lane lowered his voice. "There are a lot of things I'm willing to do. I want to keep this place open. I like it here. This might be the first really good thing I've done in years. But I have to keep paying the local law enforcement to leave me alone. Serving liquor is hard enough. Serving up men? And, more to the point, if this is the kind of place in which it becomes possible to buy a man to take home for the night, word gets out, and then a completely different sort of customer comes to this place. And that, frankly, is an element I do not want to invite here." Lane leaned back in his chair and looked around. "This place is safe, you know? It's a place men like us can go to be themselves."

"Yeah. It's great."

"I didn't want to run it." Lane glanced around and lowered his voice. "When Epstein offered it to me, I thought it was a bad idea. But he told me that I was in a unique position to understand the potential customer, which I guess I am. I understand that customer because I *am* that customer. And this place took off, which is why Epstein let me run it my way without intervention for so long. But this one cop, he sort of runs the neighborhood, he keeps demanding I pay him more to make him continue to ignore the fact that I'm importing liquor from Canada and a few other places. Thus the profits here are a little lower. Thus Epstein thinks we should do something to drum up more revenue, which includes having prostitutes here who pay us a cut. And that, frankly, is something I'm not willing to do. Why tarnish a good thing? There's no pressure here. Men can come and dance with other men, fraternize, talk, go home with, whatever, and it's good. I don't want to introduce something that could change that in a negative way."

Which Eddie understood. He looked at Lane and was in awe, to a point, because he hadn't realized how much thought Lane put into this place, or even how much it required. It reminded him, too, that Lane was already pretty heavily involved in illegal activity. Not that Eddie was a stranger to illegal activity as such, just that it hadn't registered how deep in it Lane was. Or, he'd known intellectually, but hearing Lane talk brought it home in a strange way.

"What are you going to do?" Eddie asked.

Lane pulled out his cigarette case and went about lighting a new cigarette. "I haven't decided yet. Put off Epstein as long as I can. Although he's right. If I don't bring in more income, I may not be able to pay off this cop, and then the odds of getting raided go up significantly."

"Surely there are other ways to bring in more money than offering prostitutes."

Lane raised an eyebrow. "I'm sure there are, too. I'm working on that. The trick is to convince Epstein."

Julian arrived with their drinks on a small tray. "The band tonight is hitting on all sixes," he said, placing glasses before both Eddie and Lane. "No one's dancing yet, but that'll change soon."

Lane reached over and tugged on Eddie's sleeve. "You want to show off some of those skills that got you an audition?"

"Well, maybe in a little bit."

Lane turned to Julian. "This is the good stuff, right? I told you we're celebrating."

"Yes, darling. It's the whiskey that came in the shipment this morning."

Eddie liked the sound of that. It had been a few weeks since he'd had good whiskey. Most of what had been served in the Marigold and the other Times Square clubs for the last few weeks had been gin or some other kind of unidentifiable rotgut or moonshine that didn't taste especially good but got the job done. Eddie looked at the glass and the amber color of the liquid inside and started imagining what it would taste like, how warm it would be on his tongue.

Lane raised his glass to Eddie. "Congratulations on your audition, Eddie."

"Thank you." He clinked glasses with Lane then took a sip. And immediately spat it out. "Ugh, this is awful."

Lane frowned at his glass. "Not so much whiskey as bathtub gin with something in it to make it look like whiskey. Maybe caramel?" He held the glass up and looked through it at a light.

"Well, that can't be," said Julian. "I'm sure the bottle came from one of the crates that arrived this morning. I unpacked the crate myself."

Lane shook his head. "It's not your fault, Julian. It's a bad shipment." He pounded his fist on the table. "I'm going to shoot Mook in the foot." He stood and stomped off toward the kitchen. Julian made a small squeal and scrambled after him.

Eddie sat at the table with his disappointment. He pulled an ice cube out of the glass and sucked on it. Whatever was in that glass tasted terrible. Eddie could still feel that first sip burning in his mouth. He pushed the glass aside and turned his attention to the dance floor, where a few men had started to dance. Eddie liked watching them together. One man caught his eye—he was young, maybe twenty-five, and he was wearing what looked like a modification of a sailor suit: wide-legged navy blue pants and a navy blue shirt with a tie at his neck. He had a sailor hat tilted sideways on his head. The whole affair was a costume, Eddie realized, and this man was as much a naval sailor as Etta was a woman. But the man was clearly having fun. He hung on the arm of another man who was dressed in more working-class attire, a work shirt buttoned up primly to the collar and a pair of worn-looking black pants. The two men danced with their arms tangled, and they laughed and moved in time with the music. Soon more men joined them, some of them dancing alone in hopes of attracting another man, some of them dancing together. Eddie thought about what Lane had said about this being a safe space for men like them. It was certainly a safe space for these men to act as they pleased.

Eddie watched the dancing and swayed a little in time with the music. He started to imagine dance steps that might go with the song, which was a slower ballad. He thought about the dance routine he'd use for Mr. Ziegfeld and imagined how the audition would go. It was the first bit of good news he'd gotten in weeks, it felt like, and he knew he could impress Ziegfeld if given the opportunity, although he didn't have much of a gimmick anymore if he didn't have Marian. The thought passed through his head that he could ask Marian to audition for Ziegfeld with him, but he doubted he'd be able to pull her away from her star turn at the Doozies. Or, more accurately, he doubted he'd be able to pull her away from Jimmy Blanchard.

Lane came back a few minutes later. He had a bottle in his hand and two fresh glasses. "I'm terribly sorry," he said. "I've had all of that shipment removed from the stock for the bar. But, bang it, now I'm out all that money, and I really can't afford to be." He plunked the glasses on the table. He pulled the cork out of the bottle and poured a little bit in each glass. "This is wine. It's not great. I scored it off a rabbi who is making it for religious purposes. It's too sweet, but it's not toxic. And right now, I really need to get drunk."

"Lane."

Lane placed the bottle on the table, then took a sip of his wine. He tilted his head back and forth as he considered it. "This should get the job done. Although I bet this rabbi is making this terrible wine in his bathtub. Just like everybody else is. Maybe I should start making moonshine in my bathtub because at least I wouldn't have to import my liquor through two-faced criminals like Mook."

Eddie wasn't sure how to get Lane to calm down, but part of him really wanted Lane to be as happy and carefree as those men dancing together. He reached over and ran a hand down Lane's arm. "I'm sorry," he said.

"It's all right. I'll figure something out. I always do."

Eddie believed that, or else Lane would not have ascended to the role he had in Epstein's organization.

Eddie sipped his wine, and it *was* far too sweet, but he could tell by the way it burned on the way down his throat that it was more wine than grape juice. He watched Lane and worried, hoping to ease Lane's unease somehow.

"I would like to dance," Eddie said.

Lane smirked. "Well, I would love to dance with you. Or, I'd love to watch you dance, because I have those five left feet."

Eddie stood. "Come on, I'll teach you."

Eddie led Lane to the dance floor. He did a few simple steps and got Lane to copy him. It was a little awkward, but Eddie managed to accomplish his goal, which was to get Lane to forget his problems for a little while. So they danced, and Lane stepped on Eddie's feet, and tripped, and fumbled his way through the steps, but he also laughed and held onto Eddie, and for a few moments that night, everything was perfect.

Chapter 16

"How Come You Do Me Like You Do?"

Eddie glanced out the window and saw it was a sunny day, ideal for taking a walk around the neighborhood as he continued to mentally prepare for his Ziegfeld audition. He turned back toward Lane, wanting to ask if Lane was interested in accompanying him on the walk, but feeling awkward about it.

As he tied his shoe, Lane said, "Did I tell you? Raul and Etta got into it the other night."

"Really? What happened?"

Lane shrugged and stood up. "Raul said something offhand about the necklace Etta was wearing, and I guess she took offense." Lane chuckled. "Anyway, so Etta said—"

Lane was cut off by a knock at the door.

Eddie and Lane looked at each other. The knock made Eddie's heart race. He hadn't been expecting company—the only person he would have gladly opened that door to see was standing right here with him—and the knock seemed like a bad sign. He went to the door and looked through the peephole.

Then he pulled open the door. "Marian! What are you doing here?"

"I wanted to see you," she said, shooting a long look at his chest. "I wanted to see how you were doing. I thought I'd stop by. I've missed you, Eddie."

Eddie looked down and realized his shirt was still mostly unbuttoned. He and Lane had been having a fairly lazy morning, late to get up and get on with the day. He hastily buttoned up his shirt and fumbled with an apology.

Lane cleared his throat. Eddie looked at him and Marian followed his gaze. No hasty dressing was in evidence there; Lane looked impeccable as always, dressed expensively in an aubergine shirt with the sleeves rolled up to his elbows and a pair of gray wide-leg trousers.

"Marian, this is Lane Carillo," Eddie said. He didn't explain their relationship, but he didn't think he had to. Marian was smart enough to figure out what was going on here.

She held out her hand. "Nice to meet you," she said.

Lane took her hand and brought it to his lips. "It's a pleasure, Miss France."

Marian blushed. "Well, I just wanted to say hello," she said.

"Come in, Marian," Eddie said, moving out of the way of the door. He gestured her inside and closed the door behind her. "How are things going at the Doozies?"

Marian smiled. "Great. The show is going really well. The new act was reviewed in the *Post*. Did you see it?"

"No, I haven't really been looking at the paper much lately." The truth was that Eddie had been avoiding looking at papers for this very reason; he couldn't bring himself to read about the triumph of the Doozies without him.

"Oh." Marian frowned, looking disappointed. "Well, I got some nice reviews."

"I've heard good things," Lane said.

Marian turned and stared at him. "And what do you do, Mr. Carillo?"

"I run a nightclub," he said.

"Oh."

He walked up next to Eddie and slung an arm around his shoulders. "What would you think if this fella took his act to a club instead of the stage?"

"Lane . . ." Eddie said.

"As long as he was dancing somewhere." Marian let out a breath and turned to Eddie. "I feel just terrible about what happened. It shouldn't have played out the way it did. I think Jimmy was crazy to fire you, and I want you to know that I fought for you."

Eddie smiled. He appreciated that she cared enough to apologize. He chucked her lightly under her chin with his fist. "I know you did."

"Jimmy just gets these ideas in his head, and he made this partnership with Walter Rhodes . . . I guess he thinks that Rhodes will be to him what Irving Berlin is to Ziegfeld. He wants to use a bunch of his songs in the production next year, and he's already auditioning new chorus girls and everything. I think it's presumptive of him. The Shuberts may not even invite him back next year."

Eddie nodded. They both knew there was no guarantee that Jimmy would even be able to put on the Doozies the next year if the Shubert Organization, which owned the theater, decided they wanted something else featured at the James.

She walked over to a chair and sat down. "You should know, though . . ."

"What?"

Marian clasped her hands together. "Look, Jimmy said something. He, ah, he knows. About you." She glanced at Lane. "I swear I didn't say anything. But he said that he'd heard you'd been spotted at that new club for . . . you know. The Marigold?"

Eddie looked at Lane and their gazes met. "I know," said Eddie.

"Jimmy told me basically that he probably would have let you go anyway because he wanted me to headline the Doozies, but the fact that you are . . . well, you know." She gestured between Lane and Eddie. Lane made a face Eddie couldn't read that looked like confusion, with his eyebrows knit together. "I mean, you two are . . . together. Right?"

No sense in denying it. Eddie nodded.

Marian went on. "He said that you being a . . ." She dropped her voice and whispered. "A fairy. That didn't help matters. I don't know what the truth is, if he fired you for being what you are or because of me or because of Rhodes or just because he woke up one morning and felt like it, but he did it. I want you to know that I don't bear you any ill will, and I want to be your friend still, and I miss you." She'd sounded increasingly distraught as she spoke.

Eddie walked over and pulled Marian into his arms. "Thank you."

She hugged him back for a moment before she eased away. "I hate to be the one to tell you all this."

"I realize that." Eddie smiled. "That is, Blanchard said as much to me when he let me go, so it's not really news. But I do appreciate your honesty."

"It's not the same without you, you know. The act, I mean. The whole show."

Eddie sighed. "Do you want to go have lunch or something? Lane and I were going to go to the restaurant down the block. They make a decent turkey sandwich."

"Sure," Marian said, smiling.

After lunch, Eddie bid Marian a good afternoon and walked slowly back to the Knickerbocker with Lane. It had been really nice to see her, to remember what had made them friends to begin with. They had always got along well, and nothing had changed there beyond that they no longer saw each other daily.

But even thinking fondly of Marian made him think about what she had said, what Blanchard had said, and he wondered how far word had spread. If Blanchard had talked to Marian, who else had he casually mentioned Eddie's sexual proclivities to? What other rumors might Blanchard have started? Could any of it affect his upcoming audition for Ziegfeld?

"You're thinking too much," said Lane. "I can see the little man running behind your forehead."

"What if everyone in the theater community knows?"

Lane reached over and ran a hand down Eddie's arm before retracting it again. "Half the theater community *is* queer. I've met a lot of actors in the time I've been in New York, and very few of them are the sort that fraternize with women during off-hours."

Eddie knew that was true, but he suspected that if Jimmy Blanchard could judge him and fire him for what he was, then it wasn't unreasonable that a man like Ziegfeld—a man who had made a career out of looking at beautiful women and putting them on display—would also not feel so kindly toward a queer man. "What about Ziegfeld?" Eddie said.

Lane, of course, understood, because they'd had this conversation a lot recently. He nodded. "I know you're worried, but look at it this way. If Ziegfeld already knows, there's nothing you can do except go in there and give him the best audition you've ever done. And I know you can do it, Eddie. You're a fantastic performer."

Eddie nodded. "I suppose."

"You are. You can do this. I have faith in you."

It was a comfort, coming from Lane. Eddie stopped walking and looked at him. Something passed through his chest, a warm feeling, somewhat fleeting, but then the words formed in his mind: *I love this man.*

Which was a terrifying thought. Eddie had never really been in love and didn't know what to do with these feelings. It didn't seem like it would be possible to just be in love with Lane, not considering all the mess around them.

Eddie started to panic. He turned back toward the Knickerbocker and picked up his pace. Lane had to jog to catch up. "Hey, wait. Slow down. Are you all right?" Lane said.

"Yes. I just need to get home."

"All right."

"Don't you have to go to the club tonight?"

"I don't have to be there right now." Lane frowned. "Eddie, what is it? Are you panicking about your audition?"

That was easier to explain. "Some," he said. "I just . . . I need to go over the steps."

Lane nodded, but let him go. "Sure. Go practice. Come by the club later, if you're interested. We've got Jerome Mulligan and His Orchestra playing tonight. It's going to be great."

"I'll think about it."

They parted ways. Eddie stood on the sidewalk and watched Lane go. Part of him was glad Lane was going so that Eddie could go back to his room and resume his panic, but part of him was sad to see him go, and there was even a part of him that wished they could say good-bye to each other properly out here on the street, but of course, that was impossible. Eddie wondered if a quick kiss or a hug would do much to soothe his nerves, or if it would just make everything worse.

Lane got to the club that night after a quick stop at home. He wondered the entire time he was traveling what had made Eddie's mood turn so suddenly. It was funny; Lane thought they'd gotten to know each other pretty well, but Eddie still surprised him. An unexpected mood swing like that called into question what Lane thought he knew, because he couldn't figure out what had caused the change.

Lane walked into the Marigold and was greeted amiably by his staff. He tried to push Eddie out of his mind, but found that as impossible as all things Eddie seemed lately. Eddie was so great in so many ways, but he had such a wide streak of doubt in him that Lane was worried he might sabotage his own audition with Ziegfeld. He had so much potential, but his concern that he might be blacklisted if it became public knowledge that he was queer was starting to take over. Lane wondered how much of a role he played in that mess, too, if he'd persuaded Eddie to put his own career in jeopardy just by dropping by the club. He wondered if his continued relationship with Eddie could further impact Eddie's career.

There wasn't much he could do about it when Eddie wasn't around. And maybe he was worrying over nothing. But that look in Eddie's eyes had been significant. Lane just couldn't figure out what it meant.

Julian took his jacket and walked with him to his office. "Jerome Mulligan and the band are here. They're warming up. How did you get these guys? They're spectacular."

Lane couldn't help but smile at the genuine enthusiasm Julian displayed. Lane liked Julian a little better when he dropped the act, when he stopped trying to be the flouncy, flamboyant man he thought would get him work. Lane said, "Jerome is one of us."

"He is not."

"He is. I met him . . ." Lane paused, not wanting to admit that he'd met Jerome the year before at a bathhouse and that they'd had sex once. There was very little romantic potential between them, and Lane had always held out for the real thing, but they'd kept in touch. When Lane offered Jerome the opportunity to play in the club, Jerome had agreed happily. This was quite a coup, since Jerome played plenty of more respectable clubs. "I met him about a year ago. We became friendly."

That answer satisfied Julian, who chuckled. "Well, either way, darling, it's wonderful to have a good band here. I like to see the boys dance."

"Oh, I do, too." Lane laughed. "How are things here?"

"Fine," Julian said. "Though Mook dropped by earlier. He wanted to see you. I told him to come back later tonight, assuming you'd come in."

"Thank you." Lane wondered how Julian had supplanted Raul as his right-hand man, or when exactly that had happened, but he liked

Julian well enough and when Raul had asked for a few days off to deal with some issue with his family, Julian had slid easily right into the role. He dismissed Julian, who strutted away to get ready to open the club.

Lane spent about an hour looking over the books and trying to work out how he could pay off Hardy and still turn a profit that week. The math was becoming increasingly difficult as Hardy kept demanding more and more money.

On the other hand, Hardy's reaction to their proximity that afternoon he'd paid a visit made Lane wonder if there wasn't a way to exploit the situation. Would exposing his suspicions about Hardy get Hardy to back off or would it get the Marigold shut down faster?

He ruled that this was not something he wanted to poke at just yet, though he put the thought aside to revisit later. When Lane was satisfied he could keep the Marigold open another two weeks, he walked into the kitchen and found that everyone was running around, getting ready to start service when the club opened. Everything seemed to be going as well as usual, and Lane decided to go take up his seat at his table on the floor. That was, of course, when Mook showed up again.

Mook looked awful, like he'd been in a fight: his hair was disheveled, there was a small tear in the sleeve of his jacket, and there was a bruise on his chin.

"Oh, thank God you're here!" Mook said when he saw Lane.

"What's going on?"

"It's Hardy. I was bringing you that new shipment today. Good lightning this time, not the same source as before. I was driving over here, and I saw him standing near the loading area. I wound up parking a block away, and then I walked over here to investigate. Hardy was standing there, and he made it clear he wouldn't let me deliver my shipment unless I paid him. But I couldn't pay him until after I delivered the liquor."

A shiver of panic ran through Lane. If Mook hadn't delivered the shipment, that meant they were pretty low on alcohol. "You sold the delivery to somebody else."

"It's business, Carillo."

Which Lane understood, though he was still angry. He felt some measure of panic, both because of the lack of alcohol and the situation with the police. "So Hardy is sniffing around right now?"

"Of course he is. Isn't he always? And he's looking for blood. Or a lot of simoleons. Rumor is he's already arrested three men this week and shut down a club up on Fifty-fourth."

That was not good news. "Thanks for the warning, I guess."

"I'm sorry, I really am. I gotta make dough, though."

Lane was mad, but probably would have acted the same way Mook had under the same circumstances. "I know."

"I can get something off the rum runners tomorrow, if that will hold you over. Then I have to get something new. There's a place in Kentucky that's still making whiskey for export, maybe I can make something work out with them . . ."

Lane didn't want to deal with it, especially now that it looked like the club was going to go dry later in the night. "If you can't get something tonight, I don't want to talk about it right now. You get me a shipment tomorrow or I find another supplier. You're hardly the only bootlegger in the city."

Mook held up his hands. "Of course. I'll make arrangements. I can't do much tonight, but I'll get you something tomorrow."

Then Mook was gone.

Lane walked out to the floor then. Jerome and the band got started, playing a raucous jazz number, but Lane was suddenly not in the mood. He had to come up with money enough to pay off Hardy, which was going to be hard if he didn't have alcohol to sell, and he was going to lose customers if he ran out of alcohol. Plus Eddie still played on his mind. He bunched his fists at his side.

A year ago, Lane could have made a call and had a case of whiskey at his door within the hour. He'd had connections from his early days in the family, when he'd gotten his start trafficking booze through a warehouse in Brooklyn. But all of those contacts had dried up or moved somewhere else. Three hours earlier, it might not have been an issue. He could have called in a favor or run over to Lenny's to set a plan in motion. He could have gotten Callahan to fix this, or Legs. But now he had no idea where he'd get liquor on such short notice.

He called over Julian.

"You know people, right?" he said.

Julian raised an eyebrow. "I know plenty of people, darling."

"Do you know any people that can get me a case of horse liniment tonight?"

"Can I use your telephone?"

"Yes."

Julian winked and walked back to the office. Lane waited on the floor, fretting about how the night might turn out. When Julian returned, he grinned broadly.

"I've solved your problems, darling. The fella I know will be here in about an hour. He's got a case of rotgut from some guy in Brooklyn. Maybe not great, but better than that bushwa from the other night. He wants a hundred dollars for it, though."

"Done," Lane said. A hundred dollars was nothing compared to the money they'd lose if all the customers walked out. "Thanks, Julian."

Julian leaned over and gave Lane a kiss on the cheek. "No problem, darling."

Chapter 17

"Here in My Arms"

Lane walked right through the lobby of the Knickerbocker and could have sworn one of the bellhops nodded at him, which, given how often he put in appearances here, didn't seem too odd. Lane wondered who all had figured out what his real purpose in the hotel was. It was hard to tell. In his experience, some people couldn't even fathom two men together in a romantic way, and so it never occurred to them to wonder. Some people assumed any two men who seemed affectionate with each other were lovers. Lane couldn't imagine that his coming and going at the Knickerbocker at all hours wouldn't arouse suspicion, but it didn't much matter now.

What did matter was getting to Eddie.

Lane knew something was wrong. He wasn't sure how he knew it, but that look on Eddie's face when they'd parted on the street days before still haunted him and, more to the point, Eddie hadn't come by the club at all. Eddie had been coming to the Marigold every night since he'd recovered from losing his job, and then there had been that weird moment between them, that facial expression, and then nothing for three days.

He got to Eddie's floor and took a deep breath as he marched down the hallway. He knocked on Eddie's door.

A bleary-eyed and possibly drunk Eddie answered. His eyes were wide when he saw Lane, but he didn't say anything, merely moved away from the door. Lane took that as an invitation.

"What the hell happened to you?" Lane asked after he'd walked in and closed the door.

Eddie grunted and sat on the bed.

When he didn't speak, Lane stood in front of him and asked, "Are you panicking about your audition? I know it's in two days."

"Yes," Eddie said slowly.

Lane knew he was lying. "That's only part of it. You're upset about something else, too."

Eddie shrugged.

"Eddie."

Eddie looked up at Lane with damp eyes. Then he blinked and shook his head. "This is the most ridiculous thing."

Lane considered sitting next to Eddie. He resisted his greater impulse, which was to pull Eddie into his arms. Instead he stood there and waited. He had to keep some pride. And he wanted a straight answer.

Eventually Eddie said, "Yes, I am worried about the audition. For all the reasons you think I am. Because Blanchard knows about me and has been beating his gums at anyone who will listen. Because I'm worried about flubbing the steps. Because I'm worried I'm not good enough. But . . ."

"Eddie. Talk to me." This time Lane did sit on the bed, but he didn't touch Eddie.

Eddie was silent for a long time, but his shoulders shook a little. He wasn't crying, exactly, but it was clear there was a lot of emotion moving through him. Lane didn't want to push him, so he didn't. He just sat and waited.

Eventually, Eddie said, "I love you. But that's impossible. Isn't it? How can I be in love? Especially with a man."

Of all the things Eddie could have said right then, that was pretty much the last thing Lane expected. He wanted to laugh, but fought to keep his face neutral. "Is that what you're worried about?"

Eddie squirmed.

"Eddie. Baby. There's nothing wrong with that. I love you, too." Lane ran a hand over Eddie's shoulder and was surprised that he found such comfort in the touch, in just being connected to Eddie. Eddie leaned into his hand a little. "What do you mean, it's impossible to fall in love with a man? It certainly is not. That is, can you imagine yourself in love with a woman?"

"No," Eddie said. A strange strangled laugh came out of his throat. "No, definitely not."

"Falling in love is a perfectly human thing to do. And it's a good thing. Why are you so gloomy about it?"

"I've never . . ." Eddie shook his head again. He looked at Lane. "I've never felt this before. And I always thought that . . . I mean, sex is one thing, but love? Between two men?"

"Your heart doesn't lie."

"Well, obviously." Eddie let out a soft groan, as if he were relaxing for the first time in a while. "But now? What do we do?"

Lane smiled. "Nothing different than what we have been doing. Don't worry about it. Certainly don't act like this is the end of the world, because it isn't. If anything, it's just the beginning." Lane leaned close to Eddie, so their faces were a mere inch apart. He put a hand on the side of Eddie's face. Their eyes met. "I think it feels pretty good to be in love with you."

Eddie's eyebrows relaxed. "Yes," he said, a little dreamily.

So Lane kissed him.

Heat seemed to flow through Lane as soon as their lips met. Eddie opened his mouth for Lane without much prompting, so Lane took advantage, slipping in his tongue and coaxing a moan from Eddie. Their lips slid together, saliva mixing, tongues tangling, and Lane felt his love for Eddie seeming to rise up through his chest, to pour out of him.

Eddie put his arms around Lane and kept on kissing him. Then the kiss slowed, deepened, and then it vibrated. Eddie started laughing. "Lane," he whispered. He laughed again while Lane waited for him to sort out whatever was so funny. "I love you," he said. "I love you! You're right. It feels good."

Lane pressed his forehead into Eddie's shoulder and was content to be held. "It does feel good. See? How can that be wrong?"

"It's not that it's wrong. I just never thought it was possible."

Lane kissed Eddie again—probably it was too much to hope that Eddie would spontaneously kiss him, but this still felt like progress. Lane felt giddy suddenly, and his anxiety about Eddie's mental state dissipated.

Under all that anxiety, Lane realized, was a great deal of desire. He wanted Eddie like he wanted to take his next breath.

He slid his hands along Eddie's chest, slipped his fingers under the button placket of Eddie's shirt, and started to slip the buttons from their holes. Eddie shoved his hands under Lane's jacket and pushed it off. He undid Lane's tie, tossed it aside, and went to work on Lane's shirt buttons.

They kissed and laughed and undressed each other. Eddie was something else, smiling in a way Lane couldn't recall seeing before, flailing a little in his excitement, eagerly ridding Lane of his clothes. Lane tried to hold on to him, without much luck, but he did manage to keep a hand on Eddie at all times, to keep him close.

Finally, they were naked together, and Lane said, "Make love to me. Now."

And then Eddie shocked the hell out of Lane by initiating a kiss. Lane stopped what he was doing to savor it, to memorize how their lips felt together, to just feel everything that Eddie made him feel.

What he felt now was aroused, charged. He was hard, his body bending toward Eddie, his hips thrusting against Eddie. Eddie gave it all back, running his hands all over Lane, grunting and moving, nipping at Lane's skin. Lane slid his fingers down the ridge of Eddie's spine, kissed Eddie's shoulder. He wanted to get closer. He wanted Eddie inside him.

As if he could read Lane's mind, Eddie grabbed the tub of Vaseline from the side table. "Can I?"

"Yes," Lane said breathlessly.

He lay on his back and opened his legs to let Eddie in. Eddie knelt before him, his body a wonder. The strength of his arms, his chest, his body toned from years of dancing. Lane loved it, thought Eddie incredibly sexy, and everything was more powerful now that they were deep in it, now that they'd confessed their love for each other. Had anything ever been as good as being in Eddie's arms? Was there any pleasure greater than gazing at Eddie?

Perhaps there was, because Eddie wrapped a hand around Lane's cock. Arousal and pleasure shot through Lane's body and he arched off the bed. Eddie leaned forward and kissed Lane's chest. He slid his teeth over Lane's right nipple, causing goosebumps to blossom over Lane's whole body. Lane sighed and shifted his weight on the bed a little to give Eddie better access to his body.

Eddie pulled the lid off the Vaseline and tossed it aside. He took a healthy amount from the jar and then bowed forward. He surprised Lane by taking Lane's cock into his mouth, which was hot and slick and felt like a miracle. Lane groaned and schooled himself to keep still while Eddie prepared him for their coming together. He wanted that badly, wanted Eddie near him, inside him, above him, around him. He wanted Eddie to continue to surprise him. He wanted Eddie to love him.

When Lane was ready, Eddie hovered above him, balanced precariously on one arm while he took his own cock in his hand. "I want this, Lane."

"Yes."

"I love you."

Lane smiled. "I love you, too."

A small smile crossed Eddie's face and then he pressed forward. Lane felt the familiar pressure at his entrance. He knew he must have winced or reacted somehow as Eddie pushed forward, because Eddie kept murmuring, asking if he was okay, telling him to relax.

"More," Lane moaned, wanting all of Eddie inside him.

Lane put his arms around Eddie as Eddie pressed forward slowly, started to push into Lane, waited for Lane to adjust. Lane threaded his hands into Eddie's hair and murmured nonsense love words and kissed Eddie with all that he had. Eddie gave as good as he got, opening his mouth to accept Lane's kisses and snaking his tongue into Lane's mouth. Then he was fully seated in Lane and they were together, connected, as close as two people could be.

Eddie started to thrust slowly. "I love you so much."

Lane didn't think he'd ever get tired of hearing those words. "I know, baby."

"I've never known . . . anyone like . . . you."

It became harder to speak as Eddie picked up the pace, as he thrust faster, as they moved together, everything skin and salt and sweat. Lane's heart was pounding now, his breathing to the point where he wasn't sure he could make more sounds than simple grunts, but he loved this, he loved Eddie, and he wanted it to go on forever. The pain where their bodies met was easing into a particular pleasure, one Lane had always liked but one made even better when the man above him was one he cared about, one he loved. He kissed Eddie, who sighed against his lips before returning the kiss. Eddie's cock slid in and out of Lane, accelerating Lane's pleasure, moving them both forward.

They kissed and thrust and declared their love for each other as well as they could, over and over. Eddie reached between them and wrapped his hand around Lane's cock. His hand was still slick from the Vaseline and felt like heaven moving on Lane. Lane threw his head back and cried out as everything began to feel too intense, as Lane tried to will away the orgasm to make this last longer.

Soon it became too much, though. Eddie leaned up, propped on his arms, and thrust hard and fast. Lane pulled his knees up to give Eddie room. He grabbed his own cock and started to stroke, wanting to find his release at the same time Eddie did. Eddie was close, it was clear from his facial expression.

"Lane," Eddie whispered. "Lane, Lane. I love you."

"I love you, Eddie."

Eddie went off then. He arched his back away from Lane and moaned loudly. Lane could feel him coming inside him. It was so glorious watching Eddie, watching him find his pleasure in Lane's body. That was enough to heighten everything Lane was feeling. He stroked himself, getting faster, a little more desperate, and then suddenly it was like the sun bursting through the clouds on an overcast day. Light and electricity flowed through Lane's body as he found his pleasure, and he came in ribbons over his chest.

They lay beside each other, stunned, for a while.

"Perhaps that is what people write songs about," Eddie said after a while.

"Not just songs. Operas. Novels. Great works of art. If I had any artistic talent at all, I'd be making art about us right now and it would be glorious."

Eddie chuckled. Then he turned his head and looked at Lane. "You've changed my life, you know that?"

"For the good, I hope."

Eddie nodded. "You realize that without you, I might be dead?"

"You might also still have your job." That was a deep fear of Lane's. That he'd been the reason for Eddie to come to the Marigold at all, that he was the reason Eddie had been caught.

"No. You heard Marian: Blanchard was determined to get rid of me. If I hadn't been caught, he would have come up with another reason." Eddie ran a hand over Lane's chest. "You're the reason I'm here. I'm convinced of that."

That was a heavy burden, but Lane accepted it just the same, happy to have Eddie there, happy to be the reason Eddie stayed alive. When they felt recovered, they both got up and cleaned off. Then they fell back into bed together, wrapped up in each other's arms. It seemed so uncharacteristically romantic, but Lane decided to wallow in it. He was in love, he was in bed with the man he loved, and they were wound tightly together. He knew the joy he felt in that moment was fleeting, so he decided to revel in it while it lasted.

Chapter 18

"With a Song in My Heart"

L ane couldn't remember the last time he'd seen a parade anything on this scale. It was worth leaving his worries behind for just a few hours if only to take a look at this spectacle. Confetti and streamers were everywhere, as were cars and ramshackle marching bands and people shouting. It seemed like everyone on the sidewalk was pushing forward, trying to see for themselves the man of the hour: Charles Lindbergh, back from his successful flight from New York to Paris.

"This is quite a blow, isn't it?" Eddie said behind Lane. "I don't think I've ever seen anything like this. Have you?"

"No." Lane thought about that for a moment. "I guess there was that parade last summer for the woman who swam across the English channel, but even that wasn't quite like this."

"He's touring the country," Eddie said. "Lindbergh, I mean. I suppose he means to promote aviation, but I'll tell ya, I can't imagine ever going up in one of those things. I will stay here on the ground, thank you."

"My brother wanted to fly airplanes in the war." A sudden sadness struck Lane as soon as the words were out of his mouth. "He, ah, didn't. The war ended before he got the chance." After which time Robert had moved back home, and Lane had promised he'd marry Ruthie, and instead had run to New York with Scott.

"Hey, hey," Eddie said, lightly touching Lane's arm. "What's wrong?"

Lane shook his head. "Thinking about my brother made me realize I haven't seen my family in five years. I don't know if Robbie ever got to fly, or what he would think of Lindbergh, or if he ever got married, or . . ." Lane found he had to blink away tears.

He didn't often think of his family. It had been more than three years since he'd had so much as a letter or any word as to how they were doing. Occasionally, some bit of news would trickle through the Mafia, but Lane's father had wanted nothing to do with the less savory branch of his family. When Lane had first appealed to his cousin for a job, most of his "family" in New York had been strangers.

Still, for most of his life, he'd seen his immediate family daily. He and his siblings had been close. Robbie was to be the best man in the wedding that didn't happen. Now he wasn't allowed to see them at all.

Eddie gently tugged on his elbow. "Let's get away from the crowd."

Lane nodded and let himself be dragged away until they had ducked down a side street off Fifth Avenue.

And then everything just poured out. "I sent a letter," Lane said. The street was shaded, but he was aware of the fact that they were still in public, so he blinked a few times to keep the tears at bay. "After Scott died, I sent a letter home. I told my family and Scott's family what happened. Three weeks later, I got a letter from my mother which said, basically, not to come home. I might as well have pushed Scott off the bridge with my own hands. Sometimes I think I did."

"Lane," Eddie said softly. There was a surprising amount of warmth in his voice. "It wasn't your fault. Believe me, and you know this better than anyone, but I understand that impulse, to jump off the bridge, and he must have felt he had nothing left if he went through with it. There was nothing you could have done."

Lane schooled his face, not wanting to betray how that made him feel. Hadn't Scott had Lane? He looked at Eddie, who seemed so serene, given the turmoil that Lane felt suddenly, like a whole thunderstorm had started in his chest. "Why didn't you go through with it?" Lane asked.

Eddie looked down. Lane wished he could see Eddie's face. After a long pause, Eddie said, "I wasn't completely out of hope yet. You showed up to stop me, that was part of it, but I wonder sometimes if I could have gone through with it if you hadn't gotten there. I don't know." He sighed and looked up. His eyes were red now. "But you did stop me. And if I'd jumped, it would have been a waste, no?"

Lane wanted to kiss Eddie but didn't dare out in public like this. He took a step back to remove some of the temptation and looked back toward Fifth Avenue, where the parade continued to rage.

"I miss my family, is all," Lane said.

"I know." Eddie glanced both ways before he reached over and wiped a tear off Lane's cheek with his thumb. "Are you all right now? Do you want to go back to the parade?"

"Yes, please."

So they walked back. They pushed through the crowd gathered on the sidewalk as it erupted in delirious cheers. There, sitting on top of an open-topped automobile was the man himself, Charles Lindbergh, waving at the onlookers.

Eddie laughed. "Can you believe we got to see this in person?"

"No," Lane said. "Quite an amazing moment, isn't it?"

"It's pretty swell, yes." He glanced over at Lane. Under his breath, he said, "I'm glad I got to see it with you."

Lane smiled. "I agree."

It *was* the sort of feeling men wrote songs about, Eddie thought as he walked down the street. He felt bolstered, like Lane's mere existence in his life was a cushion keeping him from falling too hard. He distracted himself by thinking up metaphors and song lyrics as he walked to the New Amsterdam Theater to meet with Florenz Ziegfeld. God knew thinking about the audition wasn't doing him any good.

He'd been nearly immobilized with fear the night before, but Lane had talked him down and just held him while he panicked and sweated. Lane had been there that morning with a hug and words of encouragement, which Eddie was surprised to find had helped him calm down.

He walked in through the stage door, and, as he'd been told, he proceeded down the hallway to the staff offices. He was greeted by a woman in a very short dress who told him they were expecting him and that he could proceed to the stage, where Mr. Ziegfeld was waiting.

Eddie hadn't anticipated having to dance on the stage at the New Amsterdam. If this went well, it wouldn't be the last time, but it was intimidating all the same. He took a moment to stand in the wing and just admire the stage, the breadth of it, and the ornate beaux-arts flourishes in the dimly lit theater. He took a deep breath and walked out onto one of the greatest stages in the city. He saw a shadowy figure in the second row.

"Hello, Mr. Cotton," said a voice—Ziegfeld's. There was another man seated next to him who was not introduced.

"Good afternoon, sir. It is a great honor to audition for you."

"Let's see your act."

Eddie had the whole routine committed to memory. It started with the grand entrance, so he walked to the side of the stage. In his act, he always wore a tuxedo, but for the audition, he'd worn a suit that he'd had tailored specifically for dancing. The wide-legged trousers that were currently in fashion were too heavy and tended to get in his way, so he'd purchased a pair of pants and had them altered so that they tapered at the legs. He did the steps out from stage left: left, left, right, right, step over, step over, pivot, turn, right, right. Every step had been agonized over and then memorized, so this was a dance he knew well. His feet made the steps without tripping or fumbling, and getting it right when he was this nervous boosted his confidence. He lifted his arms and posed to signal he was transitioning into the next part of the act.

He told a joke to get things started. "My wife Mildred came home the other night and told me there'd been a murder down the street. 'A murder!' I cried. 'Yes,' she said. 'The police found several chickens at the scene.' I thought that was pretty strange, so I asked Mildred, I asked, 'What were the chickens doing there?' 'I don't know,' she said. 'But the police suspect *fowl play*.'" Eddie heard someone chuckle in the audience. That seemed like a good thing.

Eddie then launched into what he'd always thought of as his signature song, a number called "Skies over the City," a little ditty about seeing the stars on a night when the lights of Broadway went out. It was mostly a comedic piece, light and perfectly suited to Eddie's low tenor. Then he went back to dancing. The transitions between each part of his act were a little rough, but he was hoping this was something he or Ziegfeld would refine once he was hired. Or, even better, maybe Ziegfeld had a costar in mind for him. He always worked better with someone to play against, which was why his partnership with Marian worked so well.

As he finished his act and danced off the stage, he thought that it could not have gone better. He hadn't made any major errors, he'd sung pretty well, and he'd pulled a few chuckles during the bawdier parts of the act. He came back out and bowed.

"Thank you so much for this opportunity, Mr. Ziegfeld."

"Yes," said the voice from the audience.

Eddie wished he could see Ziegfeld better. He couldn't see the man's facial expressions at all, just the basic features of his face: his eyebrows, his nose, his mouth.

Ziegfeld said, "Tell me, Mr. Cotton, what has become of Miss France?"

"She's still working for Jimmy Blanchard," Eddie said. "As a solo act."

No reaction from Mr. Ziegfeld, really. There was a long pause, and then he said, "Yes, I did read about what happened in the paper. Mr. Blanchard let you go from the show. Why did that happen?"

Eddie knew better than to bash Blanchard to Ziegfeld. "It's complicated, sir," he started to explain. Realizing that wouldn't be sufficient, he added, "He wanted to promote Marian, to make her the star of her own act instead of part of a duo. As such, he didn't feel there was a place for me in *Le Tumulte* anymore. So here I am."

"You're a talented dancer," Ziegfeld said. "Your jokes are a little stale, though. I want things that are fresh for the *Follies*, you understand me?"

"Yes, sir. Of course, sir. The *Follies* are always ahead of everyone else." Eddie stopped himself from laying it on too thick, though it occurred to him to really applaud the show. It wasn't hyperbole at all to say that the *Follies* was the biggest and best vaudeville revue in town: the one with the greatest talent, the most elaborate sets, the most spectacle. Maybe it wasn't live elephants at the Hippodrome, but it was always the talk of the city.

"Yes," Ziegfeld said. "Your singing is also not the best I've ever heard."

"I know, sir, but I believe the whole package . . ."

"I don't think you can work solo. There's not enough to catch the audience's eye."

"But, sir. Surely I can—"

"Good afternoon, Mr. Cotton. Thank you for your time."

*　　*　　*

Eddie found himself back on the sidewalk a few minutes later. Without really thinking about it, he walked to the Marigold. It wasn't open yet, but the door was unlocked, so he walked in.

Julian was adjusting tablecloths and looked up when Eddie came in. He started to say, "We're closed," but then said, "Oh, Edward, darling."

"Lane. I need to see Lane."

Julian's whole demeanor changed. He nodded and said, "Yes, he's in his office. I'll just go get him."

Eddie stood and waited. The shock was starting to wear off, and as he stood in the middle of the floor of a tawdry queer club in the middle of the day, it started to dawn on him that he'd just lost a major opportunity, and he had no clue what to do now.

Lane appeared and said, "Eddie, how did the audition—" He stopped abruptly and they stood looking at each other for a moment. "Oh, Eddie." Lane moved toward him quickly. "Oh, baby. Oh, no. No, no." Lane hooked a hand behind Eddie's head then pulled him close and into his arms.

Which was how Eddie came to be wrapped up in Lane in the middle of the Marigold in the middle of the day, and he caught several members of the staff looking on, and he would have protested more strongly if it hadn't felt so good. He pressed his face against Lane's neck and let himself be held for a moment.

"I didn't get it," Eddie murmured.

"I am so sorry." Lane tugged on Eddie. "Come with me."

Without losing their grip on each other, Lane managed to maneuver Eddie into his office and push him into a chair.

"What happened?" asked Lane.

Eddie shook his head. It barely made sense. "That was one of the best auditions I've ever done," he said. That was the truth. Eddie couldn't remember a time he'd been so technically good. "But Mr. Ziegfeld thinks I don't work as a solo act."

Lane knelt next to the chair and put his hands on Eddie's knees. "Please don't . . ." He trailed off and ran his hands up Eddie's legs. "Please don't let this upset you too much. I know you really wanted to work for Mr. Ziegfeld, but this does not mean your career is over. All right? Lately, there are a dozen new shows opening every week, it seems like. You can try out for one of those, can't you?"

Lane was right, of course. "I could, yes."

"So just—I don't know what I would do if—" Lane was interrupted by a knock on the door. "What is it?" he called out.

"Mr. Carillo, Mook is here."

Lane dropped his head in Eddie's lap for a moment. "I'll be right there," he shouted. He slowly rose to his feet. "I have to deal with this, but stay here. I'll be back as soon as I can."

Eddie realized Lane thought he'd do himself harm if left alone. But he wouldn't; that was the whole point of coming to see Lane. "I'm not going to kill myself if you leave me alone for five minutes." It came out sounding harsher than Eddie intended, and Lane winced. "I guess I'm glad of that." He leaned over and kissed Eddie's forehead. "Well, stay put anyway. Humor me." Then he left the office.

Eddie waited, strumming his fingers together. When it seemed clear Lane might be a while, Eddie looked at the desk. There wasn't much to see there except for ledgers, one of which was open, and though Eddie was curious, looking at all those columns of numbers made his head spin. Under the ledgers was a copy of a newspaper flipped open to Walter Winchell's column decrying the firing of Eddie Cotton from the Doozies. Eddie felt a warmth in his chest when he realized Lane had kept it.

The desk had three drawers. Eddie opened the first and found it was not that exciting: it contained a couple of dime novels—Lane had confessed a fondness for adventure stories one night—and what looked like half a sandwich wrapped up in paper. Eddie opened the second and was surprised by what he found there: a smattering of papers and newspaper clippings but more prominently: a gun.

That gave Eddie pause. He stared at it for a long time, but mostly what he saw was a stark reminder that this man he had fallen so hard for was still an employee of the Mob. He wondered if that gun had ever killed anybody.

The last drawer was locked.

Eddie decided to read one of the dime novels while he waited. The one he picked had a pretty lurid cover, with a swarthy-looking detective in a black coat looking shiftily at a woman in a red dress. He was a few pages into it when Lane came back.

"Sorry about that. I had a shipment come in," said Lane, walking over to the desk. He took a look at what Eddie was reading and raised an eyebrow. "I can explain that."

"This book is really terrible. Do you actually like these things?" Lane snatched it out of Eddie's hands and threw the book back in its drawer. "Thank you for going through my desk."

Eddie looked up at Lane. "That gun. You ever actually use it?"

Lane sighed. "Yes."

Eddie steeled himself for the next question. "You ever kill anybody?"

Lane raised his eyebrows. "Do you really want me to answer that?"

Eddie translated that to mean that he wouldn't like the answer. "No. Don't tell me. I don't actually want to know."

Lane slammed the drawer closed. "You knew who I worked for the first time we met. It's not like I'm hiding things from you. It's a reality of my life."

Eddie looked at the drawer that contained the gun. He knew this was the case, but it was so hard to reconcile the Lane he'd come to know—a nice, mostly gentle man—with the gun in that drawer, with the reality of his life, as he'd so quaintly put it.

Lane said, "I've got three thousand dollars in that desk, too. Is that a problem for you?"

Eddie balked. "Lane, I—"

"Yes, I've fired the gun. Yes, at people. The circumstances don't matter and it's in the past. Yes, I make money—a lot of money—selling hooch illegally and also doing odd jobs for Epstein, which, yes, sometimes requires me to use the gun. I've also fired it in self-defense, because being a queer man in the Mob required me to prove that I wasn't to be trifled with. I'll let you draw your own conclusions about that." Lane rubbed his forehead. "That is the shit I'm in, all right? That's what I do, who I am. If you can't handle it, I suggest you leave right now."

Which felt like a slap across the face. Eddie leaned back in the chair. In the first place, he didn't believe for a second that any of the Mob stuff was really who Lane was. The job was something he did, yes, but it wasn't who he was as a person. It didn't seem like the right time to argue the point, though. And in the second place, he was surprised that, after everything, Lane would tell him to leave. He held up his hands. "I'm sorry," he said. "I shouldn't have snooped. I just didn't want to think about things, and you weren't here, so I—"

"No, I shouldn't have gotten so angry, especially after your audition, I—"

"Lane. We both have difficult realities."

Lane nodded. "That is true."

Eddie stood. "I'm not leaving. I came here because I can't get through this without you."

Lane's eyebrows knitted together. "I know. And I've been doing this nonsense for almost five years, but I can't imagine tomorrow without you. How did that happen?"

"I don't know. You're the one who always has the answers about this emotional stuff. I'm out of my league." Eddie took a step closer to Lane and reached for him. He leaned close, inhaling the scent of Lane's cologne.

Then they were kissing, before Eddie had even been aware that he'd wanted to kiss. He did want to kiss Lane, though; it was a very strange idea to get used to. He'd so thoroughly convinced himself that he didn't like kissing, but he sure as hell liked kissing Lane. He loved the way their lips seemed to just fit together, the way they slid across each other, the way that the simple act of kissing could send shocks and excitement through every part of Eddie's body.

He pulled away gently and rested his forehead against Lane's. "Thanks. I love you."

Lane shook a little as he chuckled. "I love you, too. And it's just as new for me as it is for you."

Eddie didn't believe that. He pulled himself away from Lane and walked to the other side of the office. "But you and Scott . . ."

"Scott and I barely knew each other when we hopped the train to New York. We lived together long enough for him to realize he'd made a terrible mistake. I cared for him very much and I miss him, but I don't know. I loved him, but we were so young. What I have with you is different. Deeper in a way. The way I love you is different from how I loved Scott."

"Oh." Eddie scratched his head. So much of this situation just didn't make sense to him.

"Stop thinking so hard. Come on. We just got a shipment of hooch in that promises to be better than the coffin varnish we've been getting lately. Have a drink with me." Lane offered his hand, so Eddie took it and walked with him out of the office.

Chapter 19

"It Ain't Gonna Rain
No More"

A few nights later, after Lane closed the club, Eddie stood on the sidewalk in front of the Marigold and felt like he wasn't ready for the night to end just yet. There was just something in the air. It was hot, oppressively muggy in the way only New York City could be. There were still people about, lingering under streetlamps, making overtures on sidewalks. Though it was the wee hours of the morning, it seemed like a night full of possibilities.

So, he talked Lane into walking with him a little. They walked east along 48th Street to Sixth Avenue, and then they walked south a little. As they neared the Hippodrome on 43rd, Eddie thought he saw something out of the corner of his eye. He paused to look.

"What is it?" asked Lane.

There didn't seem to be anyone on Sixth Avenue within a block or two of where they stood, but they were close to Bryant Park, and Eddie knew the park was probably crawling with vagrants and prostitutes. He'd always felt some kinship with them, usually not fear. But prostitutes attracted a certain element, too, one that was angry and violent. Now Eddie worried someone who meant them harm was lurking in the shadows, lured to the neighborhood by the activity in the park. He glanced at Lane who was, as always, expensively and neatly dressed, and he considered himself and the suit he was wearing. His heart started beating faster as he wondered if they looked like men who could be robbed or, worse, that they looked like obvious homosexuals. Either status invited violence Eddie was not prepared to defend them against.

And then a kid appeared. He was wearing clothes that were out of style and too big for him, and he was frighteningly skinny. Eddie pegged his age at around seventeen.

"Can I help you gentlemen?" the kid said.

Eddie glanced at Lane. "No, thank you," he said.

The kid made an obscene gesture in response.

A funny look came over Lane's face, not one that Eddie could interpret. "Look, kid," Lane said. "We said we're not interested."

The kid shrugged. "Suit yourself. I could show you a good time, is all."

"I'll bet you could. In five years, when you're done with puberty."

"Hey, I'm old enough!"

Lane still had that inscrutable expression on his face. Eddie wondered if he was plotting something.

"You got a name?" Lane said to the kid.

"Frank."

"All right, Frank. Once and for all, we are not interested in your services. But if you want a job, a real job, come by the Marigold tomorrow afternoon." He fished through his jacket pocket until he came up with a Marigold matchbook. He handed it to the kid. "It's a nightclub. The address is on the matchbook there. Come in and ask for Mr. Carillo."

The kid shot Lane a look of such smug disdain, one eyebrow raised, but he took the matchbook and shoved it in his pockets. "Sure, fella," he said. "I'll just come to the Marigold tomorrow."

Something in Lane seemed to snap then. He crossed his arms over his chest. "You want to spend the rest of your life as a working boy, that's fine with me. I just thought I'd offer you an opportunity to try something that won't get you sick or killed. Your choice, though."

Frank let out a huffy breath. "Fine. Fuck you, fellas." He turned down 43rd Street and disappeared into the night.

"Are you sure it's a good idea to offer jobs to any vagrant that comes along?" Eddie asked.

"Eddie, that kid was crying out for someone to save him. He'll come to the club tomorrow."

"How do you know that?"

"I know."

Eddie scoffed. Suddenly the night seemed a little less open to him. "Let's just go back to the Knickerbocker," he said.

"Fine by me."

It frankly surprised Lane when the kid showed up three days later. The Marigold was about to open for the night when the kid walked into Lane's office, trailed by Etta, who was panting as she said, "I'm sorry, Mr. Carillo. I tried to stop him, but he insisted on coming in to see you."

"It's okay. Hello, Frank," Lane said, waving his hand to dismiss Etta.

"That's a man in a dress," Frank said as he looked at Etta's retreating figure.

"That's Etta, and I expect you to be nice to her if you want a job."

Frank shook his head. "That ain't no 'her.'"

"You want a job or did you just come here to beat your gums at me?"

"I want a job."

Lane stood and led Frank toward the kitchen. "How old are you, kid?"

"Twenty-two."

Lane stopped walking and turned around. "You are not twenty-two."

Frank sighed. "Fine. I'm nineteen."

"Really?"

They resumed walking toward the kitchen. As they walked through the door, Frank said, "Yes, really." He looked around. "My friend Bill says clubs like this make kids like me do the customers."

"'Do'?"

Frank made an obscene gesture.

Lane sighed. "I don't expect you to 'do' anyone. What I want you to do is bring customers drinks without spilling them. Can you do that?" He was starting to regret a little that he'd given Julian the night off; Julian would know how to handle a kid like this.

"Wait, that's it?" Frank asked. "Just bring them drinks?"

"Well, I'd like you to talk to the customers, too. Tell jokes, flatter them, make them feel comfortable here. But no sex. This is not that kind of club."

"All right, sir." There was a healthy dose of sarcasm in the kid's voice. He winked.

"What you do on your own time is up to you," Lane said. "The fellas who come in here, I'd bet they'd just love someone like you. But when you are here at work, you serve drinks and that's it. You cause any trouble, I'll kick your little behind right back out onto the streets."

"You're serious." Frank suddenly looked sober.

"Yes."

"Oh. Then that's what I'll do. I'll serve drinks."

"Good. I'd start you tonight, but you can't work the floor in those clothes." What Frank was wearing was not much more than rags. Lane reached into his pocket and pulled out his billfold. He peeled off a few bills and held them toward Frank before thinking better of it. He held his hand back. "If I give you a few dollars, you will use the money to buy a decent pair of black pants and a white shirt. Got it?"

Frank nodded. "Yes, sir." There was no sarcasm this time. "I'll use the dough to buy clothes."

"Good." Lane passed the money over. "And I expect you to be washed, too. You got a place you can take a bath?"

"Yes, sir."

"Great. Be here tomorrow at six in the evening, no later. Dressed and clean. Got that?"

"Yes, sir." Frank pocketed the money. Lane showed him out the back door and watched him run down the street, wondering if he'd made the right decision or if he'd even see Frank again.

The next night, Julian spread tablecloths and adjusted curtains and generally kept himself busy getting the Marigold ready to open.

A young man in a very stiff looking white shirt and ill-fitting black trousers came crashing through the front door. "We're closed," Julian told the kid, "but come back in an hour."

"I work here," the kid said defensively. "Mr. Carillo hired me yesterday."

"He didn't say anything to me," said Julian. This man couldn't have been much older than twenty, and he looked awkward, like his mother had cleaned him up for Sunday school. He'd missed a spot when shaving and there was a thin line of dark stubble on his cheek. His hair was messy, like it hadn't been cut in a while. And the shirt looked like it had come right off the hanger in the store.

Still, he was handsome, in his way. And clean.

"Look, I work here, all right?" the fellow said. "I bought this shirt and everything. Mr. Carillo gave me money and told me I had to."

Julian wondered if Lane adopted every hard-luck case he ran into. Not that Julian wasn't grateful. "I'll go get him."

Julian went back to the office. The door was open, thankfully. Lane sat at his desk, writing in one of his ledgers. "Lane, darling, there's a polished-up kid in the club who says you hired him."

"Frank?" Lane stood and walked over to Julian. "Good."

Julian felt bewildered but followed Lane back to the floor. The kid still stood there, rocking on his heels, looking around the club.

"Ah, Frank," Lane said. "You look great." He clapped the kid on the back. "This is Julian. He will show you the ropes."

"I will do what?"

Lane ignored Julian. "Julian is the best waiter we have. Tonight, I want you to be his shadow. Follow him around as he works and talks to the customers. Watch how he behaves. I want you to learn what he does and cater to my customers well. Got it?"

"Yes, sir," the kid said.

Lane grinned. "Great. Julian, this is Frank."

"Obviously."

"Get to know each other."

And with that, Lane went back to his office.

Julian looked at this Frank for a few minutes. "What trash can did he pull you out of?"

Frank looked down. "He didn't. He . . ." Then he shook his hands. "Nothing, it's not important."

Julian rolled his eyes and threw an arm around the kid. "Look, darling, I've seen everything. Nothing you say will surprise me. Did you used to be a working boy before Lane hired you? Did you try to solicit him?"

The kid shrugged. *That was exactly it*, Julian thought. No wonder Lane had wanted Julian to lead him around. "All right, here's what we do. Stand up a little straighter. Don't be mean or petulant. Flirt with everyone. Can you do that?"

Frank stood up a little straighter, but he still had that insouciant look on his face. He was going to be a piece of work.

And yet, two hours into his shift, Frank seemed to be a natural. He was friendly and flirty, quickly parlaying the skills he learned living on the streets into convincing the men in the club to buy drinks. Julian also noticed that, when he wasn't being surly, he was pretty cute. Frank was on the young side, sure, but still the sort of man Julian had gone for back when he'd had a choice.

He had a choice again, he realized quite abruptly as he brought a man his drink. Lane had given him that. He wasn't making as much money working at the Marigold as he'd made out on the street, but his income was regular and reliable now, and since Lane was paying his rent, he'd been able to squirrel some of his wages away. That meant that suddenly, he had a lot of choices. He had a freedom of movement he hadn't enjoyed in years, which felt like such a luxury, but, he now realized, he also could have chosen any man to go home with. There would be no more following home a john whom Julian didn't find attractive, no more pretending to lust after flesh he found disgusting, no more feigning intimacy when he'd rather be sleeping.

Lane had given him such a gift.

He led Frank around and then he shadowed him, watching him interact with customers. Frank was great; Lane's instincts had proven right again. Julian found him great in other ways, too; he liked the way Frank's body moved, he liked the spark in his eye, he liked the shape of his chest, his thighs, his ass. He had no intention of acting on his attraction—Frank was so very young, for one thing, and Julian had been enjoying the rest his body was getting for another—but it was nice to know that he *could*.

Frank walked over to a table. He leaned forward and stuck his ass out a little. He rocked his hips and shook his head and made himself look like sex on legs for the customers, who were eating it up. He was doing it for tips—Julian knew that and the men were being generous tonight—but Julian was eating it up, too. And wasn't that funny?

Feeling confident that everything was taken care of temporarily, Julian slipped into the kitchen to take a break. What he found there made his heart stop.

Lane was arguing with a man in a suit. "I've told you countless times that nothing illegal is happening here."

"And I don't believe you. I could arrest the lot of you for lewd behavior."

Julian knew that voice. *Fucking faggot fairy*, it had said to him once, before beating the shit out of him.

It was Harry, the man from the Astor.

Julian ducked into the shadows behind a set of cabinets, out of the line of sight from where Lane and Harry stood. He watched as Lane reached into his pocket and then pressed his palm against Harry's. "I don't want any trouble," Lane said. "I do my best to stay out of it."

"You disgust me," Harry said.

"Yes, well. It doesn't change the fact that I run an honest business."

"Bootlegging and letting men cavort with each other."

"So maybe if something disgusts you, don't spend so much time looking at it."

That clearly angered Harry. He reached out and grabbed Lane's tie. "Don't mock me, you fucking fairy. I run this neighborhood." He pulled on Lane's tie until the two men were pressed together.

"Sir, I—"

Both men's eyes went suddenly wide. Harry backed off and straightened his jacket. "You think you know all about me, don't you, Carillo?"

"I don't know anything."

"Keep it that way." Harry headed toward the door. "Don't think this is over. I'll be back."

"A pleasure doing business with you as always, Officer Hardy."

As the kitchen door slammed, Julian started to hyperventilate. It was like all of his airways closed up. He struggled to breathe again, but all he could see were those fists coming at his face. He didn't know what was happening here, but he knew that Lane was doing business with the man who still tormented Julian in his dreams. Just when he thought he'd escaped . . .

"Julian? Hey, Julian, are you okay?"

Lane was suddenly in front of him, easing him out of his shadowy hiding place. Julian couldn't make his mouth form words, so he just shook his head. He pointed at the door that Harry had just left through.

"Hardy? Do you know him?"

Julian nodded. He started to shake violently in a way he couldn't control.

"Oh, Jesus. All right. Come with me."

Lane steered Julian to the office. He nudged Julian into the chair. "Deep breaths," he said. "Slow down, try not to gasp."

It took a seemingly interminable amount of time, but Julian managed to get his breathing mostly under control. Lane leaned against his desk and waited patiently.

Lane said, "Client of yours?"

Julian nodded. "He's the one who . . ." He gestured toward his face, which had once been so badly bruised he'd used heavy makeup to cover it up.

Lane cursed. "I suppose I shouldn't be surprised. I had him pegged as a self-hating queer weeks ago." He sighed. "He's a self-appointed Volstead Act enforcement agent. He makes a fortune in this neighborhood from people who don't want to get raided."

Julian took another deep breath. "Hardy, you said his name is?" he asked shakily.

Lane nodded. "Yes."

"He called himself Harry when I met him," said Julian as he realized this man had been part of the fabric of the neighborhood for longer than he'd suspected. Memories suddenly surfaced of Bryant Park raids and friends getting arrested or beaten. There had been an officer named Hardy behind more than one of those incidents, hadn't there? "He's been prowling around Times Square for a while, yes? The last year or so?"

"Yes. He's a thorn in my side but a powerful one. At his word, all of this ends." Lane gestured around him. "He threatens to shut down the Marigold once a week and he could do it, too. His cronies would be in here at the snap of his fingers, and then it's over. I think if it were just the bootlegging, he'd leave us alone, but he's particularly hung up on the clientele."

"So you pay him off not to raid you."

Lane nodded. "He demands more money every week. But there's nothing I can do. He's a darling of the department because he has so many arrests under his belt. He's friendly with Mayor Walker and a number of other city officials. So I pay him and he leaves me alone."

"He's a violent man."

Lane nodded. "I was afraid that might be the case."

What a mess. Just when Julian thought he might be on the way to escaping his past, it came back to haunt him. He shook his head as he stood up.

"Are you all right?" Lane asked.

"Yes, darling. I'd like to get back to work now."

"Yes, of course."

Frank was flirting pretty heavily with a customer as Julian arrived back out on the floor. He smiled at himself, more amused by the kid's antics than he would have admitted aloud. At least it was a distraction from the very real danger Julian still found himself in.

Chapter 20

"Dark Was the Night, Cold Was the Ground"

The Marigold was having an especially good night. The alcohol was flowing plentifully—Lane had gotten a case of decent hooch at a good discount from Mook, who had responded well to Lane's threats to go to other distributors. The fact that Julian knew a guy who could get them a couple of cases in a pinch had helped, too, reinforcing that Mook was not the only act in town.

Eddie was out on the floor teaching the crowd a few steps. He got a bunch of the men at the club doing the Charleston, which was pretty funny to watch from Lane's perspective off to the side. And the club was packed, on top of it. He wasn't sure there had ever been a night this crowded in the entire time the club had been open. It was a lucrative enough night that Lane felt pretty confident he'd be able to come up with enough money to pay off Hardy and whoever else came to call.

Eddie came off the dance floor laughing. Lane caught him and put his arms around Eddie's waist. "Hey, baby," he said. "Enjoying yourself?"

"Yes," Eddie said. "What a great crowd you've got." He sighed and leaned into Lane a little. "I thought it was a silly idea, but I'm really glad that you talked me into dancing here. It keeps me warmed up, if nothing else. I have another audition next week, did I tell you that?"

"No. That's marvelous." All of it was. Lane had asked Eddie if he'd be willing to entertain some of the guests at the club, had offered to pay him even, but Eddie was doing it free of charge. It seemed to make him happy, which had been Lane's main goal, although the fact that Eddie attracted repeat customers was nothing to sneeze at. And now he had an audition? That was the gravy on top.

Eddie smiled. He put his arms more firmly around Lane and hugged him close. "Dance with me."

"Oh, no."

"Oh, *yes*. Come on, Lane." He dragged Lane toward the floor, Lane protesting and fighting him the whole way, but he let himself be led over to the crowd of men. Eddie seemed to stop traffic as he moved through the floor. Everyone applauded him.

"Well, gentlemen," Eddie said, taking a deep bow. "This here is my man, okay?" Everyone in the crowd hooted and cheered. Lane, who much preferred to be on the sidelines, felt the blush rise to his face. He did not want all this attention on him. Eddie continued, "He thinks he's not a great dancer, but I think he just needs a little practice. Am I right?"

A few of the men clapped. Eddie bowed again to the crowd, and then he bowed to Lane. "Okay, here's what you do." He took a step forward. Then he put his foot back where it had been. Then he took a step backward. Then he put his foot back the way it was. "Can you do that?" Eddie asked.

Lane felt paralyzed by all the eyes on him. It was one thing to dance with Eddie when they were just one more couple in the crowd. To be at the center of the spotlight was something else entirely. Still, he took a deep breath and tried the steps. Forward, back. Backward, back. But he tripped and almost fell. Eddie caught him.

"Okay, baby," Eddie said. He was grinning, enjoying the audience. Lane thought again about how much of a shame it was that Eddie was still unemployed. He was really born to do this, and he fed off the energy of the crowd. It bolstered him, made him smile, made Lane happy to watch. But then this was why Eddie was a performer and Lane preferred to do things behind the scenes.

Eddie had been auditioning regularly for the last few weeks but still hadn't gotten a job that lasted longer than a night or two. Watching Eddie now, it was impossible to see the sense in that. This man should have been entertaining a crowd many times larger than the small one assembled on the dance floor of an off-the-beaten-path club for queers.

"Right foot forward, right foot back, left foot back, left foot forward. Now, pay attention." Eddie lifted his arms and bent his elbows. "You get your arms in on this, too, so it looks like you're a bird."

Eddie moved so gracefully that Lane thought he looked like a lovely, beautiful bird, maybe a swan, something that moved majestically. Lane tried to mimic his movements and felt more like a chicken. Someone in the audience reinforced that by squawking. Eddie laughed and got into it. He got everyone on the floor doing the steps with him. Then it started to get wild, with men throwing their arms and feet around, moving in time with some raucous tune from the band, all trumpet bleats and saxophone melodies.

"It's jazz, baby," Eddie said to Lane as he danced. Lane tried again, feeling awkward and clumsy. Eddie took his hand and danced alongside him. Lane wasn't sure what was going on anymore, and he was sure he looked like a fool, but it was hard to deny that it felt good to be doing whatever he was doing with Eddie, and it felt great to be called Eddie's man to an audience full of other men.

The tempo changed slightly, and Lane found himself swept up in Eddie's arms. He was still awkward, but Eddie led him around the dance floor, and he found it was easy enough to follow what Eddie was doing. He stepped on Eddie's feet a few times, but Eddie just laughed.

When they were in the throes of laughing, tangled up together, Lane said, "You amaze me."

Eddie grinned. "You're not so bad, you know. I think if you danced a little more often, you'd be able to hold your own."

"Maybe I only like dancing with you. I'll practice all you want, if it's with you."

Eddie leaned over and kissed his cheek. "I love you, Lane."

"Right back at ya, baby."

They danced around the floor and Lane couldn't remember ever feeling quite so happy, or when he'd been able to just let go and have fun.

Which was why everything came crashing down the next moment.

One minute he was dancing, and the next, a swarm of cops was moving into the club, shouting and rounding up people. "This is a raid," one of them announced. He held up a piece of paper.

Lane's first reaction was pure, unadulterated panic. All the blood drained out of his extremities, his stomach churned, and a cold sweat broke out all over his body. He glanced at Eddie, who just stared, dumbstruck.

This could not be happening. Not on a night like tonight.

Lane gathered himself and pushed through the crowd of men. He was angry now. No, angry wasn't the word. Livid. Furious. Officer Hardy stood in the middle of the horde of cops, a smirk on his face, cool as a cucumber.

"Bang it, Hardy, what the hell?" Lane asked. "You told me—"

"That was before I knew about the nature of this club, Mr. Carillo." Lane knew they both knew that was complete horseshit, but Hardy said it loudly, more for the benefit of his audience than for Lane. His expression was placid, and he held out his hands, palms up, as if he couldn't be expected to do otherwise. "You have men here who are cavorting with other men. It's disgusting. I was willing to look the other way when I thought you were just selling cheap rotgut to drunkards like every other club in Times Square, but this is beyond the pale. This is sickening. So I'm shutting this place down."

Lane wanted to protest more, especially since Hardy's tone was so matter-of-fact, but the damage was done. Most of the men in the place were scrambling to leave in a hurry, running for the exits or the bathrooms. He caught sight of Etta running into the kitchen and he wondered if she would have time to change before she ran out of the club. Leaving still dressed as a woman was a good way to end up in jail for the night.

In the midst of the chaos, Lane was separated from Eddie. Somehow, not being able to see him made Lane panic even more than the raid itself did. Because if mere rumors about where Eddie spent time were enough to keep him unemployed, then surely getting caught and arrested in this raid would end his career for good.

Hardy walked up to Lane and grabbed his arm. Lane expected to get arrested now, and that was a tangible fear, too. A cold sweat broke out on his back as he pictured spending the night in jail and all of the horrific things his cellmates might do to the man who ran a notorious club for queer men and fairies. More to the point, it was bad enough to get arrested for selling alcohol; Hardy might also charge him with sodomy. Then his life would be over.

"I don't want to arrest you, Carillo," said Hardy. Lane met his eyes and saw pain and remorse there, or he imagined he did.

"Then don't." Lane used his free hand to reach into his pocket for his billfold, hoping maybe he had enough cash in it to persuade Hardy to go away. His hand closed around it and he managed to pull a few bills out. He slipped them into Hardy's hand.

Hardy closed his eyes briefly. He let out a soft breath. Time stood still a moment as Hardy and Lane assessed each other.

Lane knew it was too late to stop the raid, but he hoped he could use money and what he knew of Hardy to escape. "Listen," he said softly, "I know a man who was once employed by you. Says you beat him hard enough to kill him, but help stumbled upon him and he lived."

Hardy's eyes widened. "And you'd believe the word of a fairy prostitute before you believed me?"

"You basically just confirmed his story. I never said he was a prostitute. So yes, I believe him."

"No one else will."

"Perhaps not, but I have enough information to make a lot of trouble for you. Wouldn't your boss love to hear what you do in your off hours?"

Hardy took a step back. "This club is done," he said, "but maybe you slipped out the back before I could arrest you."

He moved away and started shouting. The kitchen staff was hauled out in cuffs, and Lane wondered if a raided club was a little like a sinking ship, if he was supposed to go down with it, but he also really needed to find Eddie. He snuck into the kitchen and then down the hall to his office, where he found Eddie hiding behind the door. Lane leaned over and kissed Eddie, because the situation seemed to call for it. Eddie kissed him back.

"What the hell is happening?" Eddie asked.

"I guess I didn't pay Hardy enough." He didn't want to get into the entirety of the situation, not yet. They needed to get out of the club and then Lane would explain.

"I can't get arrested, Lane. I cannot."

"He's going to leave us alone, but we need to leave right now."

Eddie nodded. Lane quickly gathered what he could from his desk, including his gun and his ledgers and shoved it all into a bag he kept in the coat closet. He grabbed Eddie's hand and pulled him through the kitchen and then out onto the street. Once they were outside, they ran down 48th Street.

"Now what?" Eddie asked.

"Let's go to your place."

Once they were in the heart of Times Square, it was easy enough to slip into the chaos of the crowds pouring out of the theaters. Eddie led the way, which was necessary because Lane's head was spinning so fast he didn't know which way was south. He focused on the back of Eddie's head as they walked and he tried not to think about what would happen next. The Marigold could potentially recover and reopen. But Hardy had said it was done. He wanted more than Lane could pay. Profits had been up recently, but probably not enough to make keeping the place worth Hardy's price, which Lane imagined would just continue to balloon given what Hardy could threaten Lane with. And at the end of the day, Epstein didn't care about what Lane had been building on 48th Street, about the safe space and the community and the dancing; he cared about money.

If the Marigold was really done, where did that leave Lane? He followed Eddie down Broadway and wondered what task Epstein would have for him next, or if he'd be penalized for letting the Marigold get raided. He feared both outcomes.

But they arrived at the Knickerbocker and Eddie led Lane through the side entrance.

"Are you all right?" Eddie asked.

Lane didn't—couldn't—answer. In the elevator, he hung his head, unwilling to look at Eddie, feeling like a failure, feeling doomed. Hard to believe that the place he had invested so much time in could be taken from him in an instant. He had never dreamed of running a club, and yet the Marigold had become his dream, his greatest accomplishment. It was a haven for men like him, a place he could just be. And now it was gone.

Eddie ran his knuckles along Lane's cheek. "There's nothing you can do tonight. Put it aside for now. We'll worry tomorrow."

"We?"

"I'm in this with you." Eddie slid his fingers under Lane's chin and lifted it. "Put it aside. I'll take you to my room and help you forget. All right?"

Lane nodded. "Bang it, Eddie. Just . . . bang it all."

"I know."

The elevator dinged. Eddie took Lane's hand and led him down the hall. He fished his key out of his pocket, but Lane stopped him before he opened the door.

"Thank you," Lane said quietly.

"What for?"

"You . . . tonight, you saved me."

Eddie shrugged. "If you'll recall, you saved me first. I figure I'm just returning the favor."

Chapter 21

"What'll I Do?"

Eddie woke up in his darkened room aware of two things: Lane was in bed with him and Lane was awake.

"Eddie?" Lane whispered.

Unable to form words, Eddie mumbled.

"I think I need to leave Epstein."

Eddie heard and understood the words but still wasn't all the way awake. He moved over to Lane's side of the bed and touched Lane's arm. "What? You said last night that it didn't matter, that Epstein's clubs were raided all the time."

"They are. It's not that. I just..." Lane shifted on the bed and turned toward Eddie. "Maybe this is crazy, but being with you has made me not want to be in the Mob anymore. And now everything is dangerous. My club got shut down and the cops know I'm queer. I paid off Officer Hardy, and I know his secrets, so I didn't get arrested. But the next time I go into business, he could be less charitable, and then I wind up in jail for bootlegging and sodomy. Or worse. He's volatile and dangerous. When it was just me to worry about, I wasn't concerned, but now I've got you, and I don't want to take those kinds of risks anymore."

It was a lot to take in before everything was working correctly. Eddie took a deep breath and absorbed the fact that Lane had paid the cop not to arrest him. This wasn't a game. He closed his eyes and thought about that, but then also about what else Lane had just said. Lane was part of the Mafia. Was there even any chance of leaving? Eddie couldn't have Lane making changes that crazy on his account.

Wouldn't Lane be putting himself in danger if he just left? Eddie said, "I shouldn't be the one determining how you live your life."

Lane sat up. "No. Don't you get it, Eddie?"

Lane slammed his palm on a pillow, and Eddie was definitely awake now, listening intently. And he, apparently, did not "get it." "I don't understand."

"When Scott died, a part of *my* life ended, too. For six months, he was my whole world, and then he was gone, and I was left alone in New York with no one and nothing to care about. I needed to pay rent, though, so I reached out to my cousin John. There was a family rumor that he and his brother Tony were *la cosa nostra*, but I didn't know for sure. My parents didn't want anything to do with that part of my family. All I knew was that John had a thing going at the Fulton Fish Market and I thought he could get me a job. Turns out his operation at the fish market was smuggling in liquor from the rum runners parked off the coast. So he got me a job, all right. And then I was made. Do you know what that means?"

Eddie nodded. He'd heard the term before. If Lane was a made man, it meant he was family. Part of the Mob for life. Eddie's head spun a little.

"So John got me a job working for Epstein, and I figured, I've got nothing left to lose. I liked the work well enough, but it was still the Mob. Then John was killed in some kind of dispute over a gambling operation downtown. I wasn't involved, but I was too deep in to use the circumstance of his death to extract myself from the family. And that's just it, Eddie. I'm family. My father's family came here from Sicily. My dad moved to Chicago when he was very young and opted not to get involved in the business, but his brother Joseph stayed here, ran around with gangs in the Five Points and became a *caporegime* before he was killed. John was Joseph's son."

Eddie didn't speak. He just listened.

"It's dangerous, this life, and I've done some things I'm not proud of. Still, it was work and it kept a roof over my head. I proved my worth early on and have risen up the ranks. And all that time I thought, if someone shot me in the head tomorrow, what would it matter? But everything has changed now. I have you. I could get arrested. By rights, Hardy should have arrested me last night. You know what they do to fellas like me in jail?" Lane shivered. "Or, worse, someone could get it in his head that I'm nothing but a pervert and kill me tomorrow, but I don't want to leave this earth yet. What I want is to quit this job and build a new life. With you."

Eddie found that amazing, that Lane wanted him that way. It was tempting to just accept, but he put a hand on Lane's waist and moved a little closer. "Can you do that? Can you just quit?"

Lane groaned and lay back down. "No, of course not. I've been in too long, I know too much. And Epstein, well. Epstein is not family, since he's a Jew, but he's in tight with the *caporegime* who is closest to the Boss. They're all old friends. So Epstein has a lot of power. He knows all my secrets, too. It's his money that has kept me out of jail. Epstein owns my soul. The whole Mafia does." He turned to Eddie. "What the hell am I going to do?"

Eddie didn't know much about how the Mob operated, but he knew that Lane was in trouble either way—his life was in danger whether he left or stayed.

"I don't know," Eddie said. "I don't want to lose you, either."

They lay together in silence for a long time. Eddie turned over ideas in his head—they could leave the city, they could find a way to go underground—and most of those ideas ended with his never being able to work in the theater again. He wasn't sure if that was something he was willing to sacrifice just yet. Not while there was a sliver of hope he could still dance on a stage.

"You can hide out here for as long as you need to," Eddie suggested.

Lane pulled Eddie into his arms. "Thank you. That only buys me a little bit of time, though. Plenty of people have seen me coming and going from this building. I bet most of the staff here knows we're . . . sweethearts."

Eddie laughed despite himself. The notion of them being "sweethearts" struck him as absurd. But Lane was right. If he stayed at the Knickerbocker, it was only a matter of time before Epstein found him. "Maybe that will buy us enough time to figure out what to do."

Lane sighed. "I'll have to go home eventually. I don't know that I'm any safer here, but thank you for the offer."

Lane buried his face in Eddie's shoulder. Eddie wanted to comfort him but wasn't sure how. He decided to try doing something he knew Lane would like: he lifted Lane's chin and kissed him.

Lane let out a breath but opened his mouth to accept the kiss. Their lips slid together with ease and familiarity. Eddie put his hands on Lane's back and felt the tension there ease a little. Lane pulled away slightly and said, "I love you so much."

Which Eddie knew deep in his heart. He knew that's what all this was about. "I love you, too."

Lane collapsed back into Eddie's arms and laid his head on Eddie's chest. "All of this is so crazy. How has this become my life?"

Eddie couldn't answer that question any better than he could answer how he'd gone from being the rabbi's son, the next great hope for the community, to dancing on Broadway, to teaching men in a queer speakeasy how to dance.

He wondered how much any of it mattered. He still held out hope he could get another job on Broadway, but maybe Lane meant more. Maybe keeping Lane safe—which probably meant leaving New York or at least going into hiding—was more important than Eddie's career dreams.

"You'll hate me," Lane said.

"What?"

"I can hear you thinking. And if you're thinking that you'll leave the city with me and give up your career, then you're crazy. I won't let you do that. I won't do that to you. You'd end up hating me for killing your dream. We can find another way."

"But if we can't—"

Lane held his fingers to Eddie's lips. "We'll find another way. You have so many years of success before you, Eddie. I can see you being a big name on a marquee. You'll dance and be wonderful, and I want to be there to see it."

"If only all things were possible."

Lane lifted his head and smiled down at Eddie. "With you, sometimes I think they are."

Marian knew that theater attendance was down; it was bad enough lately that she could see the empty seats when she walked out to do her performance each night. She knew in her gut that firing Eddie had been a mistake. While she was good, she was better with Eddie. The empty seats confirmed it.

She'd been weighing the idea of going to Jimmy and trying again to talk him into re-hiring Eddie when rumor started moving through the New York theater community that Eddie was auditioning all over town. He'd landed a part in a musical revue that had closed two weeks later, but otherwise hadn't made a big splash except by reputation.

Because the whole theater community was also saying Eddie was queer.

The rumor was that he'd gotten caught up in a raid at a seedy club and that he was into some pretty depraved things. That he was carrying on a lurid affair with another man. Marian knew a lot of it was nonsense—there was Lane and the Marigold, of course, but there was nothing unseemly about Eddie's relationship as far as Marian could tell. She wondered how much of a role Jimmy had played in spreading those particular rumors.

Probably it shouldn't have mattered. Marian knew full well that many people who worked in the theater were queer. She may have been baffled by why, but she knew it to be true just the same. But perhaps there was a difference between knowing the actor or stagehand you were talking to was very likely queer and seeing tangible evidence of it. There was a difference between knowing many people on Broadway were queer and the more vocal rumors connected to Eddie now, presented as if they were evidence that there was something deeply, disturbingly wrong with him.

She walked down the hall to Jimmy's office. He was there, looking at a book that she thought was maybe a ledger. That could have been a good sign for Marian's cause; it could mean that, if Jimmy really was losing money, perhaps he would be more amenable to suggestion.

Because it wasn't just that the seats in the theater were getting harder to fill. Walter Winchell and a number of theater columnists had written some scathing things about Jimmy, criticizing him for firing Eddie Cotton and for how poorly the Doozies was managed. The quality of acts had never been as good as the *Scandals*, the spectacle had never been as awesome as it was at the *Follies*, but Cotton and France, at least according to the papers, had always been the act to see, made the price of the ticket worth it. Marian had always been proud of that fact.

Still, the bad press might have been enough to make the Shuberts decide not to allow Jimmy back the next year.

She wondered as she stood in the doorway of Jimmy's office if she had let all that praise from Jimmy go to her head. Walter Rhodes, too, had told her many times that he thought she did really great things with the songs he'd written for her—there were three of them in her act now, although "My Heart Is Full" was still the crowd-pleaser—and now she wondered if she was actually good or if she'd just fallen victim to Jimmy's machinations.

She grew increasingly angry as she stood in that doorway. Jimmy barely noticed she was there. She cleared her throat.

"Just a minute, Martha," he said, calling out the name of his secretary. "Let me just finish crunching these numbers. I'll be right with you."

"Jimmy," Marian said.

He dropped his pen and looked up. "Oh, hello, dear. What is it? I'm very busy."

She wished she had a newspaper with her so that she could offer up evidence. She wanted to scream at him for the mistake he'd made. He'd done in his own production when he'd fired Eddie, and for what? For Marian to get extra attention that she didn't want? To get rid of the queer dancer in his show?

A copy of the *Evening Telegraph* was sitting on the guest chair in Jimmy's office. Marian snatched it up and flipped to Walter Winchell's column. She lucked out—Winchell had written about the waning fortunes of the Doozies in his column that very day.

"Have you seen this?" she asked. She showed Jimmy the article then she quickly scanned it herself.

"Yes, I saw it," Jimmy spat. "I'm aware of what Mr. Winchell thinks of my production, and I may just sue him for libel."

"Nothing he says here is untrue," Marian said. "Revenue *is* down. Don't lie to me and tell me that's not the case. I can see all the empty seats each night with my own eyes."

"We've had a little trouble selling tickets lately, it's true." Jimmy looked forlornly down at the ledger on his desk. "I think what I need is to pull in a really spectacular act, something that will attract people's attention, something that sizzles and sparkles, something that will really knock the pants off Mr. Ziegfeld."

Marian dropped the paper back on the chair. "What about a Cotton and France reunion?"

Jimmy shook his head. "What? Are you crazy? No. It's out of the question."

Marian pointed to the paper. "You know what's crazy, Jimmy? The way you ignore everything the press says. Winchell has been saying for weeks that it was a mistake to fire Eddie Cotton, that Eddie was half the reason anyone came to this theater."

"You're the other half!"

"Look. I appreciate the opportunity you gave me, Jimmy. I really do. It's like all of my dreams came true and I will always be grateful."

"But?" Jimmy stood up slowly and walked around his desk.

"But I'm not enough to carry the whole damn show. The songs are great and I love singing them, but they're not enough to pull people in, to hold their attention. I was better with Eddie. I was always better when I had someone to perform with, and I never had chemistry with another dancer the way I did with Eddie."

Jimmy balked. "If I didn't know better, I'd think you were in love with him instead of me."

"Don't be ridiculous. You know as well as I do that—" She stopped, realizing what she was saying. "Well, anyway. The rapport you have with someone on the stage is not the same as the rapport you have off the stage. Eddie and I were great together on stage. I never wanted him in any other way."

Jimmy shook his head. "I will not have that flaming faggot on my stage."

Marian rolled her eyes. She felt ready for a fight now. She was tired of just agreeing to everything Jimmy said, especially now that she could see his mistakes so clearly. "That's ridiculous. Do you know how many queer men there are in the theater community? If you think for one moment that you could in any way keep your stage clean of them, then you've got—"

"Shut up, Marian!" Jimmy shouted. He took a step closer to her and brandished his fist. "Shut up! You don't know what you're talking about. You're a stupid woman. Get out of my office and leave me to make the decisions. Have you ever produced a stage show? No? I've been doing it for a decade. I'll get those people back in those seats. The summer is waning now, though, so people are busy with other things. But come the fall, we're back in business. I'll get a big act that will knock everyone's socks off." He grunted. "Stop trying to run my show. I'm the producer here, not you."

"Jimmy, be realistic."

"No. I'm done. I will find the best act on Broadway, and it won't involve Eddie fucking Cotton."

Marian winced, put off by Jimmy's language.

Jimmy must not have seen it, because he kept talking. "Maybe it'll be like the Hippodrome and I'll get a few live animals in here.

Maybe I'll get some better chorus girls. I'll figure something out, and whatever it will be, it will be magical. But you are *mine*, Marian. I control *you*. You don't get a say in what happens on my stage."

"You're being ridiculous, Jimmy."

Jimmy reached forward and grabbed the collar of Marian's blouse. "No, you listen to me. *You're* being ridiculous. I'm in charge here."

The look in Jimmy's eyes terrified Marian. She thought he might hit her. She put up her hands.

"You're being unreasonable," she said.

"Am I, Marian? Seems to me you think you know better than me."

"I don't. I just want my dance partner back."

"He'll never love you, you know. Not the way I do."

"Jimmy."

She tried to get away, but he grabbed her arm hard enough to leave a bruise. She pulled back, but his grip was unrelenting. The look in his eyes was terrifying. She'd never seen him angry like this.

"I'm sorry," she said. "I'm not trying to run your show. You do a good job, Jimmy. I just think that—"

Jimmy shook her, hard enough that she gasped.

Suddenly he let go and took a step back. She took a stumbling step backward.

"I'm sorry, Marian. You know I don't mean it. I just got so angry."

He didn't look especially penitent. In fact, he still had that wild, furious look in his eyes.

Marian took a step back. "I know, but Jimmy—"

"Get out," he spat.

"Yes," she said. She turned on her heel and walked out of the office.

As she ran down to her dressing room, adrenaline kicked in and her heart started racing. She slammed the door and burst into tears.

Chapter 22

"What Can I Say After I Say I'm Sorry"

It surprised Lane that no one came. He spent a week at the Knicker-bocker after the raid, but no one found him. He went home one afternoon, and no one had been there, either. He warned himself not to get too comfortable, but things began to seem less dire as the days progressed.

Then the summons came.

He came home with Eddie after a night out in Greenwich Village and found a note had been slipped under the door. His presence was requested at Lenny's the next afternoon.

Lane glanced at Eddie.

"Epstein?" Eddie asked after reading over Lane's shoulder.

"Must be." Lane let out a breath, feeling like his holiday had just ended. "I figured it would come to this."

But when Lane walked into Lenny's at the appointed time the next day, Epstein was nowhere to be seen. Instead, Callahan and Legs Aurelio were sitting at a table eating sandwiches.

"Did you fellas summon me?" Lane asked as he stood over their table.

Callahan kicked out a chair, so Lane sat in it.

"Epstein has made himself scarce," Legs said. "So have you, actually. We just want to know what the hell to do now."

Lane looked back and forth between Legs and Callahan. "I don't know."

"That's not terribly comforting," Callahan said.

"What do you want me to say? The Marigold is done. It's over. We could reopen somewhere else, but it would only be a matter of time before Hardy found us and blackmailed us again."

"Maybe we should take care of Hardy," said Legs.

Callahan leaned back and leveled his gaze at Legs. "Not a cop, Legs. That's not how we do business."

"Besides," Lane said, "there are other Hardys. Prohibition has turned police officers into entrepreneurs. Eliminating one does not eliminate the problem."

Legs and Callahan debated this point for a moment while Lane contemplated the situation. The catch here, of course, was that Lane knew Hardy's secret and could probably have exploited it if he were to reestablish the Marigold or something like it in a new location. The prospect interested him, though continuing to work with Epstein did not. And the greater point still stood that even if Hardy could be neutralized, there were plenty of others who patrolled the area around Times Square. As an obstacle, this situation was not insurmountable, but Lane was tired.

"And," Callahan was saying when Lane resumed listening, "our next venture should be less, er . . ."

Lane sighed. "Less queer."

"Well, yes. It would certainly decrease the odds of our getting raided again."

"Then what's your gimmick? What gets people in the door? Why should anyone come to your joint when there are a hundred other speakeasies in the neighborhood?" Lane asked.

Legs and Callahan looked at each other. Callahan then turned to Lane and said, "We're not entirely sure yet. But are you in if we think of something?"

"I should check in with Epstein. I haven't spoken to him since the raid."

"Of course," said Callahan. "But if he has nothing in particular for you to do, maybe we should consider going into business together."

Lane liked Callahan and Legs both but he wasn't completely sure this was the best course of action, especially not now that Eddie was in the picture. "Let me think on it."

Legs took a big bite out of his sandwich. With his mouth full, he said, "I want to take out Hardy."

Lane considered his options. He decided he'd leave without eating and he'd take some time to figure out what to do. But he could also plant a few seeds.

"Hardy's queer," Lane said quietly as he stood. "Do with that information what you will." Then he walked out of the restaurant.

He went back home and was dozing in his bedroom when Eddie came back from an audition. Lane sat up and asked, "How did it go?"

"Hard to say. I performed well, but each of these auditions seems to go the same. I think I do well but then I don't get a call-back. So I don't know." Eddie took his hat off and tossed it on a side table. "This is kind of interesting." He held up a copy of a newspaper.

"Oh?" Lane hadn't bothered to look at a paper while he was out. Maybe it was foolish, but he had little interest in what was happening outside of his apartment.

"Apparently the police are stepping up enforcement of the Volstead Act. Nine clubs in Times Square alone have been raided in the last week. In this article in the *Times*, they interviewed a judge in Brooklyn who is irritated because he has to hear four times as many cases as he did before, nearly all of them offenses involving intoxicating beverages." Eddie handed Lane the paper. "It's not just you, I guess. I'm pretty sure three of the clubs named in the article are also owned by Epstein."

Lane looked at the article. Four of them were Epstein establishments, actually. And two of the others were owned by Lane's Mafia family, the Giambinos. He thought the other three were probably also Mob-controlled. "No mention of the Marigold," Lane pointed out. "Perhaps the fairy club is beyond the pale."

"Maybe for the best." Eddie started to change out of his audition outfit. There was a strange domesticity in the act, in the two of them chatting while Eddie went about his business. "You don't want to draw attention to yourself, right?"

"Epstein doesn't seem that determined to find me." Lane found that troublesome. Clearly, Epstein had problems of his own.

"Sure, but if not Epstein, then that cop. He *could* still arrest you if you crossed his path, right?"

"I don't think he will." Still, Lane felt grim. He dropped the paper in a wastepaper basket and went back to lying on the bed.

Eddie, down to his shirtsleeves, sat on the bed and ran a hand over Lane's hair. "I'm sorry, Lane. In my addled brain, I thought this was almost good news. Maybe Epstein will stay away if he's got this much of a mess on his hands."

"I don't see that he would go away permanently."

"No, but maybe we'll have a real plan by the time he does try to find you."

Lane wasn't any closer to knowing how to handle the hand he'd been dealt. He still wanted out, that was for certain, and he wanted to figure out how to make a life with Eddie that did not involve the Mafia or nightclubs or bootlegging or any of it. He sighed.

"Well. I hear California is nice this time of year."

Eddie laughed. "Ah, that would be the day, wouldn't it? Eddie Cotton takes his act to Los Angeles! Can you imagine? Me in a moving picture?"

"It's not too bad an idea."

Eddie shook his head and leaned down to kiss Lane's forehead. "Let me conquer Broadway first."

Lane didn't want to move, either. A fleeting thought passed through his head: his Anglophile friend Clarence had mentioned that his sugar daddy George knew people uptown. Maybe all he and Eddie really needed to do was get out of Times Square. If there was a way to get out of his problems without leaving the city, then that was what Lane wanted.

Marian pulled on the silk robe she kept in Jimmy's bedroom and walked down the hall, looking for him. She found him in his office, hunched over his desk. At first, she thought he was talking on the phone, but then she saw the receiver resting in its cradle. He must have been talking to himself. Marian figured he was looking at the numbers for the Doozies again. They couldn't have been good.

He'd come to her the night before full of apologies. Marian hadn't been inclined to forgive him for his violence the previous afternoon, but he'd brought her flowers and a gorgeous diamond necklace and he swore he'd find a way to keep the show going. She knew it was foolish, but she'd forgiven him and let him romance her back to his house after dinner, let him talk her into bed. This morning she regretted that somewhat, but she was willing to give Jimmy the benefit of the doubt, willing to accept his apology and let him make amends. Perhaps the Doozies would be better for it.

She knocked on the door frame. Jimmy jerked around and looked at her. "What are you doing here, Marian?"

"I just woke up. I thought you might like some breakfast. I can go downstairs and make something, if you want."

He grunted. "Yes, all right. I'm not sure what you will find there. There might be some eggs."

"I can work with eggs." She cracked her knuckles and smiled.

He didn't seem to be in an especially good mood. He nodded and went back to his ledger.

So Marian went downstairs. She found eggs and milk and bacon, so she went about cooking a fine breakfast. The eggs were light and fluffy, the bacon was cooked crispy, the way Jimmy liked it. She put everything on a plate and found a wooden tray. She carried the breakfast up the stairs and placed it carefully on the side of his desk.

"Eat up," she said.

Jimmy grunted again. He looked at the plate of food, and then he looked back at what he'd been working on—balancing the ledgers again, definitely—and he tossed his pen on the floor. "There's just no way to make this work." He shook his head. "I had a meeting with this fella who works for the Ringling Brothers, about possibly getting an animal for the show. A dancing horse, maybe. Wouldn't that be keen? That's the kind of thing that puts people in seats."

"You're not the circus, Jimmy. It's Broadway! Singing and dancing. Not big, smelly animals."

"What do you know about it?" he snapped.

Marian took a step back and held up her hands to show she didn't mean him any ill will. "I'm sorry," she said. "I just thought that you were serious about finding another song-and-dance act. That's what would really sell tickets, I think."

Jimmy put his hand under the tray and flipped it, sending food flying everywhere. Marian was hit in the face with a bit of egg. She took a step back from the desk. "Now, Jimmy. I made that nice breakfast for you. What are you going to eat now?"

"What are you even doing here, Marian? Why are you making me breakfast? You ain't my wife."

She grunted, realizing how false his apologies had been. Nothing had changed. "No, I'm not your wife." Not for lack of wanting. Jimmy had said he loved her, that she was his darling, his muse, the star of his show. The words had felt real. She'd been thinking for some time, therefore, that it was only a matter of days before Jimmy proposed. However, no proposal had been forthcoming, and as the Doozies' fortunes nosedived, it seemed like such a proposal was moving further and further away.

She steeled herself and said, "I thought that you cared about me, though. That you loved me. You've never objected to my spending the night before."

His face softened. "Aw, Marian. I do love you. That's why I made you the star of the show. And what thanks do I get? You can't even get people in the seats."

That made her angry enough to spit. Hadn't she told him getting Eddie back would be the trick? "That's not my fault. I told you, I'm better as part of a duo. You're the one who thought I could carry the whole show."

"I see now how terribly mistaken I was. Why did I make you the star? What was I thinking?"

He stood and he was menacing, as Marian knew he could be. He'd gotten where he was through arrogance and perseverance, traits that were good in a producer but not always so great in a lover. Marian took a few steps away, worried he might grab her and yell at her again. She said, "I'm not the person in the wrong here. I didn't mean to question you, I just think that—"

"I know what you think. That I should never have fired Eddie goddamn Cotton. I'm sick of hearing about Eddie Cotton. He's the one who caused my ruin!" He took a step closer to Marian, his face red with anger.

"Eddie did nothing. The Doozies were doing just fine before you fired him. Firing him was your decision!"

Marian felt the sting before she even realized what had happened. She put her hand to her face and felt the burn where Jimmy's palm had connected with her cheek. Shocked, she took another step back.

"Shut up, Marian! Why do you insist on continuing to babble about this nonsense? Eddie was a disaster. You know how I know that? No one else in this town will hire him. He's auditioned for Ziegfeld and every other producer in New York, and none of them has given him a job for more than a week or two at a time. You know what else I heard? That he's involved in the Mob now."

Marian stumbled, confused and disoriented by the slap and Jimmy's shouting. She shook her head and took another step back, trying to focus on Jimmy. Anger overtook her confusion. She couldn't believe Jimmy had slapped her. She couldn't believe Eddie would be dumb enough to get involved with the Mob. "That can't be true," she said. "It is true! And I can't believe that you would defend that faggot." Jimmy yelled something incoherent. He stomped his feet a few times, reminding Marian of a bull about to charge. Then he took a deep breath and, more calmly, said, "Get the hell out of here, Marian. I don't have time for you today."

She moved to leave, figuring it was best to let Jimmy cool off and to put some distance between them. But on her way out the door, he grabbed her arm and pulled her back. "No, wait a minute," he said. Then he pressed his lips against her.

There was nothing sexy or romantic about the kiss. It was angry and a little violent, and Jimmy's fingers dug into her arm. She cried out in pain, which caused him to bite down on her lower lip. She felt his teeth break the skin. She shrieked and tried to push him away. Jimmy just held on tighter and used his free hand to yank on her hair. She shouted for him to stop when he moved to pull her robe off. She scrambled and moved and finally was able to raise her knee high enough to connect with his balls. He howled in pain and backed off of her.

"How dare you!" she shouted. "Stay the hell away from me!"

But Jimmy wasn't done. He lunged forward and swung his fist. The punch connected with the side of her face and the pain was so brilliant that she couldn't see for a long moment. When her vision returned, all she saw was an angry Jimmy standing there with his fists at his side. She pulled her robe closed and ran down the hall.

In his bedroom, she tried, and failed, to keep the tears at bay as she found her clothes and pulled them on. She heard Jimmy coming down the hall, and she fought to finish getting dressed before he arrived there.

He walked into the room and said, "Marian, I'm sorry, I . . ."

"No." She pushed past him and out of the room. She found her jacket and her purse and ran outside. It was cold and rainy but it felt safer than inside Jimmy's house.

Eddie opened the door of his room and found Marian on the other side, sobbing. A large purple bruise marred her left eye.

"Oh, dear," Eddie said, the words immediately feeling stupid. He didn't know what to say or how to act, but he did know that Marian had been hurt badly. He put an arm around her and led her into the room. "Come in, come in."

Lane, who had been sitting on the bed to tie his shoes—they had no particular plans, but Lane had been going through the motions each day regardless of whether they left the room or not—sat up straight.

"What happened?" Lane asked.

"Jimmy Blanchard," Marian said with a significant amount of disdain. She pulled away from Eddie and turned toward him. "He's off his nut. Attendance is way down at the Doozies because, surprise, I alone can't sell tickets. And when I told him hiring a dancing horse is not the way to get people in the seats at the James, well." She gestured toward her face.

"Did you quit?" Eddie asked. He was appalled that Blanchard would stoop so low as to hit a woman, Marian in particular.

"Not yet, but I believe that I should. I will. The show is a sinking ship."

"I thought this might happen, but I'm surprised it went bad so fast," Lane mused.

Marian jerked toward him, as if she hadn't seen him there. She nodded. "Well, it was a second-rate show, anyway. I loved performing there, but it just hasn't been the same since Jimmy let Eddie go, and everyone knows that." She sighed. "Yes, I'll have to leave. But I could get another job. Or you and me could team up again, Eddie."

Eddie grunted. "It's not that easy."

Lane stood. "This could be your shot, Eddie. Your chance to get back on Broadway. You and Marian team up, you bring back Cotton and France, that's your ticket."

"And what about you?"

Lane shrugged. "What about me?"

Eddie rubbed his forehead. "You really want to stay in Times Square?"

Lane blinked, which made it clear to Eddie that Lane was thinking about him and not himself. By "Times Square," Eddie meant New York, because Eddie knew Lane was thinking seriously about leaving the city altogether. It was touching that Lane was deferring to Eddie, but Eddie was starting to think Lane's safety—ensuring they could continue to be together—was more important than where Eddie danced.

For someone whose best moments had all been on a stage until six months ago, the fact that all of his happiest moments lately had been with Lane seemed significant. It surprised him to realize that, but this was not the time. He schooled his features and concentrated on Marian.

"I don't think I can do it," he said.

"Hooey," said Lane.

"I'm serious." Eddie briefly touched Lane's forearm. "It's not just me anymore. If you had asked me six months ago, well, yes, I would have said me and Marian should dance our way onto whichever stage would have us. But maybe it's time to give up on that dream."

"Applesauce," said Marian. "You are a great dancer, Eddie. You're just going to give up because you haven't gotten a job in a while?"

"I'm a faggot dancer, Marian. Isn't that what Blanchard told you? Isn't that what he's told everyone on Broadway? No one will buy the husband-and-wife act anymore. And if it's not that, if that's not what Blanchard is telling everyone to convince them not to hire me, it's something else incriminating. I'm doing some of the best stuff I've ever done, I'm dancing better than I've ever danced, and I still can't get a banging job."

"Jimmy's whole production is about to go belly-up and then no one will care what he says. His opinion won't matter."

But Eddie knew that wasn't true. The way Marian hesitated before she spoke indicated to Eddie that she knew that, too. "Tell me there aren't rumors about me. Not just at the James Theater. You know lots of Broadway people. You've heard what people are saying, haven't you?"

Marian frowned. "It's just rumor. None of it means anything."

Eddie had been fishing, but Marian had basically just confirmed his worst fear. News about what he was, what he had been doing since leaving the Doozies, had probably spread far and wide by now. His career had effectively taken a bullet in the heart.

But playing along like he didn't know this as sure as he knew the sun rose in the east, Eddie turned back to Lane. "And what will you do?"

Lane shrugged. "Not sure. Go back to working for Epstein."

"I thought you wanted out."

"What's a washed-up gangster to do? It's not like I've got a lot of choices here."

Marian's eyes went wide. Eddie had forgotten she didn't know anything of Lane's background. Well, now she did.

"This stays quiet, Marian," Eddie said.

"As if I would say anything. Come now, Eddie, you should know me better."

Lane looked so sad that Eddie decided to take a chance. He walked close to him and slowly put his arms around Lane. Lane embraced him back, briefly resting his chin on Eddie's shoulder before stepping away.

"My life, it's not just mine anymore," Eddie said. "It's yours, too. And if you have to leave town, I'm going with you."

"Eddie, no. I can't ask you to give up your career."

"What career?" Eddie threw his hands up in the air, frustrated now. "I am very likely done for. Too many people have heard whatever baloney Blanchard is spreading. Maybe I'd be better off starting over in a new city."

Lane sighed. "Let's not be hasty."

Marian looked back and forth between them a few times. "So you're a real couple now, huh? Like a husband and wife, except two husbands."

Eddie and Lane both got flustered by that remark, talking at the same time and denying it. Then Lane laughed softly.

"I was almost married once," Lane said. "I love Eddie a hell of a lot more than I ever loved my fiancée. So maybe, Marian, you are not so far off the mark. This thing with Eddie and me, it's certainly something."

"I have heard of such things," Marian said.

Eddie got a good gander at that bruise on Marian's face. "What are you going to do now? You're leaving Blanchard, right? Are you definitely going to quit the Doozies?"

"I don't know," said Marian. "It's a paycheck, but I'll tell ya, if I never saw Jimmy Blanchard again, it would be too soon."

Lane put a hand on Eddie's shoulder. "Well, if you need a place to stay, I know of some good hiding spots in this city."

Marian nodded. "I think . . . yes. I think I can't go home for a little while. Can you help?"

Lane nodded. "Yes. That, at least, I can do."

Chapter 23

"I Cried for You"

The smoke in the low-rent speakeasy in Greenwich Village in which Lane and Eddie sat was so thick it hung like fog over the Brooklyn Bridge on a rainy morning. This place was sad, in Lane's estimation, dirty and dingy and lacking in life. It was the sort of saloon the Women's Christian Temperance Union decried before Prohibition reinvigorated New York nightlife, the sort of place where men went to slowly kill themselves with drink.

The hooch was the real McCoy, at least, whiskey imported from Scotland by way of the Dominican Republic, according to the place's proprietor.

Lane missed the Marigold. He missed running his own place, yes, but more than that, he missed the atmosphere. He missed the way men could openly interact with each other. He missed how happy everyone seemed there. He missed watching Eddie teaching the others how to dance.

But the Marigold was gone. Lane had gone back a few days before and seen there were chains draped across the door, secured with a heavy padlock. The city had shut it down. The Marigold was dead. Lane mourned it as if it had been a living, breathing person.

Lane and Eddie had been sleeping at Lane's place the last week without incident, which made Lane feel pretty safe there. The apartment existed outside of his association with the Mob, although he didn't doubt they knew where it was. He hadn't defected yet, though. They had no reason to come for him, he figured. When one of Epstein's associates tracked him to the Times Square cafeteria where he'd taken to eating lunch each afternoon, Lane had acted agreeable, saying he'd needed time to figure out his next move. The associate backed off, but Lane knew his summons to meet with Epstein was pending. He'd have to face it. But for now, Epstein was leaving him be.

Eddie didn't look much happier tonight, staring forlornly at his drink, occasionally tipping the glass just far enough to move the liquid without spilling it. Lane didn't like Eddie's tendency toward sadness lately. Not that it wasn't understandable under the circumstances, but Lane couldn't help but worry about a repeat of the incident on the elevated train platform.

So he asked, "What's eating you, Eddie?"

Eddie traced the edge of his glass with his finger. "If I don't get steady work again soon, I'm going to have to give up my room at the Knickerbocker."

"Oh." Lane had been so preoccupied with the crux of their situation that he hadn't given much thought to how Eddie paid his rent. He immediately regretted that, because this was an issue he should have anticipated better. "What about the shows you did last week?"

Eddie let out a huff of a breath. "You can't exactly call substituting for a sick dancer in a second-rate vaudeville show steady work. That only lasted a week, anyway." He shook his head. "Face it, Lane. I'm blacklisted. Nobody wants me. Not even with Marian back in the picture."

Lane had used his connections to get Marian a room at a hotel near Madison Square temporarily. She hadn't officially quit the Doozies yet but she'd called in sick a few times. The three of them had also planted rumors that Eddie and Marian were looking to reunite and do their act on a new stage with the hope that some producer would snatch them up. Jimmy Blanchard was reportedly furious.

"So wait it out a little," Lane said. "Broadway has a short memory. Take some time to regroup and make a comeback."

"Sure. And what do I do in the meantime? Wishin' and hopin' won't pay the rent."

The solution came to Lane suddenly. He blurted it out before he could think better of it. "Come live with me."

The look Eddie shot Lane was so astonished, Lane thought Eddie's eyes might fall out of his head.

"I'm serious," Lane said, realizing he was. "You don't have much in the way of possessions. Your clothes, your books, all of that will fit in my place. And the apartment is out of the way and it's safe. For now, at least."

"You would do that for me?" The awe still shone on Eddie's face.

"You need a place to stay. I have space and I like your company. We spend most of our time together anyway. This just eliminates the commute." Lane smiled for good measure.

"What about Epstein?"

"I'll figure something out. If I have to move, I'll take you with me. Maybe it won't come to that. But you are welcome to stay with me for as long as you need. Or forever, for that matter."

Lane didn't regret saying it, but there was something momentous about the word "forever." But that was what he wanted, wasn't it? He loved Eddie and wanted him for the rest of his life.

But did Eddie want that? Lane was sincere, but worried he'd scare Eddie. And yet Eddie leaned forward instead of shrinking away. "I . . . yes," Eddie said. "If you'll really have me, I'd like that."

"Of course I'll have you." Lane smirked. "I'll have you any way I can get you."

That finally broke through Eddie's defenses, and he laughed.

"Let's get out of here," Lane said.

Julian's hip ached and his head was bent at a strange angle and his left leg had gone pins and needles. He didn't care and wasn't inclined to move.

Frank was tucked up against him, curled into a ball with his back pressed against Julian's front. Julian curled his arm around Frank's torso and tugged him even closer. This was the eighth or ninth morning he'd woken up this way—he'd started to lose track. Frank and Julian had been hiding out in Julian's room at the boardinghouse ever since the Marigold had been raided.

They'd happened to be standing near each other when the cops barged in. Julian had simply grabbed Frank's hand without thinking and then dutifully ran to Lane's office to retrieve a sheaf of papers that were entrusted to his keeping. They'd snuck out the back together and got stuck in an alley and had to climb a fence to get to Sixth Avenue. Once they were on an elevated train, they were home free and, Julian noticed suddenly, still holding hands.

Frank, it turned out, had been living out of a sugar daddy's house on Fifth Avenue, though he had only been back to change clothes lately. Well, to change and also stuff his earnings into a mattress. He was sick of the old man, he'd said, tired of getting poked until he was sore, tired of the man's clumsy attempts at romance, tired of his life being beholden to a man who lately had come to disgust him. The man worked in the public sector, from what Julian had been able to discern through Frank's confused mumblings, a politician of some sort or maybe a judge, but either way, the sort of man who would not want it widely publicized that he was keeping house with a very young man. Frank had been prostituting himself and then later saving his wages from the Marigold so that he could get his own place and threaten this man, whose name he wouldn't say, with disclosure if he tried to start a fight.

Two days before the raid at the Marigold, though, the man had found Frank's stash of cash and stolen it. He'd yelled at Frank, furious that Frank had been sleeping with other men for money. Frank had grabbed the uniform clothes Lane had paid for and slept in the kitchen at the Marigold.

He'd explained all this in one long sentence while still clutching Julian's hand as they sat on the train downtown, so Julian did what any sensible man would do when faced with a young, attractive man down on his luck: he brought Frank home.

Frank had stayed in Julian's room without leaving for three days. Julian went out only to procure food, either from the plump Irishwoman who ran the boardinghouse or from the cafeteria down the street. While he was out, he'd grab a newspaper just to keep up with what was going on in the city outside of his block, but otherwise, his contact with the world was minimal.

Sometime on the fourth day, they went from merely sharing a bed to touching each other. By the fifth day, they were kissing. They made love on the sixth day. It was definitely love by then, at least as far as Julian was concerned, because it was the first time he'd willingly had sex in nearly a decade without being paid for it.

He felt mildly guilty about that as he smoothed Frank's hair off his baby face. Julian was not quite twice Frank's age. Something felt predatory about that. Except that Julian was coming to care for this unruly kid more intensely than he'd cared for anyone recently.

Frank stirred. Julian shifted away slightly to give Frank room to uncurl and stretch out, which he did a moment later. He looked up at Julian and smiled.

Julian smiled back and ran a hand through Frank's hair, watching it stand up before slowly falling back to his head.

"Julie?" Frank said, using the nickname that no one except Frank could have gotten away with. "Can we . . . go somewhere today? I'm getting a little sick of this room."

"Sure, sweetheart, just as soon as I can figure out how to smuggle you out of this place without Mrs. O'Sullivan seeing you."

It had never occurred to Julian to find the owners' decree against overnight guests oppressive, because Lord knew after all those years of sharing beds just to have a place to sleep, it was nice to go to bed alone for a change.

Not that he minded having Frank there with him one bit, small as the bed was.

What an odd turn Julian's life had taken.

As the bed was wedged against the wall, Julian had to roll over Frank to get out of it. Frank stretched again as Julian stood, the sheet falling away from his naked body. Julian stopped to admire him—it was nice to take the time to enjoy a man instead of convincing himself he was attracted. And Frank was definitely a man—albeit a young one, but several years older than Julian had been when he'd first engaged in carnal pleasures—which put Julian's conscience somewhat at ease.

"You . . . you don't think me some stodgy old man, do you?" Julian asked.

Frank frowned. "Hardly. You're not old."

"I'm old enough. Older than you."

"You're not . . . you're nothing like the Old Man." Frank had lately taken to calling his sugar daddy the Old Man. "You actually listen when I talk."

Julian opened one of the drawers in the banged-up dresser that sat in the corner of the room. He considered his options. Instead of clothes, he grabbed a towel, figuring he should bathe first, if only to get rid of the scent of sex and sweat that clung to his skin. Not that he didn't like it, but if they went out, he wasn't sure his neighbors would appreciate his stench.

"Also," Frank said, "you're honest. You never try to be anything you aren't."

Julian laughed softly. Perhaps not anymore, but that had not always been the case. "I'm a washed-up fairy. I don't look like I could be anything else."

"Not washed up."

Nothing on the fairy comment. Julian smiled ruefully. "Well, darling, I'd better . . ." He gestured toward the hall with his towel.

Frank nodded and stretched his arms over his head again.

It astonished Julian that Frank didn't see him as old, didn't see him as the tawdry doll he'd become. It astonished him, too, that they'd spent more than a week with not much else to do but fuck and talk and they hadn't yet grown tired of each other. Julian hadn't grown tired of Frank, at any rate.

Once he was clean, Julian returned to his room, where he found Frank wearing only unbuttoned trousers, sponging himself from the basin in the corner. His hair was still wildly disheveled. Frank had a raw, sexy quality even when he wasn't being deliberately provocative. Julian appreciated that in a much younger lover.

Julian sighed and went back to his clothes, selecting herringbone trousers and a crisp arrow-collar shirt. He tied a pink scarf around his neck like a cravat for good measure. He donned his straw boater hat and then walked over to the cracked mirror that hung on the wall. He supposed there was no need to bother with the stage makeup he kept in a box under the bed, as Frank had seen him without it plenty this week and there was no one else he felt the need to impress just then. Well, maybe he could get out a little rouge . . .

Once he was happy with his appearance, he turned to a now-dressed Frank, who grinned.

"You are something else," said Frank.

"In a good way, I hope."

"In the best way."

Chapter 24

"Fascinating Rhythm"

Lane woke up to silence. His bedroom felt like it was doused in a blanket, like the softness of the city after a snowstorm. He rolled over, looking for Eddie, and found the other half of the bed empty. That, coupled with the silence, worried him enough to force him out of bed. He was most of the way through buttoning up his trousers while simultaneously walking through the living room when the key jiggled in the lock. Eddie came in, carrying a paper sack and a newspaper, wearing a grim expression on his face.

At first, Lane was relieved that the silence hadn't meant something—be it Eddie himself or some outside force—had taken Eddie from him, but it was clear something had happened. "What is it?" Lane asked.

"You should see this." Eddie handed over the newspaper.

The headline read, GANGSTER GUNNED DOWN IN MIDTOWN.

"Has a cadence to it," Lane murmured after he read it out loud.

"Read the article," said Eddie.

And there it was in the first paragraph: David Epstein's body had been found riddled with bullets in a stairwell at the Hotel Astor. There were no witnesses that police could find, although the best theory of the crime was a Mafia turf fight.

Lane had some theories of his own. Perhaps the Giambino family was cleaning house after all the raids.

The news was a punch to the gut, but he didn't have much time to contemplate what this could mean in the larger scheme of things, because just then, there was a knock at the door. Lane pressed a hand to his bare chest and then held a finger to his lips to silence Eddie. There was another knock, followed by, "Carillo! Let me in!"

Callahan.

Lane went to the door and looked through the peephole. Callahan stood there, his hand conspicuously tucked into his inside jacket pocket. His arm flexed, revealing the butt of his gun. Lane glanced back at Eddie, his heart racing now. Eddie stared back, wide-eyed.

Lane mimicked firing a gun with his hand. He backed away from the door. "We may have been discovered," he said softly.

"Who is it? Does he have a gun?" whispered Eddie.

Lane nodded. Worried these might be his last moments, he hooked a hand behind Eddie's head, pulled him close, and planted a fierce kiss on his lips. "I love you," he said forcefully. "If something happens, remember that."

"We're in danger?" Eddie said.

Lane nodded. "I think we are."

Eddie nodded back. "I love you, too."

Callahan pounded on the door again. "Geez, Lane. I don't mean any harm. Let me in."

Lane went to the door. He opened it a crack. "Pass me your gun."

Callahan's eyes went wide. "Is that what you think of me? You think, after all the years we've worked together, I would shoot you?"

"Yes. I do think that. Epstein's dead. You come to my door and show me your gun. There's no telling what you will do."

"I didn't kill him."

"The gun, Nick."

Callahan grimaced. He reached into his coat and pulled out the gun. Instead of passing it through the door, he turned it on Lane. "How do I know you won't pull something?"

"You came to me. This is my home. I don't know if I can trust you or not. But you're accusing me of trying to pull something? You want to come in, you give me the gun. Otherwise leave."

Callahan grunted and handed over the gun.

Lane unloaded the weapon as he walked back into his living room. Callahan followed him in and closed the door. Lane glanced at Eddie, who shifted back and forth on his feet, taking in the scene. Eddie's gaze was glued to the gun.

Lane turned back around and stared at Callahan, who was looking back and forth between Lane's naked chest and Eddie. Callahan was a smart man and had spent enough time around the Marigold to know what was going on here. Lane wasn't sure he cared about Callahan's judgment.

"What do you want?" Lane asked. "I get the feeling you're not here to discuss business plans."

"Luchesi wants a meeting."

Of course he did. Beyond being the man most likely to take over Epstein's holdings, Luchesi was a distant cousin of Lane's, his highest-ranking Mafia relative after his deceased cousin John. Blood was thicker than water, Lane supposed, and nowhere more so than in *La Cosa Nostra.*

"He tell you what the topic of this meeting might be?" Lane asked Callahan.

"Nope. I was just sent to give you the message."

Lane nodded and looked at the gun. "I don't suppose he mentioned anything about his faggot cousin who ran the club for fairies and failed to pay off the local law enforcement enough to keep the place open."

Callahan glanced at Eddie. "He didn't say anything like that. He didn't say anything. I was just supposed to tell you there was a meeting." He looked at the floor for a moment then back up at Lane. "I get why you're spooked. This life was hard enough when Hardy was our biggest problem. But he's a drop in the bucket. You hear what I'm saying?"

Lane started to pace, completely unsure of what to do. Callahan was right; if the Mafia thought Lane had made a big enough mess by inviting a certain clientele to his club or not paying the police enough not to raid or, worse, that he'd betrayed them somehow by staying loyal to Epstein—who, after all, was not actually family—he was in far more danger now than he ever was at the hands of guys like Hardy. Lane knew of Mafia soldiers who had vanished for milder offenses. So Lane could go to this meeting, appeal to Luchesi's sense of family, and ask to be let go. He could go to the meeting and pretend that everything was hunky-dory, and then quietly leave the city—with Eddie, of course. He could rejoin the family business, do their bidding, go along to get along. He could run another club or take over a bootlegging operation. Or he could just avoid the meeting and let what would come next happen.

Or he could just get shot in the head.

But all of that was much easier when he had nothing to lose, when his life felt like it was worth nothing. Now it was worth something. Now he meant something to Eddie, now Eddie meant something to him. He couldn't put himself at risk like that anymore. Certainly any of those options could lead to a bullet in Lane's brain.

He paced while he worked all this out and felt both Eddie's and Callahan's gazes on him the whole time.

"He was using you," Callahan said quietly.

"Come again?"

"Epstein's not family. He grew up in Five Points and ran around with Giambino and Luchesi and Luciano and those guys and they all became friends, so when Prohibition happened and the Mafia got into the bootlegging business, Luchesi found a job for Epstein in the organization. But Epstein's not Sicilian."

Lane nodded. He knew this; despite the power Epstein had amassed over the last five years, he'd never rise higher than the rank of associate. He'd never be a *caporegime*.

"Look, I'm just a hired man. I'm not family, either. But you are," Callahan said. "You were Epstein's real link into the family. He used you to accomplish what he wanted. He wanted to supply Times Square with booze. He wanted to own the hottest nightspots. He wanted to make a fortune. So he befriended a half-dozen made men and manipulated them up the ranks so that they would do his work for him, so that his wishes would be fulfilled by family members. And you, Lane, are family. He basically made you a *capo* so that you could do his bidding."

"But I didn't want—"

"It never mattered what you wanted. You were Epstein's eyes, ears, and arms in the family. And whoever killed him will probably come after the people he used next. You're not safe."

"Shit," said Lane, rubbing his forehead, knowing that what Callahan said was true.

Callahan glanced at Eddie again. "What you do on your own time is on your conscience, but you know that Luchesi is a religious man."

Callahan's implication was clear as day to Lane: Luchesi would not be supportive of Lane's relationship with Eddie. This was not news to Lane. "When is the meeting?"

Callahan let out a breath. "Week from tomorrow. In Brooklyn." He gave Lane the details.

Lane's instincts told him this was bad. "You think Luchesi had anything to do with what happened to Epstein?" What he was really asking was whether this was a setup, because that was how it felt. Lane had been to plenty of these meetings with the head of his family, usually there as extra muscle to shake down somebody else. Lane had always toed the family line and had never done anything to earn the organization's enmity; except now, he'd run a club for Epstein that the family did not approve of. If the perception was that Lane was Epstein's patsy, the warehouse in Brooklyn to which Lane had been called would be a good place to take care of him. So to speak.

"I honestly don't know if Luchesi's involved or not in what happened to Epstein," said Callahan. "Cops think it was a rival family. The Masseria family wants a piece of Times Square."

But that wasn't necessarily the real explanation. Lane knew better than to think it was that easy. Yes, it could have been a rival family who took out Epstein in order to get a hold of his turf. There was a lot of money to be made in Times Square. But it could also be a member of Lane's own family, Luchesi or Giambino one of the other bosses who thought Epstein was getting too powerful. If this was the case, Lane might have been okay, as a bona fide member of the family— family took care of their own. But would they take care of their queer cousin? Lane was not sure of that.

"Thank you, Callahan."

Callahan stepped toward the door. "You going to give me my gun back?"

Lane's own weapon was locked up in the closet, but Callahan had a better piece. "I think I'll keep it."

Callahan grimaced. "Fine. I've been instructed to escort you to the meeting next week, so I'll meet you here an hour before. All right?"

"All right." Although Lane wasn't at all sure he'd be there to meet Callahan.

"Be careful, Lane." Callahan nodded once and then let himself out.

Chapter 25

"Someone to Watch Over Me"

There was so much trash in Eddie's room at the Knickerbocker that he began to suspect he could get everything that actually mattered into one box.

He supposed it didn't help much that the room had been ransacked while Eddie had been away. Someone had left a Bible on the desk opened to the relevant passage in Leviticus about man lying with man. Eddie had been so furious when he'd seen it that he'd slapped the book closed and pushed it onto the floor. It fell, and Lane had spent a good minute staring at it.

"What?" Eddie had asked.

Lane just pointed. The book had fallen open to the title page, where someone had written in pencil, "Property of Tony Carillo."

"Another cousin of yours?" Eddie asked.

Lane nodded. "Guess they know about us."

Eddie hated the situation. He'd been jumpy for the last couple of days, expecting some member of Lane's "family" to appear with a gun. Eddie no longer had that death wish that had plagued him after he'd lost his job with the Doozies, which made the situation all the more alarming. Even riding the elevated train up to 42nd Street had been a little scary, with Eddie worried any of the men in coats too heavy for the weather could be holding the gun meant to be fired into Lane's skull. And Eddie could not imagine what he would do without Lane. If Lane were gone, Eddie's life really would be nothing.

Lane kept saying he wasn't bothered by the situation, but Eddie didn't believe him. Lane had been short with him lately, quicker to anger. They'd been going to sleep earlier and turning the lights off in the apartment often, perhaps to fool anyone who might be hovering outside into thinking that they were hardly ever there.

After a few days of that, Eddie realized that his life had turned a corner. It would never be what it was. Maybe he'd get a job dancing, but it would never be in one of the big shows, not if he stayed in New York. And God knew he couldn't stay in Times Square, not with the stress of wondering who was about to do in Lane. And as for Lane, well, it turned out Eddie loved him even more than he loved performing. If he broke his leg tomorrow and could never dance again, well, he'd get by, but if he lost Lane, Eddie would be lost for good.

So he couldn't keep on as he was. He couldn't keep pretending that his lot would improve, that there would be an opening in the perfect show, because as more time passed, that was less likely to ever happen. So now he had a choice: stay with Lane and make some significant changes to his life or leave Lane and go back to trying to get a job. It wasn't that hard a choice in the end.

Now Eddie watched Lane fold and neatly stack his clothing into an old trunk for a moment. He was about to turn back to his piles of sheet music when there was a knock at the door.

A jolt of fear went through Eddie, like maybe one of Lane's Mob pals was here to get his Bible back. He went to the door and looked through the peephole. Not mobsters, but Julian and that working boy Lane had hired for the Marigold. Eddie let them in.

"Eddie, darling, thank God you're here." Julian buzzed into the room, the kid on his heels.

Julian looked his age, was Eddie's first thought. He wore a worried expression and no makeup. His hat was tipped at a precarious angle, but it hid his dyed hair. Eddie had never seen him this naked; he'd seen Julian's naked body, of course, but he had never seen Julian dressed this plainly, with no makeup mask, no affected airs.

"I wasn't sure where else to go," Julian said plainly, and there was something different about his voice, too. It was flatter, the sing-song quality gone.

"What happened?" asked Lane.

Julian looked startled, like he wasn't expecting anyone else to be in the room. He nodded and said, "The O'Sullivans are kicking me out because I've been letting Frank stay with me, which I knew was against the rules. I have until tomorrow morning to find another place to live."

Eddie looked at Lane, already knowing what he would do. Lane pursed his lips and looked at the half-full trunk. Then he sighed and pulled a scrap of paper out of his pocket.

"Are you . . ." Julian looked around the room. "You're leaving, too," he said to Eddie.

Eddie nodded. "Can't afford to stay here anymore. Not if no one will hire me."

Lane handed the piece of paper to Julian. "That's my address. You come there tonight and we'll figure something out."

Eddie laughed, though he didn't feel much mirth. That was exactly what he'd expected Lane to do. "Your apartment will become Lane's Home for Wayward Queers."

"We'll figure something out," Lane repeated.

Lane didn't want to leave New York. He had only been there for five years, but it felt like his home in a way Illinois never had.

So maybe instead of fleeing the city he could hide in plain sight.

After he and Eddie got all of Eddie's things moved into Lane's apartment, Lane excused himself to make a phone call. The connection took so long Lane was convinced it wouldn't go through—he hadn't had a phone long and still found the technology a little suspect—but then Clarence was speaking.

"Your George. He knows people," Lane said after they greeted each other.

"What do you mean?"

"Up in Harlem. At the clubs and speakeasies up there. When we went to the Doozies, you said George knew people, that he could tell me where to go."

"Do you want to go up to Harlem with us? Is that what you're asking?"

"Not exactly. Let's just say . . . I haven't been in a while. But maybe we can go before the end of this week." That seemed to be the date of Lane's death sentence. The more time passed, the more Lane was convinced no one intended for him to leave his meeting with the Giambino family heads alive. "You and George, me and my . . ." He wasn't sure what to call Eddie.

Clarence gasped. "You have someone!"

"Well, yes. I literally just moved him into my place."

"Oh, that's delightful news. I can't wait to meet him."

"Later this week?"

"Yes. Let me consult with George. I'll get word to you. There's this marvelous little hooch parlor on 132nd Street. I think it will be right up your alley."

Lane had the beginnings of a plan by the time Julian and Frank arrived that night with their few belongings.

He'd piled blankets on the floor, thinking Julian and Frank could fashion a pallet of sorts to sleep on, at least for that night. Eddie hovered, and Lane could feel his disapproval. He opted to ignore Eddie and made sure Julian and Frank were comfortable.

"I really do thank you, Lane," Julian said, his face composed in a way it wasn't usually, a furrowed-brow serious expression that was markedly different from the carefree, nothing-can-get-me-down grin he usually wore. "I don't have the words to express my gratitude at everything you've done for me. I truly thank you."

"It's not a problem," said Lane, feeling a little bashful at the compliments.

"You guys are really great," Julian went on. "You too, Eddie, though you continue to scowl at me. I love you as a dear friend, you know, even if you are a grump."

Eddie crossed his arms over his chest and *humph*ed. "Yeah. I guess you ain't so bad."

That was as close as Lane thought Eddie would get to telling Julian he cared.

"All right, boys. You need something to eat or drink, there's the kitchen. There's not much, but help yourselves. Water closet's over there. You need anything else?"

Julian fussed with the pillows and blankets while Frank stood there rubbing his eyes. "No, darling," said Julian "This will be fine."

Lane chose that moment to retire himself, dragging Eddie to the bedroom with him.

Eddie said sternly, "No funny business out there," to Julian before Lane closed the bedroom door.

"I know it's not ideal," Lane said once they were alone, "but I don't have a better solution. Do you?"

Eddie frowned. "It's not just Julian. I don't like any of this."

Lane understood. It had felt lately like the whole city was falling down around them. "What if we left?" he said, mostly as a way to test the idea, to throw it out there, to see how Eddie would react.

"What?" Eddie said, his eyes wide.

Lane was so tired of all of it. "Bang Luchesi. Bang the Knickerbocker. Bang the all-holy New York Police Department. Bang New York City. Bang it all. We can get away from everything, you know. We can go to Boston, Chicago, California, anywhere. What's holding us here? Families that don't want us? Jobs that fired us?"

"Are you serious?"

"Yes." Wasn't that the easiest solution? Getting out of New York, changing their names, escaping the Mob. Maybe Eddie could be in moving pictures, dance on the big screen. Maybe Lane could run a legit restaurant. Maybe they could do something else entirely with their lives. That was a whole lot of maybe, but it was better than the certainty that their lives as they had been in New York were falling apart. "I am dead serious, Eddie."

"How can you think about leaving New York? How could I? I've lived here my whole life. This city, it's my home, my life. I can't just pick up and move."

"It's not that I want to leave—"

"And what about Marian? What about the clowns in your living room? We can't just take off and leave them here."

Lane couldn't help but smile at the conviction in Eddie's voice. Despite his disapproval, Lane knew Eddie had a bit of a soft spot for the men currently making the most of the hard floor of Lane's living room. "We take them with us. All of them. Julian and Frank and Marian, too."

Eddie's jaw dropped. "Can you afford that?"

That reminded Lane that Eddie was almost out of money. Lane wasn't, but paying Hardy not to arrest him hadn't helped matters. "Probably not. It was just a thought. I have another idea."

Eddie's eyes went wide as he stared at Lane. "My head is spinning. Another idea? What ideas could there be? Your family is coming for us."

"I know what I just said, but what if we . . . hid? Here in New York."

"Is that even safe? With your family members leaving Bibles for me in my own home? Jesus, Lane, you as much as told me you think they intend to kill you at this meeting. Do you want to stay here waiting around for them to do that?"

Lane paced a little, taking the time to gather his thoughts. "You know, the one thing the Mob always emphasized was family. You're a member of the family, you belong. You've got a job if you need one. I don't think they *want* to kill one of their own. But Epstein, Luchesi? Even Giambino or Tony Carillo? Those guys? None of them are really my family. We've got the same blood, maybe, but I was always the cousin from the Midwest whose father didn't want to be part of the family. Plus I'm the queer one." He took a deep breath. "But you, Eddie, you and a couple of the guys I've worked with over the years and even Julian, the people I worked with at the Marigold, the friends I made. You guys are my real family. We're the way a family is supposed to be. We care for each other without needing anything in return. And Marian is your family. I know she's like a sister."

Eddie let out a huff of a breath. "That's a nice speech, but it doesn't solve the problem."

"I thought maybe I could keep working for the Mob. I could negotiate something to keep us safe. But we'd never be safe and that's no solution. One bad business deal, and that's it, we're facing the muzzle of a gun again." Lane took a deep breath. "But if we find a new place to live, even if it's in the city, if we stay away from the police and stay away from the Mob, we might be all right. It's not . . . it's not a perfect solution, but it's the best I can come up with."

Eddie looked at him warily.

"And," Lane continued, "anyone who needs a home, anyone who needs a family, they can come with us wherever we go. Together, we'll figure it out."

Lane turned to look Eddie in the face. Eddie glanced toward the door and then looked back at Lane. Their eyes met. Eddie sputtered before he spoke. "Well, all right. I'll bite. Where is this magical hidden place in the city you have in mind?"

"I'm still working on that, but it's definitely not Times Square. I've been calling people I know. We could go to Harlem or Queens. We can get lost in the queer communities there. Those neighborhoods aren't as conspicuous as Times Square, not nearly as Mob-controlled. These places have opportunities for us."

Eddie frowned. "All right. If you think so."

Not the enthusiastic response Lane had been hoping for, but it was something. Lane made himself smile. "It's not a perfect solution and there will still be danger for us, but I don't want to leave New York either, and this is the best I can come up with. *La Cosa Nostra* may decide that if I disappear, it's good riddance."

Eddie looked up, his gaze meeting Lane's. His eyes were a little red. "I just . . . if I lost you, I don't know how I would . . ."

Surprised by the sudden display of emotion, Lane reached over and put his arms around Eddie. "Trust me, Eddie. Trust me to keep us safe. I'll find a way."

Eddie hesitated for a moment, but then he put his arms around Lane. "All right. I trust you."

Lane knew how hard it was for Eddie to trust him, and he appreciated the sentiment all the more for it. "Tell me you love me, Eddie."

Eddie laughed softly and shook his head. "I love you, Lane. I'm a goddamn fool to love you, but I do anyway."

Lane closed the space between them and pulled Eddie into his arms. "That's all that matters, you know. Here, Harlem, even California, as long as we're together, nothing else matters."

Eddie pressed his face against Lane's neck. Lane savored the feeling of their bodies pressed together. "I do love you, Lane. More than I ever thought I could love anyone."

"I love you, too, Eddie, you old fool."

Epilogue

"Rhapsody in Blue"

Spring, 1929

There was no small amount of joy in watching Eddie dance. Lane sat at a little table off to the side of the dance floor, alternately crunching numbers and watching Eddie rehearse with Paul. Paul was a brilliant choreographer in his own right, and the two of them kept shouting at each other to try different moves. Paul was burlier than Eddie and nearly six inches taller, thus not quite as light on his feet, but there was strength and grace in his dancing that Lane admired. The two of them looked spectacular together, which Lane had no problem admitting because Eddie still came home to him every night.

Actually, Lane knew he should start calling Eddie "Elijah," since he'd dropped the stage name. Lane had never quite acclimated to the name change and still called the man he loved "Eddie," and pretty much everyone else did, too.

They were in the basement of the Odd Duck, the speakeasy Lane had opened six months before on 136th Street, deep into Harlem. It occupied the basement of the row house Lane and Eddie had bought together the previous fall with earnings from a year of working quietly in the Harlem nightlife scene. Eddie had been choreographing dance routines for small clubs all over the city and Lane had been lending his considerable expertise to a club on 127th Street, which was how he'd met Paul.

Paul was a dark-skinned, self-taught dancer originally from Alabama who fled to New York when it became clear to him that his family didn't understand his more artistic nature. When the club on 127th had found out Paul was cohabiting with a white male poet in a more-than-roommates arrangement, they'd promptly let him go, despite his obvious talent. When Lane opened the Odd Duck, Paul was one of the first people he had contacted.

In the six months the Odd Duck had been open, it had become a club for misfits. White patrons mingled with black ones, men with women, and nearly all of the clientele was queer. It was off the beaten path enough—and had tight enough security—that it had so far escaped the notice of local law enforcement. Well, aside from the cop Lane saw sneak in about once a week to dance with his male sweetheart; Lane had seen him on patrol often enough during the day that he knew without a doubt that this man was a police officer.

Not that everything was swell all the time. Customers sometimes got drunk and surly. Just the previous week, Lane had had to break up a fist fight. More to the point, getting liquor into the club without attracting attention was a constant challenge, particularly since the Mob controlled most of the bootlegging business in the city. As long as he didn't announce his presence in Harlem and was careful about who he let in the club, the Mob left him alone. There was a rumor, even, that he had died in 1928, and Lane was content to let his "family" believe that.

Still, the Odd Duck was a modest success, and Lane couldn't have asked for more.

Lane put his pencil down and openly watched the dancing continue. In the time since Eddie had started choreographing his own dance routines, he'd changed his style somewhat. The bowler hat he'd worn to hide his identity when they'd first moved to Harlem had become an integral part of every routine. Eddie would doff the hat, let it slide down his arm, catch it, toss it in the air. It was a prop the way his silver cane had been when he danced in the Doozies. He had lately been playing around with slower movements, too, with rolling his shoulders and adding a fluid quality to the movement of his arms. It was fascinating to watch the way Eddie's mind worked, the way he honed a particular style of dancing that perfectly complemented the shape of his body. He'd been teaching that style to Paul, who had picked it up easily, and sometimes the two of them could move together in near perfect synchronization.

Eddie and Paul finished their rehearsal with a handshake and a promise to make that night's performance a spectacular one. Lane stood and moved toward Eddie to catch him before he went upstairs to eat dinner and change for the night.

Eddie grinned when his gaze met Lane's. They walked toward each other and kissed briefly. It was nice to work in a business where there was no pretending, no subterfuge, no secrets. Everyone who worked for Lane knew he and Eddie were together, that they lived like husbands in the residence upstairs. Anyone who had a problem with that was promptly shown the door.

"Good rehearsal," Lane said, reaching over to rub Eddie's arms.

"Yes, I think tonight's show will be one of our best. Assuming Paul remembers to do the kick turn instead of that silly do-si-do thing he keeps doing."

Lane smiled. "He will."

Eddie reached over and ran his fingers over Lane's tie. "Can you take time away from your empire to have dinner with me?"

"I think so. Let me just grab my ledgers."

A few minutes later, as Lane unlocked the door and led them into the residence, Eddie said, "Did I tell you I got a letter from Marian?"

"No. When?"

"Earlier today. She finished filming that movie."

"Oh, good."

"And . . ." Eddie stopped at the foot of the steps that led up to the kitchen. "She eloped with Bert."

Lane laughed. That seemed like good news. Just before she had absconded from New York in favor of Los Angeles to make moving pictures, Marian had reconnected with Bert, once a stagehand at the James Theater, and the two of them had quickly become inseparable. Eddie had said at the time that he liked Bert, that the man was sweet and seemed to genuinely care for Marian. When she left for California, Bert had tagged along.

"I'm happy for them," Lane said.

"Me too."

They climbed the stairs together. Eddie walked toward their new electric refrigerator, a strange luxury for two men who had for a year lived in the only rental they could find after moving out of Lane's place downtown. That place had been on the third floor of a crumbling house in the shadow of the Third Avenue El, which rumbled past their windows so often Lane sometimes worried they'd both go deaf from the sound. Still, it had been cheap, and it had given them time and opportunity to save enough money to buy the house they now shared.

They ate turkey sandwiches and chatted about music and dancing and what sort of entertainment was scheduled for that evening. Halfway through his sandwich, Eddie paused and said, "It's quiet."

"For a change," Lane said, rolling his eyes.

"No, I mean, where's Frank?"

"Back at Julian's, I imagine. This morning, he insisted it was real this time and packed all of his things into a box. I told him I'd keep clean sheets on the guest bed. Just in case."

Julian was still Lane's right-hand man, serving drinks at the Odd Duck and coming up with clever door passwords, which changed weekly. He'd found an apartment in a building three blocks south of Eddie and Lane's place, which seemed to suit him. Frank bounced back and forth between Julian's bed and Eddie and Lane's guest room, depending on the week and whether he and Julian were speaking to each other. Theirs was the sort of passionate affair in which they fought as often as they made love, and though Lane found them entertaining to watch, he was glad his relationship with Eddie was much calmer.

After dinner, they changed and went back down to the club. Julian was laying out clean tablecloths on the tables. Lane approached him cautiously, wondering if Julian would be angry or pleased that Frank had moved back in with him.

The ear-to-ear grin seemed to indicate pleased.

"That trumpet player is a dishy number, isn't he?" Julian said to Lane.

Lane glanced back toward where the band was setting up. Eddie was already deep in conversation with the bandleader, probably trying to work out a tempo for the number he planned to dance with Paul. And, yes, the trumpet player was quite handsome, if you liked them with slicked-back hair and thin mustaches. Not quite Lane's cup of tea. "He's ducky, sure. But last time I checked, a certain boarder of mine became your problem again."

Julian shrugged. "I'm just looking, darling. No harm in that, is there?"

When Lane was satisfied that the club would open on time, he retreated to his office. He picked up the newspaper he'd left there earlier. The front page article declared that the stock market had hit another all-time high, but just below it was an article about how farmers in Iowa were struggling to make ends meet. It was a troublesome juxtaposition, one that made Lane think the recent growth in the stock market was temporary rather than the signal of a new era of prosperity as some seemed to think. Lane knew better than to think the good times could last—his experience at the Marigold had taught him that, if nothing else—but he did intend to enjoy what he had as long as he had it. And, he figured, if he lost all of this tomorrow, he'd still have Eddie.

He walked back out to the main part of the club a short time later, as the band was just starting to roar and the opening act—a group of black chorus girls in sparkly costumes working their way through a kicky routine Paul and Eddie had created for them—earned delighted applause from the assembled crowd. It wasn't quite packed, but there were enough people seated around the dance floor that Lane knew he'd turn a profit that night. He smiled to himself and walked over to where Eddie stood at the edge of the dance floor.

"Julian said to tell you we're getting low on gin," Eddie said.

"We always are. We'll make do."

Lane slipped his hands around Eddie's waist and rested his chin on Eddie's shoulder. Eddie sighed, let out an appreciative murmur.

"You ready to debut the new routine?" Lane asked.

"As we'll ever be. Paul is still trying to make changes."

"I'm sure it will be wonderful."

The chorus girls all cried out "Woo!" and spun around, which distracted Lane for a moment. Eddie extracted himself from Lane's arms. "That's my cue."

"Break a leg," said Lane. "I love you."

Eddie smiled. "Love you, too." He gave Lane a quick kiss on the cheek and then snuck behind the bandstand.

He emerged with Paul a moment later, and the two of them immediately launched into a left, left, right, right, kick routine, with the steps gradually becoming more elaborate. The mixed crowd hooted and clapped enthusiastically. Lane sighed happily. It was a strange space, this club, but it was Lane's and it was perfect.

Keep reading for a special sneak peek of Kate McMurray's next historical romance, *Ten Days in August*, coming in March 2016 . . .

Day 1

New York City
August 5, 1896
Temperature: 89°F

A small black dog with wild eyes ran up Broadway, snapping and snarling at passersby. As women shrieked and men hopped out of the way, a cry of "Mad dog!" echoed through the crowds out strolling, trying to find relief on a hot day.

Jerry the dog was well known to saloonkeepers and police officers from City Hall to Houston Street; Jerry would wag his tail and beg for scraps and get his head patted before jogging from one saloon to the next. Most considered him a harmless little tramp. But today, something was wrong. He ran for the open front door of a bank, alternately panting and growling. When the attendant tried to kick Jerry out of the way, Jerry bit his foot and ran inside. Someone said, "Look out, Mac! He may be mad!"

The panic inside the bank caught the attention of bulky Officer Giblin, who hauled out his gun and eyed the little dog. Jerry's gaze darted around the room as he slobbered all over the floor.

Officer Giblin brandished his gun, but didn't want to do anything rash. He poked at the dog with his nightstick, trying to ascertain if he was really mad. The dog snapped and lunged for the nightstick. That was all the evidence Giblin needed. He aimed his gun.

"Not in here!" one of the clerks shouted. "Think of the ladies present!"

Giblin nodded. "All right, you mangy rascal." He chased Jerry out of the bank. Once they reached the street, Giblin aimed his gun and fired. The little dog rolled over dead instantly. The crowd cheered. Giblin bowed and walked away. Hank Brandt watched from a few feet away with some amusement as Officer Lewis ran across the street. He fired his own gun into the dog's head.

"Thank you, Lewis," said Hank, pulling off his hat and wiping the sweat from his brow with his handkerchief. "He was just as dead before you fired, but we appreciate your attention to detail."

Lewis thrust out his chest. "I just dispatched with a mad dog in *my* precinct."

"So you did." Hank wasn't completely convinced the little dog was mad so much as suffering from the effects of the day's extreme heat, even more relentless than it had been the day before. "Congratulations, Lewis. You killed a dead dog."

Lewis muttered an oath and walked away from Hank, so Hank decided to continue on his way to the precinct house.

"Extra, extra! Heat wave taking over the city!" crowed a newsboy, thrusting a paper at Hank.

"I'm living it, kid," Hank said. Still, he tossed a nickel at the newsie and took a paper. The unbearable heat dominated the headlines, though there was a story below the fold about Police Commissioner Roosevelt blustering about saloons being open on Sundays again and an update on the trial of a woman accused of chopping her husband into bits before dumping the remains in the East River. *The World* had no qualms about declaring her guilty.

Hank had some doubts, given that he'd worked the case. He still suspected her lover, a married man who delivered ice. Maybe the city had decided the ice was too valuable to spare him.

Hank was sympathetic. Dear lord, it was hot. The air around him was thick and rancid. Simply being outside was like walking around with eight blankets draped over his shoulders. The street smelled of rotting food and horse manure.

Ah, New York in the summer.

He arrived at the precinct house on East Fifth Street, where the whir of the overhead electric fans drowned out all other noise, and still the fans weren't doing much beyond blowing papers around. The smell was slightly better inside, but it wasn't any cooler.

"Brandt."

Hank wasn't even at his desk yet and already someone was trying to get his attention.

He sighed and turned his attention toward his colleague and sometime partner, Stephens, who stood there with his arms crossed.

"Would you *like* for Roosevelt to give you a lecture?" said Stephens, glaring at Hank's bare forearms.

Hank had forsaken a jacket and rolled up his shirtsleeves in an attempt to escape the oppressive heat. Not that it worked. Stephens, of course, was in his full uniform. The collar of his coat was soaked with sweat. Hank wondered what Stephens hoped to achieve by suffocating under all that wool.

"It's amusing to me that Commissioner Roosevelt thinks any man could wear a coat in this weather. If he wants to discuss proper attire, he can do so when the weather cools off." Hank pulled his handkerchief out of his pocket and mopped his brow again.

Stephens balked, but recovered quickly and said, "We have a new investigation. That is, now that you've decided to grace us with your presence."

"It is too hot for sarcasm, Stephens. What is the case?"

Stephens puffed out his chest and made a show of pulling a wad of crumpled paper from his jacket pocket. He consulted his notes. "Murder at a resort on the Bowery."

Hank glanced back toward the front entrance to the precinct house. Taking on a case would mean investigating, which meant going back outside. That was about the last thing Hank wanted to do. Not that the precinct house was cool and comfortable as such, but Hank had reasoned that if he sat very still, he might be all right. He turned back to Stephens. "Which resort?"

Stephens looked at his tattered papers. "Club Bulgaria."

Hank schooled his features so that Stephens wouldn't detect his reaction. He wondered if Stephens knew of the reputation of this particular club. Not that Hank had ever been there. He'd merely been tempted.

"Any other information?" Hank asked.

"Not much. Officers who arrived at the scene first talked to the club owner briefly, but he didn't seem to know anything. The body is still there. A few of the staff from the club have been made to wait there for our arrival."

Hank could only imagine how putrid the body must smell in this heat. "Well," he said. "No sense standing around here dripping. Let's go."

Nicholas Sharp—stage name Paulina Clodhopper—stood outside Club Bulgaria in his street clothes, smoking the last of a cigarillo. It was doing nothing to calm his nerves. He tossed the butt of it toward the street and rearranged the red scarf draped around his neck. It was too hot for such frippery, but he had an image to maintain, and besides, the police were on their way. He wanted to look somewhat respectable. Really, though, Nicky would have much preferred a long soak in an ice bath while wearing nothing at all.

The sun blared down on the Bowery and it smelled like someone had died—which, Nicky acknowledged, had happened in truth—and it was nearly unbearable, but he could not stand inside any longer. Not with Edward laid out on the floor like . . . well. Nicky did not want to think of it.

A man in rolled-up shirtsleeves and an ugly brown waistcoat, his hands shoved in his pockets, walked down the street toward Nicky. He was accompanied by a man who must have been boiling inside his crisp police uniform.

The man in uniform looked Nicky up and down with an expression of deep skepticism on his face. "Are you Mr. Juel?" His tone indicated his real question was, *Are you even a real man?*

Nicky bristled. "No, darling. He's inside."

The man in shirtsleeves said, "You work here?"

"Yes."

This man was really quite attractive, in a sweaty, disheveled way, though Nicky supposed there was no way around that in this weather. The man pulled a handkerchief from his pocket and then pulled the dusty bowler hat off his head, revealing dark brown hair cut short. He wiped his whole face from his damp forehead to his thick mustache before he dropped the hat back on his head. There seemed to be a strong body under the wrinkled clothing, but it was hard to tell. Still, Nicky was drawn to this man. His companion in the uniform was blond and bearded and looked considerably more polished, but in a bland way. The disheveled man was far more interesting.

"I'll take you in to see Mr. Juel," Nicky said. "That is, if I could have your names."

"I'm Detective Stephens," said the uniformed man briskly.

"Hank Brandt," said the man in shirtsleeves.

"Acting Inspector Henry Brandt," Stephens said. "Honestly, Brandt, there are protocols."

Brandt grunted and waved his hand dismissively at Stephens. To Nicky, he said, "And you are?"

"Nicholas Sharp. Come with me."

He led the police officers inside. Julie was waiting in front of the door to the ballroom. He stepped forward and introduced himself, standing tall but fussing a bit more than was necessary—"This is *such* a terrible tragedy, nothing like this has *ever* happened here before, I am still in such a state of shock!"—his voice growing increasingly shrill as he spoke. Nicky might have believed him if this had been the first act of violence perpetrated at Club Bulgaria.

"Can you tell us what transpired, Mr. Juel?" asked Detective Stephens, the picture of proper politeness, though it was Brandt who pulled a pad of paper and a pencil from his pocket.

"I did not know the fate of poor Edward until I arrived this afternoon."

Nicky glanced at Brandt to ascertain his reaction. Julie was lying just as sure as he had a receding hairline; he rarely left the club. Nicky knew for a fact that Julie had been sleeping in his office at the back of the club for nearly a week, ever since his lover had thrown him out of their Greenwich Village apartment. Nicky didn't know for certain, but he also suspected poor Edward had been lying on the floor of the ballroom for some time before Julie had deigned to notice him.

"And where were you through all this, Mr. Sharp?" asked Brandt.

Nicky adjusted his scarf. "I went home just after midnight last night. I arrived back at the club about an hour ago, where I was confronted with Mr. Juel and the news that poor Edward had departed the earth."

Brandt nodded. "What exactly is your occupation here?"

"I entertain the guests."

Brandt pursed his lips. "You entertain them."

"I sing," said Nicky.

Brandt's eyebrows shot up. "Right. So. This Edward. Is he a friend of yours?"

Nicky kept hoping Julie would intervene, but he stayed resolutely quiet. Nicky wasn't quite sure what the best answer to these questions would be or how much information he should give away willingly. He said, "He also entertained the guests. In a somewhat different capacity."

Brandt turned toward Stephens and said, "Would you go take a look at the ballroom? I will follow along in a moment."

Stephens nodded and proceeded into the ballroom. Julie trailed after him.

Nicky shivered, alarmed now that he was alone with Mr. Brandt, who removed his hat and took a step closer to Nicky.

"Tell me honestly," said Brandt. "Edward was a working boy."

Nicky sucked in a breath. Brandt stood close enough for Nicky to smell him, and it was a sour, earthy scent, the fragrance of someone who had spent too much time stewing in his own sweat on a hot day.

"Yes," Nicky whispered.

"And you are as well?"

"No. I only sing."

Brandt grunted. "I'm not here from the vice squad. I do not wish to toss anyone in jail unless they killed your friend Edward. Do you understand me?"

"Yes. And I am being honest. Edward was a working boy. I sing on that stage a few times a week." Nicky pointed toward the ballroom. "That's all."

"You sing."

"Yes. And to answer your next question, last I saw Edward was last night. He was entertaining a guest. They went to the back. I do not know what happened after that."

Brandt must have been astute enough to discern Nicky's meaning, because he jotted something down on his pad. "What did this guest look like?"

Nicky closed his eyes to try to picture him. "He had dark hair. He was quite tall. Thick mustache. A very fine suit of clothes, much nicer than the sort the guests here usually wear."

Brandt scribbled all that down. He said, "Would you recognize this man if you saw him again?"

"Yes, I believe so."

"They went to the back and never reemerged?"

Nicky didn't quite know what to make of these questions. Clearly, Brandt was worldly enough to know how a club like this worked, so he must have known that the back rooms behind the ballroom at Club Bulgaria were where men went to have sex with each other. Edward would have sidled up to a man like the one Nicky had seen him with last night and seen the money dancing before his eyes. He would have taken the man in back for a . . . financial transaction. And then?

"I'll be honest and tell you I didn't think much about Edward hanging on the arm of some man from uptown. This fancy dressed man was slumming, which is hardly a novel occurrence. Usually the bourgeoisie come down here to gawk and feel superior, but occasionally one of the boys here does get his claws in one. It wasn't strange enough for me to take note."

"Except for his clothes."

"Yes, well. I quite liked the cut of the man's jacket and spent a brief, wondrous moment imagining I could afford to purchase such a thing."

Brandt nodded. "In other words, Edward may just have emerged from the back room unscathed after entertaining this man, but if he did, you did not see it." He stepped toward the ballroom. "Come with me."

"Oh, no, darling. I couldn't possibly. I've spent far too much time with poor Edward today as it is."

"Fine. Stay here, then. Don't leave. I'm not done talking to you."

"Your wish is my command."

Brandt narrowed his eyes. Probably he didn't appreciate Nicky acting flippant, but there was no other way to manage such a situation.

Nicky watched Brandt walk into the ballroom. When the voices of the men inside rose, Nicky found a spare chair to sit in. There was nothing to do but wait.

Kate McMurray has published several best-selling male/male novels, including Rainbow Award winner *Show and Tell* and *Across the East River Bridge*. She has been writing stories since she could hold a pen. She started writing gay romance after reading a book and thinking there should be more love stories with gay characters. Her first published novel, *In Hot Pursuit*, came out in February 2010, and she's been writing feverishly ever since.

When she's not writing, Kate works as a nonfiction editor. She also reads a lot, plays the violin, knits and crochets, drools over expensive handbags, and is a tiny bit obsessed with baseball. She lives in Brooklyn, New York and is active in the Romance Writers of America.

CPSIA information can be obtained
at www.ICGtesting.com
Printed in the USA
LVOW12s1952160516

488473LV00001B/25/P